A Land To Call Her Own

Julie Pollitt

This book is dedicated to my sister Cathy.
I couldn't ask for a better friend or sister.

For information contact:
tallgirlwriting@gmail.com

Follow Julie on Twitter:
https://twitter.com/julieepollitt

Check out Julie's website:
http://www.juliepollitt.com

Find Julie on Facebook
Author Julie Pollitt

Cover design by Lynnette Bonner of Indie Cover Design
http://indiecoverdesign.com/
Images copyright: The Killion Group Image #INS0267

Chapter One

Denver City, Colorado Territory
Autumn 1865

Tess Porter stared out the window at the darkened sky over snow-capped mountains from inside the Overland Express way station. She pressed her hands together, interweaving her fingers. More than once her grip grew tight. She drew in a deep breath and reminded herself she could now relax.

Tess again studied the vast open land, which held a freedom only she could understand.

A scant amount of people dotted the sidewalks in town, a vast difference from her New York City. She searched the faces for her father, but he was not among them. The fall winds snuck through the cracks around the door and a chill prickled up her spine.

Her eyelids closed, she drew in a deep breath and pictured Franklin Shepherd. A small wave of guilt coursed through her for recanting the arranged union on the morning of her wedding ceremony, only weeks ago. She'd wrestled with the decision to marry Franklin, knowing he would take good care of her. Before leaving her native city, her respect mounted for the man, but never once did her love.

"Miss?" A man's shrill voice echoed through the empty room, intruding into her thoughts. "Who you waitin' on?"

"My father. He promised to meet me here," she said, backing away from the window. She ran her fingers across his worn letter in her pocket. Perhaps something on the ranch kept him.

"Seems like there ain't nobody else comin'. Maybe you best get a room at the hotel 'fore too long," the tall, lanky stagecoach clerk said, as he shuffled behind the counter. "I'm lockin' the door soon."

"He promised. He'll be here." Her voice echoed confidence, if only the rest of her would agree.

"Who's your father?"

"Ed Porter."

The clerk's eyelids fluttered as if surprised by his name.

"Do you know him?"

He paused a moment before speaking. "Yes'm."

"Do you know where he is?" She lifted her eyebrows in question.

The clerk swallowed, his Adam's apple sliding down and back. He lifted his arm and slowly moved his finger out, pointing across the street. "He's... he's over there."

She walked back to the window and looked out. "The church?"

"Yes'm," he said as he nodded.

She tugged at the edges of her white gloves and lifted her small pocketbook into the palm of her hands. "I'll return for my trunk."

Why was he at the church? She bit her bottom lip and creased her eyebrows. He'd known for some time she was coming.

The clerk remained silent. He followed her to the door, closing it behind her.

Each of the wooden steps creaked beneath her. She eyed the street before crossing, and dodged the piles of steaming horse droppings. Tess pinched her nose with her thumb and forefinger to lessen the stench.

The jangle of a harness forced her attention up, and she stopped to let a wagon pass in front of her. She lifted the hem of her dress to avoid some of the mud puddles scattered across the dirt road running the length of town.

Three wagons were hitched to a wooden post on the side of the red brick church. She squeezed her hand around the knob of the church door and pushed it open. She stuck her head through the opening in the door and decided it was all right to enter the foyer. A small handful of people were gathered in the first few pews singing a hymn. Her heart fluttered in her chest, knowing her father had to be close. Tess hadn't allowed herself to get excited, until now.

So many times in her childhood, Tess and her older sister, Francine, peered out the front window of her grandmother's sitting

5

room. They waited for their father's promised return after months of absence. Having memorized his figure, Tess would press her nose against the glass and refuse to leave her post until he came into sight. The two young girls would throw open the front door and leap off the steps into his arms, hoping to be held as long as he stayed. Now Tess, her sister Francine, and her family would be joining him out west.

Tess slid into the back seat and tried to remain inconspicuous. She studied the back of each man in the room, slowly trying to recall her father's posture and mannerisms. None looked familiar.

The music ceased. The preacher walked up the stairs at the front of the sanctuary and stood behind the unadorned wooden pulpit.

"Please be seated." He waved his hands, motioning for everyone to sit down. They complied with the exception of five men, huddled toward the front of the sanctuary.

As they parted, they revealed a long wooden box on top of a table. A casket. Her eyes traced the familiar outline of the man's face lying inside the simple pine box. Tess stood up and moved closer. The man's nose protruded slightly at the bridge, just like her father's. Could it be? Her knees trembled at the thought.

"We are gathered here today to honor the life of our dear resident, Ed Porter," the preacher said, confirming her worst fears.

"No!"

Her echo rang across the church. As people turned, a multitude of faces pressed on her, like a weight. Tess swallowed hard. She took a deep breath and gripped the back of the pew with her hand to steady herself. Her feet inched slightly toward the aisle.

As she neared the casket, she looked inside the pine box at her father. The man who always used his hands when he talked, spoke without reservation, and loved without apology, lay motionless in front of her. The air left her lungs like a blow to the stomach.

"Miss?" the preacher said, standing in front of her. "Miss?"

Tess tipped her head up and turned her gaze to meet the preacher's face, ignoring everyone around her. Her lips parted, but nothing came out. She looked back down at her father and tears stung her eyes.

6

"Are you okay?"

Tess felt a young woman pulling her to the side. She led Tess to sit on the front pew. Numbness covered her. The woman's voice came in a delicate whisper. "Do you know this man?"

Pa. The word reverberated in her head, but she couldn't speak. She drew in a breath hoping she could fill her lungs and nodded her head.

"What's your name?" The woman rubbed her arm in a soothing motion.

"Tess… Porter." She bit her lower lip and tried to keep the tears from pouring out. It was no use. She covered her face and sobbed into her hands.

"Your father?" the woman pushed a handkerchief into her folded hands and curled her fingers around it.

"How can this be?" Her words were barely a whisper as Tess looked up at the preacher. "He sent for me. He can't be dead." She studied the casket again.

The woman slid her arm around Tess, squeezing her shoulder. Tess pressed her eyes shut and tried to will away the fact that her father was dead.

"What do we do now?" Someone whispered.

The preacher knelt down on one knee in front of Tess. "Should we go on with the service then?"

Her mind felt as though she were lost in a dense fog, drifting at sea.

She paused for a moment as she stared at him. "What else is there?"

Francine. Her sister entered her thoughts. How would she tell her? Francine, her husband Luke, and daughter Lizzie would be arriving soon to finally live together as a family.

She wanted to start a new life with her father. Tess had felt a freedom arise in her heart when she broke the engagement with Franklin. Now, she was away from her belittling, contemptuous grandmother and the possibility of a loveless marriage.

When her father wrote to her, desperation filled his letters. He wanted her to come and live with him and create the family they were meant to be so many years ago.

He rarely came to visit. When he did, words were rarely spoken between him and his own mother, Eliza Porter.

7

Francine and Tess lived with their grandmother while he wandered from place to place—always with a jug of whiskey in his hand. This letter seemed different and more caring. Sober.

Tess wiped her eyes with a soft handkerchief. Now she would never know what drove him to send for her. The relationship she had dreamed about for so long slid through her hands like water. Her hopes lay drenched and gone on the church floor in front of her.

The pain of his death felt like a thousand bee stings. Tess concentrated on breathing, pulling air into her lungs, just to survive the moment.

A chorus of voices singing startled her from her thoughts and she glanced up. A man picked up the lid to place it on the wooden casket.

"Ian, wait," the preacher said, holding out his hand to stop Ian from covering Tess' father for eternity. "Let her look... one more time."

How could this be true? Tess hadn't seen his face in years and now she had to look at him for the last time. Sadness engulfed and pressed in on her, and her father couldn't wrap his arms around her to give comfort. She needed his shelter. But it was gone.

Tess stood to her feet and peered into the casket. His aged face was identical to her loving grandfather's. Memories flooded back into her mind of her father's whiskered chin tickling her soft cheeks. Her eyes traced his face, trying to memorize every feature.

The black suit he wore had to be a gift. The sleeves stretched down past his knuckles. She couldn't recall a time he dressed so fine.

Years of whisky abuse and solitary life were evident in his face. His cheeks were thin and the sun parched his skin. The evidence of time was written around his eyes and mouth.

Her knees trembled and she wondered if her legs would hold her. She'd never see his smile or feel the weight of his arms around her again. She held in the tears and the pain burned within her. His low, soothing voice would never course through her ears again.

Why Lord? Why are you letting this happen?

Tess took a step back and looked at the men standing around the casket. The man who held the top of the pine casket stared at her with his ocean-blue eyes, waiting for her approval to lay it on top of her father.

For a brief moment, as he watched her, she felt a covering of peace. Tess turned her face away from his penetrating glance. She wanted nothing more than to be alone. The intrusion of people around her suffocated her thoughts.

He set the wooden lid on top, scraping it against pine beneath. As they hammered the nails, it felt as though someone were hammering the finality of his life into her soul one nail at a time.

* * *

"Will you be all right out here on your own?" Catherine Bishop, the preacher's wife asked, jarring Tess back to reality. "We can stay out here at your father's... I mean, your cabin, a spell longer."

Tess smelled the cornbread Catherine placed on the table inside of a small basket. Her stomach grumbled in protest, but she ignored it. "I'll be fine."

Thomas, the preacher, came through the door with an armload of wood and set it down next to the hearth. He made a pile of twigs in the bottom of the fireplace before setting larger logs on top. He struck the match against one of the rocks lining the fireplace and held it underneath the stack until a small flame flickered. The fire grew and warmed her skin as the heat traveled across the cold room.

"I've put your trunk next to the bed," he said.

Catherine placed her hand on Tess' arm. "What else can we do?"

Bring back my father. Tess took a deep, shuddering breath, knowing it was impossible. "There's nothing you can do."

"We hope to see you in church on Sunday," Thomas said.

"Right. Church." Tess looked around the room at her unfamiliar surroundings. The cabin should've felt comfortable and inviting, but she missed her father. Fear churned in her gut. Nothing felt the same.

Catherine wrapped her arms around Tess. "The Lord will watch over you. He won't let you down. Even in the midst of your grief, He will be there."

Tess knew the truth in that statement, but God felt farther away that moment than ever before. A twinge of anger rose up inside of her. She knew He wasn't to blame, but where was His control?

She never understood how people could doubt God and His plans, until now.

Catherine and Thomas left, closing the door gently behind them. Tess heard the jingle of the horse's harness pulling the wagon away, and the sound of clomping hooves drowned in the distance.

The one-room cabin was far from the comforts of home and the finer things she was accustomed to. The bed was merely feet from the rickety table in the middle of the room. The table looked as though it was made from scraps of wood. Rust crawled up the edges and the sides of the old black cooking stove.

Her mother's faded yellow patchwork quilt lay across the bed. *Pa wanted this family to work.* She covered her mouth with the palm of her hand to stifle the cry that threatened to come out.

Tess gazed around the small room. On the mantle, above the crackling fire, sat a framed picture of her family taken almost twenty years ago. She stared at it. In the black and white Daguerreotype, Tess rested on her mother's lap and her older sister Francine stood next to her. As usual, her father was absent.

Footsteps on the porch pulled her from her thoughts. Before she could move, hinges on the door squeaked, and she watched it creak open one inch at a time. A stream of light filtered into the room and spilled on the floor.

A man in a stiff stovepipe hat entered the cabin. Once inside, he looked around the room until his eyes fell on Tess. His mouth twitched in surprise.

"Who are you?" Tess demanded.

"What are you doing here?" He asked. His robust shape filled his meticulously-ironed jacket.

"This is my father's cabin," she said. "You didn't answer my question."

Clearing his throat, he pressed his fingers along the front collar of his suit jacket. His chest rose. "I'm Henry Barrington. I own the ranch north of here."

"Why are you here?" She stammered to find the right words. Tess started to remove her dust-covered gloves, but changed her mind. She kept her eyes on him.

"I came to check on the place." He said.

"You've heard my father is dead?"

He nodded.

"Do you know how it happened?" Tess asked.

"No. Someone found him dead. He must have fallen."

She recalled the strangers staring at her during her father's funeral, shaking their heads, murmuring they were sorry. What had happened? When she asked, no one seemed to know.

"I offer my deepest sympathies, and I am terribly sorry for your loss." He removed his hat and held it under his arm. Lines from his comb had drawn tiny furrows though his silver-streaked hair.

"Thank you." Tess said.

"Please, sit down." He pulled out one of the chairs and held out his hand for Tess.

She took his hand and sat down.

"Can I offer you a clean handkerchief?" He reached into his inside pocket and pulled out a folded, pristine white cloth. He unfolded it, handed it to her, and smiled sympathetically.

She took the handkerchief and dabbed it against her eyes. "I'll never get to see him again."

"Death of a loved one is never easy, Miss." He spoke quietly. "It takes time to grieve."

She pressed her lips together and nodded her head.

He offered a few moments of silence. "You'll probably want to head back home," he said, the words sliding off his tongue like butter.

Tess wasn't sure how to respond.

"I can help you sell the place," Henry said. "You could make a healthy start for yourself back home, where it's more comfortable," he paused for a moment. "In fact, to help you, I'll buy the place, take it off your hands. It's not necessary for a young woman like you to get your silky white hands dirty with ranching. A nice lady like you needs the finer things . . ."

Sell the place? Was he serious? She just arrived and this stranger had no inkling of what she needed.

She couldn't go back to the possibility of a loveless marriage. After her grandmother practically threw her out, Tess knew the possibility of going back to New York City was out of the question. Her chest tightened and her hands shook in her lap. She intertwined her fingers hoping he wouldn't see her shaking.

Tess slipped her hand into her skirt pocket and felt her father's letter crinkled inside—the letter she'd waited so long to

11

receive, asking her to join him out west, to live with him as family. But it was just a letter. Her father was dead. He couldn't protect her now.

"You have no need of this land. There are vast amounts of fresh water here for my cattle."

Tess felt her insides twist with anger. How could he make such an assumption? He knew nothing of her situation.

"This property is not for sale." She stood up so fast her heels came off the ground.

He narrowed his eyes and shot her a look that would stop a train dead in its tracks.

"You'll get a fair price," he said. A twitch replaced the crooked smile.

"It's not for sale," Tess said through gritted teeth. She looked him in the eye. "My father had a plan for our family."

Henry stepped closer. Her cheeks flushed as he drew even nearer. His nostrils bulged. His lips tightened. The wrinkles around his mouth turned white. "Your father's cattle are unhealthy. You've no hay in the barn. Winter is coming and the Colorado Territory is harsh and unforgiving. The barn was barely finished after he wasted all his money in the brothels… when he wasn't too drunk to walk."

"How dare you speak of him in such a manner." Her body stiffened and her voice grew deep. Deep enough to scare herself.

Yet what he said was probably true. Her father's drinking followed him, alienating him from his children and all he ever held dear.

"There's no way you can run this ranch by yourself, Miss Porter. "

She knew he was right, though she dared not tell him so. She'd never been out of the city. She knew about parties and school, not running a ranch.

Her lips pressed together. "I will find a way to run this ranch successfully." She'd read about families who'd gone west to start a new life. Women died everyday in this land. The odds were against her.

"Those animals will either freeze or die of hunger—that is if nothing were to happen to you first. You're quite a spunky young lady," he said, sarcasm dripping off his words. He took one step forward and she could feel the vibration of his heels scraping the

12

floor. "Spunk will not get you far in ranching. It takes guts, knowledge, and money."

"I will not sell. This is still my father's... my father's land." A lump formed in her throat and she swallowed hard and blinked back the tears.

Henry slapped his hand around her wrist and squeezed, pulling her body toward his. His teeth clamped shut, but the words came slithering through. "Mark my words, it will belong to me."

"Let go of me." Tess pulled her arm back with all her might, but she was unable to free herself. This time she used her body weight to pull back. He tightened his grip, pinching her skin between his fingers. Spit rolled off his bottom lip as he laughed.

"Let her go Barrington." A deep voice accompanied the crack of a rifle cocking across the room.

Chapter Two

Ian Bidwell stood in the doorway of Ed Porter's cabin. He tightened his fist around his rifle and gripped it tight. "The lady told you this place ain't for sale." He knew the kind of harm Barrington could selfishly dole out. He'd witnessed it firsthand.

"What do you think you're doing here?" Barrington said through gritted teeth. Before letting Tess free, he glanced at her, and then shoved her down like a rag doll.

She dropped to the floor with a thud and crawled backward until her back met the wall.

"I saw you comin' this way and I knew you were up to no good," Ian stepped close enough to Barrington to see the new whiskers on his face. The older man took a few steps backward, almost tripping over his own heels.

Barrington's nostrils flared and he looked back at Tess like a man bent on revenge. "Mark my words Miss Porter, I will own this ranch. One way or another."

Barrington clinched his fists together as he stared at Ian. The man's futile attempt at assertiveness was lost on Ian.

Ian's eyes burned with fire as he gazed at Barrington, refusing to give in.

"Think about what you're doing," Barrington said, his voice sopping with a salty sweetness. "Come back to the ranch. We work well together. You know I have a lot to offer."

Ian's teeth clenched together and the muscles around his jaw tightened. "Don't count on it."

Barrington took a deep breath and exhaled a cloud full of steam before spinning on his heels and stomping out the door, disappearing from sight.

Ian stood in the doorway and kept his eyes pinned on him as he rode away, praying he didn't turn around and do something stupid. He knew the man's capabilities, but more than that, he knew his own and didn't want to have to shoot a man. Again.

Tess muffled her sobs in the folds of her dress, pulling his attention away from the door.

Ian leaned his rifle against the wall—close enough to grab—and knelt down next to her. She buried her face, and her shoulders shook.

"You okay?" Ian held his hand above her shoulder. He wanted to touch her, comfort her. But he curled his fingers into his palm and pulled his arm back.

"No," Tess said, sitting up and smearing tears across her face. "I can't do any of this. Especially without my father."

"I'm sorry." He pulled his dusty hat off and placed it on the table, then thought better of his manners and laid it next to his revolver on the floor. "Your Pa was a good man."

Her eyes grew wide and she drew in a quick breath. "You knew him?"

He nodded. Ian knew Ed well. The loss ground at his aching heart each time he thought of his friend. Tears stained her cheeks. As she looked at him his heartbeat raced, and he turned his head away.

Tess pulled her father's letter from her pocket and ran her finger across his name on the envelope. "He promised me," she paused for a moment, "Francine, and her family a new start in this place. I spent the long trip west planning the conversations we would have as father and daughter." A small giggle erupted. "This was going to be my opportunity to get to know what it was like to have a real family. At least a family that loves unconditionally."

She sighed and the soft, supple skin on her forehead pressed together and wrinkled.

Ian wanted to help in some way, take away her pain. But since the loss of his mother, he knew all-too-well grief had to be worked out on its own.

"I never got the chance to tell him good-bye." Tess pulled off her gloves and wiped her tears with the edge of her finger.

He studied her trembling hands for a moment.

"I'm sure he knew you loved him," Ian said. "He talked about you and your sister often."

15

Tess grabbed the corner of the table to stand, but her legs melted beneath her. Ian lunged forward and slipped his hands under her arms. They lingered a moment as she regained her strength. They stood up together.

Tess turned toward him with her face only inches away. A gentle smile crossed her face.

He pulled in air more than once to catch his breath. She was the most beautiful woman he'd ever laid eyes on. Her eyelashes were long against her hazel eyes. Wisps of light brown hair fell against her cheeks. Ed mentioned his daughters were beautiful, but Ian never guessed Tess would render him speechless. Ian desperately wanted to stay there in her midst. He fidgeted, searching for a place to put his hands.

She looked again into his eyes for a brief moment. He turned away, afraid she would see right into his soul.

"Thank you for your help, Mister… ?" she said, breaking the silence.

"Bidwell. Ian Bidwell." He extended his arm. She slipped her soft, warm hand into his and shook it.

He watched her facial expression change. Her soft features tightened and her eyebrows met. Tess' hand stiffened before she pulled it away.

"Are you here to buy the land or push me off of it?" She said, standing up straight and crossing her arms in front of her chest.

He laughed. She didn't mince words. "Neither. I saw Barrington comin' this way. I came out to make sure you were ok."

Tess remained silent for a minute and Ian wondered if she was pondering his answer for truth. He wasn't surprised. Quite a few folks in town questioned his newfound honorable actions, especially after he spent the last few years bent on ruining lives, including his own.

"How do you know my Pa?" Tess' question broke into his thoughts.

"I met him in town a few months ago. He helped me see things differently." If only she knew. Watching her father transform from a drunk to a man of God made a life-changing impression on him.

Ian stared out the window before looking back at Tess. He smacked his pant leg and his cheeks warmed as dust floated out in a

16

small cloud around him. "Ranching takes hard work. You need help."

"I don't know what to do." Tess wiped a tear from her cheek and shook her head.

"You can't run this place alone—"

"I can't afford to pay anyone. I've got no choice," she said, straightening the folds of her dress. "I'll do what it takes."

She was determined. But he knew Barrington could wear a person down. And fast.

"You know Mr. Barrington well?" She asked.

"He's my… uncle." He wasn't proud of what he couldn't change.

"And you worked for him?" Tess tipped her head forward and looked up.

He nodded. He regretted every minute of it. So many lives were ruined trying to make his uncle's better.

Ian glanced out the open door. "I best be getting gettin' back to town 'fore it's too dark to see," Ian said. He wanted her to know as little as possible about his mistakes. They were hard enough for him to swallow.

"Thanks for your help," Tess said.

"I only did what any civilized gentleman would do." Ian chuckled.

Tess smiled.

"Miss Porter, I know Barrington well." Ian placed his hat back on his head. "Be careful." Ian would give anything to go back and change his past. His skin crawled when he thought about how many times he broke the law working for that man, all in the name of money. None of which he had to show for now.

"Thank you for your concern, but I doubt he'll be back."

"He'll do what it takes to get his way. Stay on the lookout."

Ian looked down at his boots and returned his gaze to Tess. "Miss Porter, this here's unsettled territory. There's Indians roamin' the prairie just out your back door. And there's lots of folks around who can't be trusted. Just be wary of who you share your business with."

"I appreciate your concern, Mr. Bidwell. However, I believe I know how to take care of myself."

"I'm sure you do." He liked her fearless attitude, but would it survive the Colorado Territory? "Do you have a gun?"

She shook her head no. "I'd never know what to do with a gun."

"If someone's comin' through that door, you'd figure it out pretty quick. Better bolt the door when I leave. Take some care." Ian reached for his rifle and walked out the door. He wanted to stay and protect her—protect Ed's daughter. But he couldn't interfere where he wasn't wanted. He'd wait for the right time to try to help her.

***

Tess wanted Ian to stay longer. His presence made her feel like a child safe in her father's arms. When he lifted her off the floor, she felt a rush of shivers race through her.

His blue eyes held her gaze so tight, she couldn't look away. His presence, just like at the funeral, gave her a sense of peace.

But was this all part of a plan between him and his uncle? Were they working together to get rid of her? If only her father were still alive.

Was he even telling the truth about her father? Were they really friends?

The painfully-loud silence in the room made Tess ache more for her pa. She started to offer a prayer, but instead, anger rolled through her. An accusation took its place. *Why did you take my father?*

She couldn't—no, wouldn't—go back to her grandmother. The woman's abuse came in forms unseen to the eye. Her efforts at matching Tess with Franklin, were nothing less than an attempt to pawn her off once and for all. Since her grandfather died, Tess knew nothing would stop her grandmother from ridding herself of what she considered a thorn in her side.

Tess spent her life wondering why her grandmother held her in such contempt. Her intolerance alone gave Tess reason to question her self-worth more than once.

Tess left New York City with a small sum, knowing she couldn't afford to return. The long, arduous trip wrung out her funds fast. And what she had left would barely be enough to pay for food, let alone hire someone to help out on the ranch.

She couldn't help but humanly wonder if God would stay by her in the middle of a ranch on the lonesome frontier. Would the

God her grandfather preached of remain by her side without wavering?

Tess walked outside. The immense scrub oak tree she sat down underneath cooled her in its shade. Glitters of light reflected off the vibrant green and yellowing leaves, dancing in the wind.

As she gazed at the mountains, a strong breeze sent tiny wisps of dust whirling in front of her. Tess ran her tongue across her chapped lips in the dry air. Jagged mountain peaks in the distance stretched toward heaven, higher than any she'd ever seen.

What would her sister Francine do? Would she and her family stay on the ranch, or leave for a better life? Tess wanted a relationship with the sister she now barely knew. Everything felt so uncertain, as though it was all spiraling out of control.

Knowing her father died alone ground at her emotions. More than once, he had made her feel insignificant and unworthy of his love. His choice to keep alcohol—instead of his family—at his side still soured Tess. But he didn't deserve to die alone.

When he decided to go west she'd felt remorse that they would never be a family. She agreed to Franklin's offer of marriage, believing at the time it was her only hope at a better life away from her grandmother.

When her father's letter arrived it promised a new beginning for Tess, Francine, and her family. Her heart soared with a newfound freedom. He'd acquired some land, and Tess saw it as a sign that healing had begun. Surely this land would keep them together.

Her feet pressed against the ground beneath her. Ed Porter was six feet under, dead, gone. Nothing could help her now.

She pulled her legs toward her chest, bent her head down, and rested it on her knees. She tried to recall the words to "Amazing Grace." After humming the first few notes she sang faintly, "Amazing grace, how sweet the sound, that saved a wretch like me. I once was lost but now am found, was blind but now I see."

Tears streamed down her cheeks in a river. Tess knew everything now depended on her trust in God. Only He could see her through.

Her heart allowed the weight of sadness to engulf her.

***

The setting sun warmed against Ian's back as he rode toward Denver City. Tess' face burned into his memory. He'd only just met

19

her, but he could tell an artist every line, every curve of her features. Emotions tore at him when he thought of her grief at her father's funeral. He hadn't wanted to place the top of the casket over him.

Lord, give her strength to get through this time in her life. Watch over her at the ranch, and keep Barrington far from her.

Ian found himself praying more often since he turned his life over to Jesus a mere three months ago. Tess' father, Ed, told him it was just like havin' a conversation with someone, only it's God. If the Almighty didn't expect too many fancy words, Ian could give it a go.

Watching her father's transformation from a drunken mess to a wholehearted Christian gave Ian the desire to follow Jesus. He laughed when he thought about his Mama's repeated attempts to get him to pray each night as a child. Like a typical rebellious boy, he spewed his prayers as fast as he could get them out.

Now that his Mama was gone, he figured she must be up there talking to God herself, puttin' in a good word.

His thoughts returned to Tess and how she looked so refined at the funeral before the news of her father hit her ears. When she walked through the church doors his heart jumped in his chest. When he saw her again at the cabin, it took every ounce of his strength not to embrace her and try to comfort her in her sorrow.

Tess' grief made him think about his own hollow spot in his heart. Ed had become his closest friend. But how did he die? No one could explain it. Ian had his notions that Barrington had something to do with her father's death he just couldn't prove it. He'd kept the idea to himself knowing the sheriff took payment from Barrington, and it wouldn't do any good to go to him. Ian knew about the sheriff, because he'd carried him payments more than once. Many times Ian had suspicions the man was so crooked, he'd do it for free.

Ian hoped Barrington would stay put. He'd seen far too many range wars to know Barrington was planning one.

***

Tess curled up on the bed in the cabin. Through the window she watched the sun pass behind the mountains and a faint orange glow break through the looming gray clouds on the prairie. Before long the clouds swelled and shot pounding rain mixed with small pellets of hail on the roof. The hammering sounded like the nails driven into her father's coffin.

Closing her eyes, Tess recalled one of the rare times as a child when she climbed into her father's lap. She felt the warmth of his neck and the vibration of his voice telling a story. Unfortunately, far too many times during her growing-up years, he'd failed at being the father she so desperately longed for.

Tess turned over in the bed. The storm outside began to subside but the storm in her heart continued to rage.

Her eyelids felt as if they weighed fifty pounds. The morning would bring its sorrow soon enough. Finally giving in to exhaustion, she fell asleep.

Tess awoke to the thunderous sound of hooves pounding the earth. The sky was still as black as sin. Unlike the earlier hail, the sound resonated through the house. When she set her feet on the floor of the darkened cabin, the throbbing intensified. At once silence stifled the noise. A drop of moonlight crawled across the floor.

How foolish! I didn't bolt the door. She sat up and ran to the door, fumbling with the latch. Her hand slipped. *Why didn't you listen and lock the door?*

She stopped. Tall grass swished outside. Someone or something inched toward the front of the cabin. Her hands grabbed at the latch again. She struggled to hook it. Her fingers felt clumsy. *Impossible.*

They moved onto the front porch. *Maybe Ian was right about having a gun.* But Tess knew she'd never be able to point it at another human being and pull the trigger.

Her hands were swift in searching for something— anything—to use as a weapon. Her toe bumped the corner of the stove, and a bolt of pain shot through her. She bit her lip to keep from screaming. Her hand ran along the cold hard steel stove until she felt the cast iron skillet. Her fingers wrapped tightly around the handle, scraping the rusty metal grate as she lifted it.

She drew in a breath as the unseen terror inched closer. The wooden stairs bowed and squeaked under feet. Hairs on the back of her neck and arms prickled against her skin.

Whispers from the intruders made it evident they were men. How many, she could not be sure. One leaned on the door, pressing hard against the latch. He tried again and Tess dug her nails into the palm of her hand, lifting the skillet up in front of her.

Silence. Her breath became the loudest noise in the room as her breathing intensified.

The door burst open and moonlight spilled onto the floor. The shadow of a large, bulky man stood inches from her, followed by the stench of body odor. Tess lifted the skillet and held it up above her head. She swung hard, missing the man.

A strong arm caught her neck and slung her to the ground. The skillet hit the floor and ricocheted across the room.

"Don't hurt her too bad. Just get the point across," one of the men said. The gruffness in his voice drove her heart to pound faster.

One of the attackers yanked her wrists behind her, pressing his knee against her back as he tied them with a knotted rope. The pressure from his weight shoved her ribs into the wood floor. She screamed in agony.

He lifted his knee off her body and Tess caught her breath. She sucked air into her lungs. Rolling onto her knees, she peered through the darkness. She saw the silhouette of a slightly-overweight man in black clothes, rummaging through her things. He ripped lids off of pots and slung jars to the floor, sending shards of glass skipping across the room.

The other man snuck up next to Tess, leaned in close, and whispered, "Be quiet and no harm will come to you."

Tess craned her neck to see his face, hoping to find some identifying feature, but could not see. His voice burned into her memory.

He stormed out of the cabin, kicking furniture and belongings out of his way. The other man continued his frenzied search of the room. Fearing he would attack her again if she moved, Tess remained crouched in the corner.

His boot caught the corner of her Saratoga trunk by the bed. He stopped and the room fell silent. Laughter rumbled up through his gut and echoed through the cabin as the lid creaked open. Shivers itched across her skin.

Pulling her garments out of the trunk, he tossed aside each item until Tess heard the clunk of change against a metal box. *Not the money*. Her breath caught in her throat and she held it.

The box rattled all the way to the table. He flipped it upside down and scattered the contents. After picking the bills out of the pile of coins, he crammed them into his pocket, never once looking in her direction. He slid the small amount of change off the table into his palm and wrapped his fingers around it.

Returning to the living room, he knelt beside Tess. A wave of body odor and alcohol mixed together slithered into her senses, gagging her.

"There'll be no more ranching in your future." His voice was low and slurred. His belly jiggled against her arm as he laughed. She curled her upper lip in disgust. Tess caught a glimmer of the revolver in his hand just before it hit the side of her head and all went black.

Chapter Three

"Well my, oh my. Ian Bidwell."

Ian froze. The hairs stood up on the back of his neck. He knew the deep, cocky, Southern accent well. Too well.

"Josiah King," he whispered between his teeth. The black night around him closed in and suffocated his thoughts. He swallowed, but the lump in his throat refused to go down.

He'd already put his horse up for the night and thought a stroll through town would be a nice change. Until he heard Josiah's voice.

Ian's insides turned, pushing up on his stomach. He wanted to run, but the fact that Josiah snatched him from death, only a couple years ago, made it impossible to walk away.

"I thought you mighta done come down to these parts to seek out your uncle." Josiah had a snicker that could irritate the skin off a snake.

"For a spell." Ian didn't want to share anything about his business with a man that knew too much about his past. Would he ever be able to escape it?

"How's that leg of yours?"

Josiah lit a match and held it up to his cigar.

In the small flickering light, Ian could see that Josiah wore a pressed suit, with a crisp white shirt. His meticulous appearance might fool others, but not Ian.

"It's pretty well healed up. Hurts now and again." Ian rubbed his thigh. He'd yet to have full feeling return to the area where a bullet struck.

Hearing Josiah's voice brought back the memory of the shoot-out at the saloon like it was yesterday. They'd refused to pay for their liquor. The bartender, tired of freeloaders, decided he would take matters into his own hands. He pulled out a gun and aimed the barrel right at Ian. A shiver shook his shoulders at the memory.

Just before the bartender pulled the trigger, Josiah lunged toward Ian, knocking him out of the way, causing the bullet to miss Ian's head. Instead it hit his thigh, nicking an artery. Josiah stopped the bleeding and carried him to a doctor. Without him, he'd have a tombstone above him.

"I figured you'd have yer pockets full of gold and spirits by now." A laugh bellowed out of him and clouded the air with whiskey so thick Ian could almost taste it.

The stench of the past closed in around him. "Josiah, what business do you have here in Denver City?"

"Me and my brother got us 'nough gold dust to buy a general store. We bought out Simon's. Might turn it into a hardware store. Figurin' with all the buildin' goin' on in town, we might could make us a little bit of money. Sure 'nough." He lifted his hand and pointed in the direction of the old store across the street.

"I figured you got itchy for the frontier," Josiah said.

Ian wanted to ignore him, walk away. Everything in his body revolted at the reminder of his past.

"You there? You always did get that fer-off look." Josiah snapped his fingers in his face. His rotten jagged teeth stuck out underneath his fat lips. Laughter boiled out of him. It was the kind of laugh that would make the devil nervous.

"I best get home. I've got friends waitin' on me."

Josiah jutted his hand out in front of him. "Don't keep yourself from comin' 'round."

Ian shook his hand and turned to walk away. He refused to reply to his invitation. He would do everything in his power to stay away.

Ian couldn't help but question why the Lord allowed Josiah, of all people, to show back up in his life. It had been several years since the two tried their hand at panning gold, but later parted ways. He'd grown weary of Josiah's drunkenness. Was God testing Ian's newfound faith? God probably didn't have much trust in him, knowing he'd go right back to his sinning ways.

A chill in the air brought Ian back to the present. He'd learned to see things in a different way. His thoughts turned to Tess.

She would never have interest in a man with such a past. Ian didn't deserve such a beautiful, innocent woman.

He wanted to know more about her, but he stopped himself from thinking about something that would probably never happen. Her father spoke of her purity of heart, something Ian was trying hard to gain himself. Ian wondered if God really was big enough to help him overcome his past. Even if He was, Ian wasn't sure he'd ever be able to get over it himself.

***

Sunlight spilled through the window and warmed Tess' face. For a moment she forgot she was still on the floor, after being attacked the previous night, until the pain shot through her head.

She pulled the ropes that bound her wrists. They poked and scratched her raw skin, like needles chafing her arm. After tugging at the ropes for a few moments she slid out her hands.

She shuddered at the thought of the men ransacking the cabin. Nothing felt safe.

The right side of her head throbbed. She reached up to touch it. Pain sliced across her skull and she yanked her hand away through matted hair. Her fingers got caught in the tangles, sending shots of pain through her head.

She blinked her eyes several times, trying to free herself from dizziness. Her dresses sat in a jumbled heap several feet from the open trunk. Slivers of broken glass lay scattered around the floor, glittering in the sunlight shining in through the dirty window. She thought of those horrible men and what they'd done. Deep down she wondered if Henry Barrington sent them to get rid of her.

Oh Pa, I need you now. She looked down at the blisters forming on her wrists from the rope burn. Would this have happened if he were here? Tess sighed. She couldn't torture herself with the questions.

Supporting her weight against the chair next to her, Tess struggled to her feet. She stepped toward the trunk intending to neatly fold the dresses and put them back. She picked one up and ran her hand along the ripped and tattered seams, wondering if they could be mended. They were all she had as a reminder of her former life in the city.

She dropped it in her trunk and turned to walk to the door, kicking pieces of glass across the room. Her image in a small mirror

26

on the wall stopped her. She peered at the strange woman staring back at her. Her face didn't look familiar like the beautiful, elegant woman she used to be. Sadness pulled at her shoulders, weighing her down.

Tess walked outside and sat on the edge of the well behind the cabin. She lowered the bucket into the well until it slapped against the water, sinking as it filled up. The muscles in her arms shook as she pulled it back up and set it on the edge of the well before dipping the ladle into the water.

The icy water burned against her chapped lips as she sipped. A chill worked its way through her body leaving rows of goose bumps. She dipped her handkerchief in the water and placed it on the side of her head hoping to ease the sting out of the cut.

Pull yourself together Tess. Her sister Francine, husband Luke, and Lizzie were on their way to the ranch. She had to be strong.

Tears welled up and she cringed at the thought of telling her sister about their father's death. Would they stay in spite of his absence? Tess didn't want to think about the possibility of being left alone again.

The idea of going back to marry Franklin entered her thoughts. Just as quickly as her thoughts settled on Franklin, Ian came into her mind. His arms felt secure when he lifted her from the floor. Her heart never felt the rush of butterflies as it did when his hands slid around her waist. When he pulled back, she wanted his hands to return. To stay.

Tess had never thought of a man in such a manner, but Ian seemed different. *What am I thinking?* She had to put him out of her mind. He worked for the man trying to push her off his land. Even if he quit, they were blood. Nothing separates blood.

Luke would arrive soon and know what to do, unless they decided not to stay. So much uncertainty made her heart swell up and ache.

She still carried some resentment toward Francine. Her sister had married at sixteen and left her behind with their grandmother. Tess tried to maintain a close relationship with her through the passing years, but Francine always stayed at arm's length.

Tess hoped Francine's arrival out west would offer the chance to renew their relationship. But for now, that hope lay shattered with all the glass on the cabin floor.

Tess' anger boiled against the man who'd stolen her money and even more at the man she knew must have sent him. Henry Barrington probably had a pocketful of thieves to put up to anything he wished, including ransacking a dead man's cabin. Ian's face entered her mind again. She must stop thinking about him once and for all. Tess refused to give in to Henry Barrington, or any of his relatives.

***

Francine Stratton smiled at Lizzie as the four-year-old slid her tiny fingers into her mother's hand. Her daughter never failed to be a comfort.

The stagecoach swayed as Francine leaned into her husband Luke's shoulder. She rubbed her stomach and the baby inside kicked.

Atchison, Kansas was bigger than she imagined. Brick and wood buildings lined the wide, dusty streets. Rows of slatted-board sidewalks poked out in front of the businesses, bowing slightly in sections. A group of ten wagons gathered in a circle in the center of the street near one of the corrals. Their canvas tops flapped in the wind. She breathed in the excitement of the frontier.

"I wonder what Denver City will be like," Francine said, running her hand down her husband's arm and intertwining her fingers with his.

The stagecoach came to a halt and continued to rock.

After a moment Luke opened the door, stepped down and stomped his brown leather boots against the ground, trying to rid them of accumulated dust. He held out his hand for Francine. Lizzie leapt from inside and into his arms, giggling.

"That's my girl," he said.

Francine looked up at the top of the stagecoach. She regretted that their entire lives were held in those little bags and a trunk strapped to the roof. But the trip would have been far too expensive with a great deal of luggage and furniture.

"I'll have your belongin's delivered after I eat my dinner, if that's dandy with you?" The coach driver said. He spewed a brown stream of spit between Francine and Lizzie.

28

She shoved her daughter out of the line of fire, gave a sigh of relief, and said, "That'll be fine. Can you point out a decent hotel for us?"

The driver nodded to the end of the street. A large sign in front of one of the buildings jutted out and read, "The Peachtree Hotel."

"That one'll be good 'nough for you and yer family."

"Thank you." Luke stretched his hand up, tipped the driver, and they headed in the direction of the hotel.

Francine's emotions rolled like the mountain passes they'd traveled over. One moment she felt low as a valley, as though she'd left a piece of her heart back in Boston. The next, she soared on the mountaintop with the glow that their lives were starting over fresh. All in all, making the move west would finally bring her family together. She was ready for a renewed relationship with her father and Tess.

"I'm gonna get us a room so I can lie down," Luke said as he pulled little Lizzie close to his side. "I'm not feelin' too good."

Francine glanced at her husband. A pasty sweat covered his face. "You okay?"

"Just needin' some rest." He held her hand and squeezed it.

"How much longer, Mama?" Lizzie asked. Her blonde ringlets bounced up and down with every step. The trip had failed to wear her out. She grew more excited with each day of travel.

"We'll be there soon. I know Papa will be excited to meet his first granddaughter." Francine traced her finger along the young girl's chin line and smiled. "Once we arrive at Papa's house, we won't move again. We'll be home for good."

"I'll get us settled at the hotel," Luke said. "Why don't you take Lizzie to the restaurant we passed down the street? Get her some fixins. She deserves a treat. I'll find you after I get some rest."

Francine stood on her toes and pressed her lips against Luke's. Her heartbeat always fluttered at his touch. She took her daughter's hand before crossing the street. Her hopes soared with expectation of their future.

Atchison bustled with sidewalks full of shoppers and workers. "Look at all the stores, Lizzie. I bet they have a special treat waiting for you at the diner."

As they reached the end of the street, a man ran up behind her and smacked her on the shoulder several times.

Francine spun around. "What do you think you're—"

"Ma'am?" the man said.

She looked around him, searching for Luke. He'd make sure the man kept his hands from her. Francine rubbed her arm before turning around to walk away.

"Ma'am? I'm talkin' to you." His voice grew deeper and more stern.

She turned to go back across the street, hoping he would leave her and Lizzie alone.

"Wait a minute," he said, staying close behind.

"Luke?" As Francine yelled his name her voice cracked.

She tightened her grip around Lizzie's hand and pulled the child closer. Her feet moved fast beneath her, tripping her. Francine lifted her arm, pulling her back up to a standing position.

"That hurts Mama. Why you pullin' me?" Tears formed in her eyes as Francine dragged her back toward the hotel.

Her eyes ran down the length of the buildings, reading every sign. *Where is the Peachtree Hotel?*

"Lady… that man you're with… " She could hear his footsteps slamming down on the ground behind her.

She scanned the crowd, looking for Luke. His tall, wide-shouldered build would stand out above the crowd. But, he was nowhere to be found.

"Ma'am! Look." He ran up beside Francine and pointed across the street.

Her heart pumped so fast it made her head pound.

"That your husband?"

A small grouping of people gathered around someone lying on the ground. She could see a pair of brown leather boots, still covered in dust. *Luke.*

She dragged Lizzie back over to the sidewalk, and pushed people to get through the crowd, but it was useless. She gripped the arm of one of the men and shoved him out of the way. Luke was sprawled out in front of her, unconscious.

"Luke?" Francine begged. She looked up at the people standing around her. "Get a doctor!"

"Luke, honey? Talk to me." Francine lowered her ear over his open mouth. She waited to hear breathing. Nothing. "Is anyone a doctor here?" She screamed out, glancing up at the sea of strange faces. No one answered. They were only staring at Luke lying on the ground.

"Someone help us!" she cried. Her face flushed with heat. Her heartbeat thumped in her ears.

"Luke. Talk to me," she begged, pushing her hand against his unmoving chest. His head rolled to the side, and a long breath of air escaped from his mouth.

"Breathe, breathe." Her words escaped between sobs.

"Move aside, move aside." A man's voice carried through the crowd. "Let me get to this man." He knelt down next to Luke. He moved the tips of his fingers around the side of his neck, searching for a heartbeat. He held them steady and threw his eyes up to meet Francine's gaze.

"Is he... alive?" The word stuck to her tongue. She wanted— no needed—him to wake up and tell her everything would be okay.

The doctor looked down at Luke and back at Francine.

"Is he?" She choked out.

Chapter Four

Visions of the two men breaking in and tearing up her father's cabin the previous night raced through Tess' thoughts. Broken jars and torn pieces of clothing lay scattered around. The patchwork quilt her mother made was bunched up in a pile on the floor. What did the men want? Were they after just money, or did Henry Barrington send them as she suspected?

Little bits of hair got tangled in the brush as she tried to remove dried clots of blood. Pain shot through her. Hoping to ward off the feeling of nausea she drew in some air. Tess ran the brush through again, this time with ease.

Fear billowed through Tess every time a creak in the cabin sounded or the horse made a noise out in the corral. Were the men coming back to finish what they started, and kill her? Tess peered out the window and scanned the horizon. No one in sight. She held her breath for a moment before exhaling a chest full of fear.

The sound of glass breaking still rang in her ears. She ran her finger across the small scratch on the palm of her other hand where shards popped against her as the men raged and tossed things about with such anger and intensity. Glass ricocheted as far away as under the stove, against the hearth, and close to the door.

Her plan to come west had felt safe and easy. The hardest part, she believed, would be the long and arduous trip. She'd been in Denver City one night and already her world seemed smashed to bits.

As Tess peered out the window she was reminded of the scripture verse in Second Corinthians, *"We are troubled on every side, yet not distressed; we are perplexed, but not in despair."* She repeated the words aloud, as if trying to convince herself.

Lord, You are my rock, but I feel as though life has withered beneath me. Extend Your mercy to me. A tear ran down her cheek and she pressed her lips together trying to keep the rest from overflowing. Maybe selling to Henry Barrington and going back to New York City was the answer. He was right, she didn't belong here.

***

Ian lifted the broom in his hand and swept the accumulated dirt toward the back of the sanctuary. He'd enjoyed helping Thomas at the church, especially since he and Catherine had been generous enough to let him stay in their home when he made the choice to follow Christ. When he did, he had to leave his uncle's house. He could no longer swim in the sin he'd created for so long.

Disgust filled his gut when he thought about his former ways, all to please his uncle and shove bills in his own pocket, which usually ended up sliding across the bar at the saloon.

He had nothing to show for his behavior. Of course, many times Ian realized if he had kept the money, he'd have a tough time spending it. It was tainted with sin.

Threatening others, sometimes following through, just so his uncle could have more land, or women he fancied, defined his life. Not now. Not after Christ's mercy and grace saved him.

So many times he thought he wasn't good enough to be forgiven. How could God forgive him for his sins? They were so many.

"Who do you think you're kidding?" Barrington said.

Ian jerked his head up and gripped the broom handle. "What're you doin' in here?"

Barrington sauntered toward Ian. "What was that show yesterday?"

"I don't know what you're talking about."

"I know you," he said. His lip curled up. "I've known you all your life." He lifted his hand and pointed around the church. "Do these people know the real you?"

"They don't care about my past," he said, shifting uncomfortably. Only Pastor Thomas truly knew his past. The other parishioners had accepted him, or so he believed.

"You'll never win over that girl. She's too good for you." A crooked smile crept across his face. "If she knew anything about you, she'd run the other way."

He might be right, but that didn't mean he would go back to his sinnin' ways.

"Besides," Barrington continued, "she won't be around these parts too long."

"I know what you're gettin' at." Ian's voice grew stern, echoing through the church. "You'd better leave her alone." Anger boiled up inside of him and he took a deep breath to keep it down. He wasn't about to lose his temper over his uncle.

"I usually get what I want." Barrington smiled.

Ian couldn't contain his disgust. Anxiousness rose up inside of him. He wanted out of his presence.

"I'll always have a place for you," Barrington stretched out his hand.

Ian stared at it. He didn't flinch.

"You're like a son. You'll be thankful one day when I'm gone and all that I have will become yours… if you come with me now."

"I don't want anything that belongs to you." Ian couldn't think of one thing Barrington had that didn't come from his wrongdoing.

"Just remember who you are and where you came from," Barrington said. "You don't belong here." He looked around the church before he turned and walked out the door.

***

The Atchison air felt stifled as more people gathered around Francine and her husband Luke, lying on his back on the wooden sidewalk. She glued her eyes to his chest searching for any movement.

"Please God," she said through gritted teeth. She laid her hand on his chest, held her breath and waited for it to rise. Still nothing.

"I'm sorry Ma'am. But your husband is dead." The doctor placed his fingers over Luke's eyes and closed them.

She glared at the doctor, "That can't be. We talked just a moment ago. He said he wasn't feeling good, but he can't be dead." Her body shook as she sobbed over the devastating news.

"What happened Mama? What's wrong with Daddy?" Lizzie pulled at her mother's sleeve. She tugged again, this time harder. "Mama?"

Francine buried her face in Luke's chest. "It can't be. It can't be."

"Ma'am, you're gonna have to get a hold of yourself. If anything, for your daughter's sake." The doctor placed his hand on Francine's back.

Francine lifted her head and wiped her tears on her sleeve. She looked down at the face of her husband.

"Mama?" Lizzie screamed. "What's wrong with Daddy?"

Francine turned away from her husband and looked at her daughter. Tears streamed down Lizzie's twisted face. She wrapped her arms around the young girl, pulling her into her chest and running her hand through her blonde curls.

"Daddy went to be with Jesus," Francine said, trying to grasp the notion for herself.

"When's he comin' back?" She tilted her head up to look her mother in the face. Her eyes hot with redness.

"He's not... coming back." A sore lump slid down Francine's throat as she tried to swallow.

Francine looked back at the doctor through a cloud of tears.

He placed his hand on hers, "I'll get him to the undertaker. You may go by there in a while."

Francine nodded. The doctor and several men standing nearby helped lift Luke up and carry him away. She watched helplessly as her husband left her sight. It took all her might not to scream out his name. It had to be a dream. A sick, twisted dream. Francine hated the fact that it wasn't. A stifling, dense fog lowered around her.

***

Tess poured the last pan of boiling water into the oversized bathtub in the center of the room. Steam rose up and evaporated into the cooler air. She kept the fireplace burning in an attempt to keep some of the warmth in the room long enough to take a bath.

Tess continually glanced at the door. This time, she bolted it shut. To make it even more secure, she slid her trunk in front of it, hoping the weight of it would keep someone from trying to bust through the door. She wasn't about to take a chance on another intruder. Tess didn't like moving the trunk back and forth out of the way, but at least it would give her a little bit more sense of security.

Keeping a gun had never been an option before now, but after the intruders the other night she figured she didn't have a choice. She'd have to learn to protect herself. At least until Francine and Luke showed up. Then Tess would let Luke worry about how to protect them and the ranch.

Suddenly, the wood creaked outside on the front porch. Tess moved backward, tripping on the table and falling face first into the tub, splashing water on the floor around her. A scream erupted. She tried to sit still as the water waved back and forth against her body. Her muscles tightened and heat ran into her cheeks.

"Everything okay in there?"

Ian! "Yes, yes of course," she yelled loud enough to be heard through the door.

Tess lifted herself from the pit of the tub and stood up. Water poured off her dress and hair like a waterfall.

A towel. Tess glanced around the room searching for something to dry off her body. She couldn't believe the impropriety of the situation. She'd have to change her clothes. But how could she with Ian standing on the other side of the door?

"Tess?" Ian said again.

"Just a minute!" She yelled. "Can you go wait down by your horse, or something?"

Ian didn't respond. *He must think I'm crazy.*

"Uh… sure."

She waited to hear movement, but there was none. He was still right on the other side of the door.

"I'm fine," she hollered back. "Just go wait somewhere else."

She could hear his footsteps walking back down the front porch stairs.

Shivers ran up her spine. She had to change from the sopping-wet dress into a dry one. The first dress she lifted from the trunk was ripped. She dug through several until she found one that looked as though the intruders had not torn it.

Tess searched for a towel, but found nothing. She grabbed her mother's quilt and dried her body. She raced to put on her corset. Tess buttoned her dress in a fastidious manner and slipped her feet back into her shoes.

Tess leaned over and pushed the trunk out of the way of the door and opened it.

Ian stood down at the bottom of the stairs, petting his horse.

"Sorry. I was… I was just taking care of some things."

Ian's jaw fell open and his eyebrows rose. "I see that."

Tess felt the front of her dress to make sure she buttoned it correctly. She looked down at her shoes to find her dress tucked into her boots. She immediately pulled it out and straightened it.

"I didn't mean to interrupt. I—"

"It's fine. I mean, you're fine." *What is wrong with me? Why can't I talk?*

A smile grew wide across his face.

"What is it? Do I have something hanging off of me?" She truly hoped her corset was tied tightly enough.

"Your face. It's red. But your sopping-wet hair seems to distract from it." He laughed out loud as he walked back up the stairs.

Tess lifted the palms of her hands to the sides of her cheeks and felt the warmth in her face. She hadn't even thought to brush her hair after she dried it off. *I must look a freight.* She grabbed her long, brown hair and twirled it around, hoping to tie a knotted bun at the nape of her neck.

"What happened to your head?"

Without warning, Ian moved so close to Tess she could feel his warm breath on her face.

Tess blinked several times at his presence. The hair on her arms rose and tickled her skin. Her stomach fluttered and she bit her lip.

He reached up to touch her hair, but stopped himself, and pulled his hand back by his side.

She had forgotten all about the wound when he came to the door.

"Some men came—" She squeezed her eyes shut for a moment, remembering the glass shattering through the cabin, and opened them back up again. Looking at his face gave her an unreserved sense of peace. A days worth of stubble covered his cheeks and chin. His blue eyes dove into her, warming her insides.

"Why didn't you come tell me? You should've come and told me."

What could she say? She lowered her gaze to the ground and then lifted her eyes to meet his, still on her face. A feeling of comfort washed over her, even in the silence.

"You need to get the doc to look at it."

She shook her head. "I'm okay. Just shaken up." She said in a soft, gentle tone. "I don't believe the cut is too deep."

"I'll bet Barrington had something to do with this." He stomped his foot on the porch.

She agreed wholeheartedly, but kept her thoughts to herself. She couldn't let him know too much. What if he is still working for his uncle?

"You need someone protecting you."

Tess longed for security. "My brother-in-law, Luke, will arrive soon."

"You need someone now."

"I've already told you I can't afford someone." She thought for a moment. "Besides, it's inappropriate for a man to live out on the ranch with me. What would people think?"

"What if Barrington sends his men again? What then? You shouldn't be concerned about what others think. You might end up dead." Ian turned and looked north, toward Barrington's ranch.

The land was wide open, with only patches of trees. She couldn't see his house, but the fenceline her father erected was still in place, not far from her own cabin.

His voice softened. "I know your father would want someone to watch over you. If he knew what happened to you . . ."

"I just can't—"

"I'll get my things and bring them tonight."

Her voice rose to a high pitch. "You can't move here—"

"I'll stay in the lean-to."

"What will others say?" Her stomach wadded up in to a knot at the impropriety of the situation. But, she was surprised at the rush of excitement that coursed through her at the idea of someone—no, Ian—living so close. She'd have someone to protect her.

Her worst fears settled in just as fast. What if he's part of the plan to get her off the land? Was he forcing his way in, only to get her to move out? *That's it.* He wanted her out. Well, she would show him. Tess would stay right here. He wouldn't get her off this land by creating an improper situation. She'd let God judge the people who thought poorly of her.

He started to walk to the side of the porch, to look out at the mountains. It was the first time she noticed his limp. Her eyes focused on his struggle to move like a normal, whole man.

"Did they take anything?" He asked.

"Money," she said.

Ian shoved his hands into his pockets. The muscles on his forearms tensed and relaxed. "Barrington will do anything for this land."

"Why here? He has plenty of land." Tess cast her eyes on the vast prairie that stretched for miles, up to the base of the mountains.

"Your father has some precious land. You're covered up with a mighty stream of water that veers through the property. Barrington doesn't have much of a water source. His cattle will drink his water dry in a short matter of months. When there's not enough spring run-off, his cattle have nothing to drink. It keeps him from getting a larger herd.

"He wants the water," she repeated.

"Enough to kill for it."

Chapter Five

"We must have some rules. That is if you plan to stay here. Well, not here. Not in the house, but in the lean-to," Tess said. Her voice cracked and she took a sip of water. She wondered how long her nerves would distract her. She didn't like the kind of nervousness that seemed to creep up every time he came around.

"What kind o' rules you got in mind?" His lips shifted in to a crooked smile.

Tess held a coffee cup in front of him. "Sugar?"

"No. I'll take it black." He held his hand up in front of him.

"That's good, because there's not much here."

Ian put his lips against the cup and took a sip of his coffee.

"You living here without… supervision, could come across as, well, improper."

Ian laughed. "What kind o' supervision you talkin' about?"

Tess set her hands on her hips. She knew he teased her. Her grandfather might understand the situation, although he always demanded another person accompany a couple if unmarried. Her grandmother, on the other hand, would make her out to look as though she were a harlot if even talking alone with a man.

But her grandmother had never been faced with the possibility of losing her home. Tess wasn't about to go back to New York City and beg to live in her grandmother's house again. Not now.

"You must always stay outside," Tess said to Ian. "Unless I summon you inside. I'll bring your meals to you outside. We'll put one of the chairs out back for you to sit in while you dine. If someone were to show up, what would they think?"

"Fair enough."

"No peeking in the windows." She spit the words out quickly, as if they were unsuitable. She felt her cheeks flush the moment the words left her mouth. She would absolutely die if a man peeked in the windows, especially Ian.

"What else ya got in mind?"

"If you need me, you may stand outside and call my name, or gently rap on the door." Tess straightened her dress and stood up straight, as if she were a schoolmarm. "I don't believe it matters if you talk loudly. That is, as long as you are outside."

"That's good, 'cause I like to whoop and holler all day." It was obvious he was still teasing. She could tell as he pressed his lips together to keep his laughter from boiling over.

"I'm aware you are mocking me, Mr. Bidwell. But if you demand that you stay here, it will be with my rules."

"Any others?"

"I suppose that's all. For now." She tipped her head to the side and stared at Ian.

"Well, I have a few myself." He took another sip of coffee.

"You do?" Her eyebrows pressed together.

Ian nodded.

"Well, what could they be?" She couldn't imagine what kind of rules Ian might demand upon her.

"If you plan to stay here and learn how to work on a ranch, you gotta follow my lead, without questions. I can't stand a woman that asks too many questions or doesn't do what she's told."

"Is that so—"

"See there, you're already doing it." He pointed to her. A smile formed across his mouth.

She pulled her head back and crossed her arms. She could tell he was still trying hard not to laugh.

"I want you out of bed and dressed before the sun rises."

"I suppose I can follow those rules. They aren't so hard to abide by."

"You need to get rid of that dress and put on a pair of your Pa's pants—"

"I'll do no such thing!" How could he say that? He talked about her clothing as if he were familiar with her.

"You can't very well ride a horse with that get-up on." He pointed to her clothing.

41

"I can ride side-saddle."

His laughter finally made its way out. "You're gonna get awful tired of ridin' a horse sittin' side-saddle. All the gals out here ride astride. You're gonna be one of 'em."

"I can't wear my Pa's pants. He was larger than I."

"Get one of his belts out and cinch it tight. I'll knock a few extra holes in it, so you can keep yer britches up."

Tess' mouth dropped open.

He was having quite a time with this conversation. She just knew it. A man had never touched a garment she was going to wear. Especially not a man she barely knew.

"I just can't—"

"The way I see it, you don't have too many choices, Tess."

She hated to admit he was right. She didn't have a choice. If he didn't stay until Luke arrived she'd either get killed by Barrington's men or lose the ranch. A pair of men's pants wouldn't kill her. She just hoped no one saw her riding.

Ian started for the lean-to.

"Fine. I'll wear his pants. But you must call me Miss Porter."

Before he reached the lean-to, he turned around and faced her. A dangerous smile crept across his face. "Nah. I like Tess better." He smiled again so big she wondered if he planned to keep it there awhile.

Tess stomped her foot on the ground. "Oh, he's so ornery."

"I heard that." He yelled through the lean-to wall. He paused for a moment before adding, "Tess."

Tess crossed her arms and puckered her lips. She liked the way he said her name—even if it was a bit improper.

***

The wagon wiggled inside the ruts as Tess rode toward town. None of the papers proving Tess and Francine were to inherit her father's property were inside the house. Several times the thought crossed her mind that it was possible the men who ransacked her house stole them. That would explain Barrington sending in his men.

She hoped the bank would be able to provide a safe deposit box holding something of her father's that would prove their inheritance.

42

The rumble of the wheels softened as the path grew larger and more accommodating to the wagon, allowing her to hear the thunder of hooves in the background.

As she looked over her shoulder, two men stormed in her direction, and a frenzied storm of dust kicked up behind their horses. Her heart must've climbed into her throat and she eyed the road ahead of her wondering how long it would take before she got to town. In the distance, the rooftops were still small.

She flipped the reins, snapping them against her horse, forcing her to go faster. "C'mon, Lady." The horse picked up a faster rate, now in line with Tess' heartbeat.

She peered out of the corner of her eye at the men now staying several paces behind her. They rode along Barrington's fenceline. The men were far enough away that she couldn't get a good look at their faces. Were they the same men who ransacked her father's cabin? She didn't want to take a chance on getting close enough to find out.

As Lady picked up speed, the wagon lurched to the side, sliding out of the ruts. It moved back and forth, putting pressure on the wheels, creaking and moaning as it swayed in the dirt. The wagon wheel slammed against a rock, shoving it to the side. The bump thrust Tess forward. Her hands fumbled to catch herself, but she slid forward toward the back of the moving horse.

Her fingers wrapped around one of the front boards on the wagon and she pushed herself back up. She reached around and grabbed the seat, shoving a splinter into the supple skin in her palm. The movement allowed her to hoist herself back into the seat. She pressed her feet against the footboard, assuring an upright position.

The men rode alongside the fence, directly across from her. She looked over, this time trying to make out their faces. These men were lean, unlike one of the men from the cabin the other night.

Denver City loomed in the distance and Tess let the wagon maintain its speed, fearing another incident. As she looked again at the men, one slid his hand down his thigh and placed it on a shotgun, still hooked in his saddle.

Lord, make these men turn around. I don't want to die this way.

At that very moment, the men turned their horses and rode in the opposite direction.

Tess arrived on the outskirts of town. She exhaled a breath of fear that felt as though she'd been holding it since leaving the cabin.

How long would she have to live wondering if she would make it through another day?

"I need to talk to the sheriff," Tess said, closing the door to his office behind her.

"I'm the sheriff." He pointed to himself.

She glanced at his badge, shiny, without any scuff marks. His clothes were pressed and neatly tucked in.

"I just had some men follow me into town," she said, still trying to catch her breath.

"What do you mean? There are men ridin' 'round these parts all the time."

"I know when I'm being followed."

"You new in town?" One eyebrow rose up on his face. He set a cigarette on the tip of his lip and let it dangle from his mouth as he talked.

"Yes. Why does it matter?" Her heart hadn't decided it was ready to slow down to a normal pace yet. She took a deep breath, trying to convince herself to settle down.

"Lots of folks come out here thinking the West is a wild place full of violent men."

"I don't have any preconceived ideas about the West. I know when I'm being followed." Frustration wormed its way inside of Tess. She had a few words she wanted to say, but held her tongue.

"Lots of stories have been written 'bout people coming out west and getting killed by some gold-crazed lunatic."

"My fears haven't risen from a story I read. I know—"

"Miss," he said, interrupting her. Sarcasm fell out of his mouth with ease. "You seem like a right nice gal. Don't you have better things to do with your time than run around worrying that other men are followin' you?"

Tess gritted her teeth and groaned within. "You are the sheriff, aren't you?"

He nodded and got up from his desk. He walked across the room and stood by the window looking out. "Denver City has its moments of crime and trouble. But it ain't much."

"I know who's following me." Maybe getting more to the point was a measure she had to take.

"Now you know who it is?" He turned and faced her.

"It's some of Henry Barrington's men. I know it is."

He laughed. A snide look twisted the features of his face. "Henry Barrington?"

"Yes," Tess said, clearing her throat. Although she felt certain it was Barrington's men, his stare made her nervous, and she wanted to crawl under something.

"Why would he send men after you?"

"He wants my land." Tess took a deep breath again, hoping more confidence would come with it.

The smile disappeared from his face. He swallowed hard and didn't answer.

"He's trying to scare me off the land," she said, trying to diffuse the thick layer of tension in the room.

"You're Ed Porter's kid?"

She nodded. "Why?"

"No, no." He wasn't as quick to answer. "I didn't know he had a daughter."

"He has two," Tess made it clear she wasn't going to be alone.

"And the other girl, where is she?"

Tess frowned at his question. Why did he care about her sister and her whereabouts? "She and her family are on their way out west to live here with me."

"It ain't Henry Barrington. I assure you."

"I know it's him. He came to the house the other day, threatening me," she added, speaking quickly.

"Henry's a good man. He's an upstanding citizen in this community."

"He—"

"It had to be Indians. There's lots of them scaring folks 'round here. They want us out of Denver City."

"It wasn't Indians. The man was violent." Tess accentuated each word, trying to get her point across.

"They're still mad about the Sand Creek incident last year."

"Sand Creek?"

"They wouldn't go peacefully, so we wiped out some of their people, making a point."

Nausea overwhelmed Tess at the thought of a massacre. "It wasn't Indians."

"Henry Barrington wouldn't hurt a fly. I can't do anything for you Miss. Have a good day now." He walked to the door and opened it for Tess.

She stared at it for a moment, wanting to say something. But she knew he wasn't going to do anything to help her.

As she reached the sidewalk, she glanced down the street. How much crime went unnoticed under this sheriff's eye? She wasn't planning to live in fear. She'd live on the ranch, no matter who got in her way.

Sunlight reflected off the windows on the Bank of Denver City building and spilled onto the dusty ground. Red bricks covered the two-story structure. A sign in the window read "Gold Dust Bought & Sold."

Tess opened the door to the bank and walked into the foyer. Two men in black suits were standing at the counter waiting on the teller.

Standing in a bank lobby in a search for her father's will had not been on her list of things to do when she arrived in Denver City.

"Miss, can I help ya?" The teller said, standing behind the counter.

"I am looking for my father's things," she said, "Ed Porter. I am hoping he had a safe deposit box."

"It's a fine day for a walk." A crooked smile formed across this face.

"Pardon?" She crinkled her eyebrows together.

"Denver City is growing into a metropolis right before our eyes."

"Yes sir, but I just want to retrieve my father's items."

"This is a bank," he said, pushing his glasses up the bridge of his nose.

"I'm looking for my father's papers. Do you have safe deposit boxes or not?

"Excuse me for a moment," he said. He looked at her before his eyes shot down to the floor. He walked to a back room and disappeared.

46

Did he not understand her question? The bank either has the boxes or they don't. If not, she would go to the next bank and continue the search.

Another man, taller and dressed in a more crisply-ironed suit, appeared in the doorway. She had a sense that someone was talking to him, behind the wall, out of her line of vision. He stared for a moment, shook his head, and vanished again.

Tess looked around the bank. Two customers were wrapping up their business in the next line. They stuffed money into their inside coat pockets and walked out together.

The second teller walked to the back of the bank, leaving Tess alone in the cold lobby. She fiddled with her gloves for a moment and hoped the men would return soon.

The taller man returned and came to the counter. "What is your name?"

"Tess Porter."

"How are you related to Ed Porter?" They obviously knew something. Otherwise the questions would be avoided.

"He was my father," she said. "Is there a problem?"

"Your father did bank here."

So what was the problem? He didn't turn around and go toward the back of the bank to retrieve her father's papers. He stood behind the counter and just stared at her.

"Did my father leave anything here or not?"

He cleared his throat. "Someone else came to get the papers."

"Who?" He didn't have family here. Tess was the first to arrive. Francine wouldn't arrive for at least another week.

"A young man."

"What did he look like?" Why did she even ask? She didn't know a soul in town, with the exception of Henry Barrington, and he had to be at least fifty. Could it be Ian?

"Perhaps sixteen or seventeen."

That ruled out Ian. He was clearly in his twenties, maybe even thirty at most.

"Did he tell you who he was?"

"No, but he'd been in with your father. At least twice."

It didn't make sense. Who did her father bring into the bank with him?

47

"What kind of bank is this? You don't find out the name of people who gather very important documents and carry them off?" This indiscretion could cost her everything.

"I cannot help you."

"Do you know where this young man might have gone?" She lifted her hands in question.

"We don't know anything." His lips tightened.

They knew something. They were hiding it. She could almost be sure of it.

"When did he come in to get the papers?" Tess was growing weary of trying to get information from the man.

"Just after your father died."

"Thank you." Tess stormed from the bank. *Impossible.*

"Miss Porter! Miss Porter!"

A muffled voice sounded in the distance, accompanied by the sound of rapping against a glass window. She turned around to face the building behind her, and see who was trying to get her attention.

The stagecoach station keeper, who told her of her father's whereabouts the day she arrived, tapped again on the glass. "Miss Porter!"

He lifted his index finger in the air, and then disappeared out of sight. A few seconds later, he opened the door to the home station and walked out on the sidewalk. "I'm so glad I found you."

"What is it?"

"The telegram office has been looking for you. Your father has a telegram."

"My father?" Her mind raced with possibilities.

He nodded and pointed down the street. "The office is right around the corner."

What could it be? Her grandmother was all too happy to get rid of her and sever ties with her father. She wouldn't dare spend money on sending him a telegram.

The wooden-slat-covered telegraph office sat tucked in between two brick buildings. Tess opened the door and walked in. A man sat behind the counter, tapping away at the telegraph. He stuck one finger in the air as he finished typing out a message.

When he completed his task, he pushed his chair away from his desk, stood up, and walked to the counter. "Can I help you?"

"I'm looking for a telegram for my father, Ed Porter."

48

"Ah, yes. The station keeper said you were here in town. Sorry 'bout your Pa. Didn't know him, but it's never easy to lose somebody you love," the man said. "I've got the telegram right here." He shuffled through a few papers and held it out in front of her.

"Thank you," she said, taking it from his hand. Tess walked over to the bench against the wall and sat down to read it.

Her father's name was written across the top, along with the date and time.

"We are in Atchison. Stop. Luke died. Stop. Will arrive in Denver City in two days. Stop. Francine. Stop."

A flood of emotions filled Tess. She felt a pinch in her nose as she tried to keep the tears from falling.

Francine's husband dead? Tess read the telegram again. Each word sharpened the pain. How? When? Her heart broke for her sister. Oh what she would give to be by her side to lend her comfort.

Now that Luke was gone, who would run the ranch? Her entire life crashed down around her. She couldn't expect Ian to help her now that Luke was gone. She still didn't know if he worked for Barrington. She had to find the man who stole her father's papers.

***

Isaiah Porter sat down under one of the oak trees on Henry Barrington's property. One of Barrington's other hands, a man he could barely tolerate, rode up and slid down off his saddle.

"Gimmie one-a them cigarette's you been totin' 'round," Joe said.

He pulled out a cigarette paper, placed a wad of tobacco inside and rolled it up, twisting the ends. He handed it to Joe before repeating the process with his own cigarette. He struck a match and lit the end. The paper at the end turned bright orange.

He puffed on the end for a moment and leaned back against the oak tree shading him.

"Looks like somebody done moved into your Pa's old cabin. Guess you weren't fast 'nough to get there."

"I'll get it. It's my sister." He patted his jacket and felt the papers he had placed inside his pocket. He'd been to the bank just after his father died. Knowing Tess and Francine were on their way, he wasn't about to take a chance on losing the homestead. If he got the papers and waited long enough, staying out of sight, maybe Tess

49

and Francine would leave town. He could sell the property to Barrington and the two women wouldn't even know they had a brother. He could get outta town and quit working for a man he could hardly stand.

"Well, shoot. I didn't know ya had sisters." Joe slapped his leg with his free hand. He lifted his cigarette and took another drag.

"They don't know it, either. My Pa never told 'em 'bout me."

His father's face appeared in his thoughts. His anger still seethed that his father didn't care enough about him to even tell his sisters that he existed.

"Best to stay that way, too. If ya know what I mean," Isaiah added.

"I won't be runnin' over and tellin' yer sisters 'bout nothin'. As long as Barrington doesn't send me that-a-way." He laughed.

He figured his sisters wouldn't want anything to do with him, if they knew about him. But a part of him feared for their lives. He didn't like ransacking his father's cabin. Barrington said he'd make it worth his while, but he'd yet to see anything stem from that promise.

When they broke into the cabin, Isaiah felt a connection he couldn't explain. He'd never seen her before in his life. But something inside of him wanted to protect her from harm.

When Marcus hit her upside the head with his gun, it took all he had to control his anger. He wanted to pummel the man, but they had to leave. Isaiah came back later that night, snuck back in, and loosened the ropes around her wrists. He had to make sure she was still breathing. Relief flooded through him when he discovered she was okay.

He'd hang on to the papers before selling. Hopefully Tess and Francine would realize how hard ranching life is and want to move on, especially without their Pa.

Isaiah would never tell Francine and Tess about the papers. He couldn't trust them. After all, they were from the same father. He was untrustworthy himself. How does he know they won't take the papers, sell the ranch, and skip town? He couldn't stand to live another day penniless.

His father left his mother penniless all those years. He wanted that land. It was rightfully his. His father owed him the land, and would make darn sure his sisters would never get it.

Chapter Six

Tess cradled the telegram in her hand as she walked outside. Her heart broke for Francine. Luke was gone. Now, how would her sister take the news of their father's death? *What grief she must feel.*

Helplessness settled on Tess. There was nothing she could do but pray for Francine and her daughter Lizzie. She hoped the remainder of their trip west would be an easy one, without her husband. Tess knew all-too-well the dangers lurking on the wagon trails.

The road was fraught with Indians, indecent men, and plenty of opportunities for a woman to be compromised. Tess hoped and prayed for Francine and Lizzie's safety.

Tess crossed the street and stepped up on the sidewalk. She paid no mind to the bustle around her. She felt it only right to thank the preacher and his wife for their overflowing generosity on the day she arrived. Her heart was still so heavy, but she knew God provided them to take her to her father's cabin safely.

As Tess rounded the corner, she spotted Ian standing in front of the grocers. His back was leaned up against one of the wooden poles on the outside of the building. Henry Barrington stood across from him, just mere steps away.

Her heart raced as she thought about her feelings the previous night when Ian informed her he would be staying. She wanted him to stay and protect her. A weight had been lifted from her shoulders. The fear she held onto for the short time since she arrived was now dwindling. But she had to continually remind herself that he used to work for his uncle, or was this an indication that he still did? She couldn't let her feelings get the better of her and fall for a man who might be trying to steal the very land she was trying to protect.

51

Maybe he is warning his uncle. Could it be? Would he protect a woman he just met, from his family? She couldn't take any chances. Tess determined she'd stay on the alert at all times.

Men killed each other in the West over gold, or even a dollar. Could he be trusted? Was he truly friends with her father, or just wheedling his way into his heart and now hers, for the sake of stealing their land?

I must contain my heart. She couldn't take a chance on losing everything because she had fleeting feelings for a man who might be connected to shady dealings.

Tess was determined she wouldn't lose the land. She wasn't about to let the two men intimidate her.

She hurried toward the grocer's. As she neared, Ian stepped away from the pole. Barrington spotted her coming toward him and kept his eyes focused on her.

"Mr. Barrington," she said, tipping her head forward in a curtsey.

"Miss Porter." The two exchanged pleasantries and Ian stood between them, silent.

If Ian were truly helping his uncle, she'd make it as uncomfortable as possible for the man.

"I didn't realize you were in town," she said to Ian.

"Had to tend to a few things."

"Quite a fine thing he's doing for you," Barrington interjected.

"Pardon?"

"Taking care of a woman who just lost her father. That's a large task for someone to take on."

She opened her mouth to speak, but Ian slid his hand under her arm and pulled her around the corner. What was he doing? *How dare he pull me away.*

He dragged her several feet and pushed her up against the side of the grocers. Before speaking, he looked back in the direction they came from.

"I don't believe you should pull me away while I am having a conversation with someone."

"You don't need to be doin' any conversing with that man. I keep tellin' ya that he's trouble." The inflection in his voice rose higher. "You need to understand how dangerous that man is. I don't

52

want you anywhere near him." His eyes narrowed and he leaned in close.

"I don't like the man any more than you do, but I am not going to cower away from him." She was somewhat stunned by his demands. Tess pressed her back against the wall and tried to stand up straight to appear taller, but he still had several inches on her.

Was this part of the plan between him and his uncle? She tried to read his face. He truly looked like he wanted nothing to do with his uncle, but would she ever be sure he was only trying to protect her?

"I know what he's capable of," Ian said, barely moving his lips. "Stay away."

Tess stared into his eyes, but didn't answer. Time would tell.

"Did you hear me?"

"Of course I heard you. How could I not? You're right here." She crinkled up her face to match her emotions.

"Next time, please answer me. You sure do know how to rile a man."

"Well, you need a few lessons on how to treat a lady," she quipped.

Ian nudged Tess against the wall again. His words came out one by one, and she could sense his frustration with her. "I know how to treat a lady."

As Ian leaned in closer, he placed his hand against the building behind her. Tess blinked several times. His eyes locked onto hers. Not speaking a word, he just stared.

Tess felt as though her feet were weighted down, and she didn't move. She felt like a little girl on the school playground as her heart pattered against her chest.

Anger burned in his eyes, but not the kind of anger that would evoke a fight. Perhaps his fear for her life spoke through the deafening silence.

His lips parted and he sighed his frustration with her.

At once, he pulled back and slid his hand underneath the delicate part of her arm with gentility and walked her back to the wagon.

No words were spoken.

***

"My apologies Ma'am," the doctor said, standing just inside the doorway of the small infirmary.

"Your apologies won't get my money back," Francine said. Her emotions fluctuated between anger and grief. She didn't know if a cry or a scream would burst forth when she opened her mouth. "How did this happen?"

The doctor shook his head back and forth. "We brought your husband to the undertaker and two of the men promised to sit with the body until you arrived—"

"There were no men at the undertaker when I got there."

"They must've taken the money from your husband's pocket when I left." He lifted his hand to his brow and scratched it.

"To steal money from a... a dead man." Francine couldn't believe thieves would stoop to such a level.

"We must find them," Francine said, pleading.

"I didn't... I didn't know the men. I've never seen them before today."

None of this would've happened if not for the death of her husband. Was God to take everything precious from her life? Francine held Lizzie's delicate hand in her own, and squeezed a little tighter.

"The stagecoach driver brought some of our luggage to the hotel. Now the clerk will not allow me into the room unless I pay. He said he lost customers saving the room for us. What are we to do?"

"I wish I could help you," he said. "I myself just arrived in town and cannot afford a place of my own. I am fortunate for the generosity of others that I may stay in their home. Small as it is."

Francine could no longer hold in the tears. Like a spring, they could not be stopped. She rested her face in the palms of her hands, no longer knowing what to do.

"Please don't cry," the doctor whispered. "I don't really know... what to say." He pulled a handkerchief from his pocket and dangled it in front of her.

Francine grabbed it from his hand and wiped her tears, which were still flowing.

"Look," the doctor paused. "I don't have any money to give you. I barely have enough for myself. I shouldn't do this, but I will let you and your daughter stay here tonight."

Francine lifted her head. "Oh, thank you. Thank you."

"You must remain hidden. Do not let others see you. I'm new and I don't believe the townsfolk would allow me to board anyone—especially strangers."

"We will, we will." Francine took a deep breath.

"I can't bring myself to turn a woman and her child out on the street."

"Thank you, sir," Francine repeated several times. *Thank you, Lord.*

"As for your luggage, maybe the innkeeper will have pity on you."

Although their stomachs were empty, Francine was grateful they would not have to endure both starvation and cold. At least the two could huddle together and lie on one of the infirmary beds for a decent night of sleep. It had been quite a while since Francine could remember having any privacy since taking to the trail. One night would be a blessing.

***

"I'm hungry, Mama," Lizzie said through a yawn while resting on the infirmary bed.

Francine pulled the curtain to the side and looked again out the front window, trying not to be seen. She glanced across the street, waiting until the restaurant closed. She didn't want to dig food from their trash, but she knew it might be a long time before the two could eat again.

"We'll get something soon. I promise." Francine walked back to the bed and rubbed her daughter's back, hoping she could keep her happy just a little longer.

Francine had never stolen a thing in her life. She didn't want to start now, but she couldn't see making her daughter go hungry because the clerk wouldn't let her get to her luggage. She knew a few dollars were stashed down in the trunk. Enough to get a decent meal or two before the stagecoach took off. Francine hoped the clerk wouldn't rifle through her things and find the money. Luke had her stitch money underneath the material lining. No one would guess where the money was hidden. She prayed.

The light in the café dimmed and Francine walked around to the backside. The air felt crisp and she removed her shawl and placed it around Lizzie's shoulders.

55

"What're we doin' here, Mama?" Lizzie's blue eyes lit up, even in the darkness.

"We need somethin' to nourish our bodies. We don't have any money and this will get us by." Francine leaned in the trash and pulled out scraps of food left in the bin.

"It's not very good," Lizzie said, as her face twisted into a strange shape.

"No, but it will give us something to fill our tummies until tomorrow." She was grateful the baby was still inside of her. It could continue to nourish off of her, even if she missed a meal or two.

Francine was glad her husband had paid the ticket all the way through to Denver City. At least she wouldn't have to worry about getting to her father's place.

***

Tess awoke to a loud crack outside her cabin. A fire raced through her and she sat up in the bed, listening for the source of the noise. The sun had not even started over the horizon.

She turned the knob on her lamp, illuminating the room with a warm glow.

Maybe Ian arose before the sun. Tess knew fear would've gripped her if he weren't outside in the lean-to. She flipped her legs over the side of the bed and stood up. Her robe hung on a nail, sticking out of the wall near the door. As she lifted it up and slid her arms into the sleeves, the horse whinnied. Tess walked to the window to look out.

Tess dropped to the floor and her heart jumped into her throat. Two Indians rifled around on the front porch. Where was Ian? She couldn't scream or they would hear her and come rushing in. Would they kill her? She looked over at the lamp and wanted to kick herself for turning up the light. They had to know she was inside.

She squeezed her eyes shut and hoped she didn't make too much noise. Would they think no one was home and move on? She'd heard reports the local Indians had raided some of the ranches, looting and killing homesteaders.

She put her hands on her legs to keep them from shaking. Would she be next? A hush fell across the room. Were they gone?

She lifted herself up to look out the window, not spotting either man. Without a window in the back of the house, Tess had no idea if the men were still outside.

56

As Tess took a step back, she bumped into the table, scooting it across the floor. The scraping noise echoed through the house.

The door on the barn slammed shut, sending a chill straight through Tess. Where was Ian? At this point, she didn't care what the men took as long as they left her and the horse alone.

She sat down on the floor and pulled her legs toward her chest, holding them tightly against herself.

The men must've pulled on the well rope. The familiar squeak penetrated through her and she lifted her fingers to cover her ears. She could only guess what they were doing. The bucket must've been dropped, banging against the sides of the well all the way down to the bottom.

The interspersed moments of silence tortured her. She waited, hoping the men would leave.

Chapter Seven

Ian rode along the fenceline searching for open spots where cattle could escape. At least he knew the enemy well enough to know his habits. He would stay one step ahead of Barrington's plans.

Ian's mother flashed through his mind. In the few days he knew Tess, she had reminded him more than once of his Ma. Not only did her light brown hair share the similar color, but her quiet, reserved way of talking made him nervous. Not the kind of nervous that scared him, but the kind of nervous that made his heart ache for home. Home that left with his childhood innocence.

Hooves, pounding in the distance, alerted him to an oncomer. Ian knew the movement of the horse, the way it ran. One of Barrington's stock. He lifted his gun from the holster making sure he had plenty of bullets, and slid it back in.

As the rider neared, he took his hand off his revolver. Ed's son. He knew he'd not try anything stupid with Ian. He could take the boy down faster than he could get off his horse.

The young teenage boy rode up and stopped next to Ian. He sat up straight on his saddle as if trying to intimidate Ian.

"Isaiah, what happened to your nose?" It looked as though someone had hit him with more than a fist.

The boy lifted his hand and gingerly touched the bruise on his face. "What're you doin' out this way?"

"Looks to me like someone got a hold o' you," Ian said. "Your nose broken?"

"This ain't your property," Isaiah said. He tugged at the top of his hat, pulling it down on his forehead.

"Ain't yours either." Ian thought he'd stop Isaiah in his tracks, making things clear. "Your sister is here. Or do you know that already?"

"You can always come back to Barrington's ranch, ya know. Things ran a lot smoother with you 'round." Isaiah paused for a moment. "At least you had a code in your dealings."

Ian knew what he meant. "Easy, Slater." His horse moved beneath him, like he knew what it was about, too. He made his choice to follow God. He'd been tempted plenty of times to go back, he hated livin' off the preacher. Felt like he was a beggar. But he couldn't go back to Barrington's. He couldn't live such a violent life.

"Why don't you leave?" Ian asked.

"I can't leave. I ain't got nothin' to go to."

"You've got Tess and Francine."

"They don't even know I exist. Pa never told them girls a thing about me. Just proves how little he cared."

"He did care. He wanted to tell her and Francine when the time was right," Ian said. "It just never came."

Ian wanted to tell Tess, but he couldn't. Ed asked for his confidence in the matter and he swore he'd never tell. Now with him gone, it was up to Isaiah to let his sisters know he was their brother.

"You treat them right, or you'll have me to deal with," Ian said. "Don't you go and do somethin' stupid for Barrington. You'll regret it."

"I don't regret nothin'. Not even this." He pointed at his nose. "Earned it fair."

"Gettin' your head knocked around to prove you're a man ain't fair. It's senseless."

The boy needed to get away from Barrington. He would turn Isaiah's life inside out. Barrington would let the kid take the heat and go to jail for him.

"Don't forget. Barrington would be happy to have you back runnin' things," Isaiah said.

Ian shook his head, pulled on the reins, and rode away. He just had to remind himself of the regret he'd feel if he ever went back to that man. When he found Christ, not all his desires flittered away. He thought they would, considering Ed stopped drinkin' the minute he asked Jesus into his heart. He struggled at times, but knew God promised him each day would be a little easier. He just had to remind himself of that fact.

Ian loathed Barrington, but he still reacted the same way he used to—with violence. His temper erupted too fast. Praying for a release from it became his first priority.

***

The cabin door creaked open. Tess swallowed hard. One of the Indian men moved through the door with ease, eyeing the room. Tess stayed on the floor with her legs pulled to her chest.

Feverishly, she prayed he wouldn't notice her on the floor.

"Woman!" The man stopped the moment he saw her, turned back to the door, and shouted at the other.

The other man burst through the door. They both stared at Tess sitting on the floor. Her heart raced faster than thundering hooves.

"Why you here?"

"I," Tess' voice cracked as the words eked out. "I live here." *Where is Ian?*

To her surprise, one of the men wore a white, long-sleeved suit shirt. His pants were like nothing she'd ever seen before—a dark leather material of some sort. His black, shiny hair reached his midsection, flowing freely. He had a ring that looked like a shade of copper on his right hand.

The other man wore a similar shirt with a black vest. Their faces were a darkened brown, evidence of so much time in the sun.

Tess remembered that she still had on her pink nightgown and robe. But, somehow, being dressed inappropriately at the moment didn't seem to matter right now.

"Are you hungry?" Tess asked the men, hoping it would show a sign of friendship.

"Hungry?" One of the men repeated.

Tess rose to her feet. Her knees shook as she walked toward the stove, forcing her to move closer to the men. As she neared them, her nose twitched from the scent of a dark, musky smell. Tobacco, she guessed.

One of the men chattered to the other in their language. The swallows and clicks in their voice were unfamiliar, yet she marveled at the sound.

Their voices grew louder and sterner. Not wanting to interfere, she just watched. Were they fighting? Their hands joined the conversation, swinging back and forth. One of the men slammed

60

his hand down on the table, not noticing Tess jump at the sound, which felt as though it reverberated through her entire body.

The older-looking man swung his hand in a straight-across motion and the conversation ended. Tess took several deep breaths, hoping it wasn't a fight about her or her home. She simply wanted them to leave. But how?

She placed her hand on the oven, opening the door wide.

"No!" One man yelled.

Tess jumped, hitting her hand on the top of the stove.

"No weapons."

She shook her head back and forth. "No, no weapons. Food."

The Indian moved closer to Tess and bent over to look in the oven. Her breathing intensified. His breath reeked of smoke, but she couldn't stop staring at him.

"Get food." He pointed toward the oven and allowed Tess to pull out the sheet of left-over biscuits from the night before.

The plate shook as she held the biscuits out in front of the men. She tightened her grip, trying to hold the plate still, but her nerves would not allow it. "Take one. Please."

Each man reached over and grabbed a biscuit and crammed it into his mouth. "Good." One of the men smiled and reached for another one, but paused before he took it.

Tess held the plate up higher, letting him know the freedom she was allowing for him to take it.

This time, after he grabbed the food, he ate it more slowly. Tess set the plate on the table and backed up slowly, hitting the wall.

The larger man nodded his head as if approving Tess' offering. He stared at Tess for a moment while chewing.

The moments before the men left without word, Tess stayed against the wall for what felt like an eternity. When she sighed, it felt as though death escaped her.

She placed her hands on her still-wobbling legs before struggling to get over to the door. Once she reached it, she opened it and watched the two men ride off, away from the cabin. What she would give to crawl back in the bed and wish away the fear that consumed her. How could she ever live in such a wild place, fearing each day for her life?

***

61

"What happened?" Ian asked Tess. He'd only been gone a short while. He thought for sure going before daybreak would not pose a safety problem.

When she didn't answer, his heart began to pound against his chest. At least he could see she was physically without harm. He flung his leg over the saddle on his horse and dismounted. He dropped to the ground and half-heartedly threw the reins across the railing, that stretched the length of the cabin.

She stood at the top of the stairs on the front porch and cupped her hands over her mouth. Tears streamed down her face.

Tess barreled down the stairs and into his arms, pushing him back. She wrapped her arms around his neck. Her tears felt wet against his face. Ian drew his arms around her waist and embraced her sobbing body.

"Are you hurt?" He struggled to pull her away, to see if she'd been hurt, but her grip stayed tight. Resigning to her was not going to be a problem for Ian.

Her head moved back and forth against him.

"Was it Barrington?" The anger welled up inside.

Her scratchy voice cracked, "No. Indians."

His heart started to pump faster. He knew most were harmless, but after the Sand Creek Massacre last year, they were rightfully angry. They'd been known to go up and down the frontier raiding houses and sometimes killing innocent women and children.

On several occasions he talked with some of the Arapaho men. They were harmless, loving people. Until last year, when their families and village were destroyed by the White man.

That was it. He wouldn't leave her side again. For the first time in his life, he didn't have to conjure up the grief he would feel if Tess were no longer in his life. How could he go on?

"Did they hurt you?" Ian knew Tess' fear, but he wanted to hold on to her, and comfort her. She ran to him for comfort, and he would provide it. At the thought, he tightened his grip around her waist.

She pulled away, out of his grasp, and looked down at the ground. He couldn't see all of her face, just enough to know she was pained by the situation.

He placed his finger under her chin and lifted it up. Tess' face was inches from his. Ian drew in a deep breath as their eyes met. Every fiber of his being wanted to embrace her again.

Tears continued to stream down her cheeks. Ian reached up and wiped one away. He kept his palm against her warm face. Her lips moved into an understanding smile.

Would he ever win her over? He couldn't imagine a day when he would deserve a woman like her. Tess lifted her hand and rested it in the fold of his arm. Her tears stopped and they moved closer.

As he moved his face closer to hers, she pulled his arm down and stepped away. That's it, he'd crossed the line. He chided himself for trying to kiss her. Who was he kidding? He didn't deserve her.

"Tess?" Her refusal to look at him drew worry, and she stared in the distance, refusing to turn her head.

She squinted her eyes. "Look, someone's coming."

Ian turned around to see a wagon heading their way. He pulled his rifle from his saddle and tipped the top of it across his shoulder.

A lone man rode in the wagon. As he neared, Ian could see his attire didn't match that of a man familiar with the territory.

He looked over at Tess, wishing he could read her unmoving features. Did she know the person?

The wagon came to a halt. The man at the reins looked to be around forty-five, perhaps fifty.

"Who you lookin' for?" Ian asked. The man said nothing, only climbed down from the wagon and walked toward Tess.

"I believe I have found whom . . ." the man paused and looked at Ian, "I am looking for."

Ian walked closer to Tess. She was his charge until her brother-in-law arrived. He swore to protect her.

"What are you doing here?" Tess asked, not moving.

"I see your arrangements aren't quite what you were offered in New York City." His eyes traveled the length of the cabin, and he turned around to view the property. "Although I must say you have quite a view of the mountains."

She nodded, still remaining quiet.

"Have you been crying?" He asked. "Is this man hurting you?" He turned and a scowl formed on his face.

"No. No, he would never hurt me." Tess reached out her hand, pointing to Ian. "He's been watching over me the past few days. My father… he's gone. He died."

"That explains the tears." He walked closer to Tess and wrapped his arms around her.

Ian didn't like the familiar way he touched her. Although Tess remained stiff as he held her.

Ian interrupted their embrace. "You her brother-in-law?" Ian asked.

"I'm sorry," Tess said. "How rude of—"

"Franklin Shepherd. Her fiancé," he said, interrupting Tess. He kept one arm wrapped around her shoulders and reached out his other hand to shake Ian's.

Ian looked at Tess. He swallowed hard. "You're engaged?"

Chapter Eight

Ian wasn't prepared for the rush of jealousy that flooded through his veins. *Engaged?* Why didn't Tess tell him?

"I had no idea you were to be married to another man," Ian said, knowing he almost kissed her moments ago. He knew the Lord would want him to apologize for his behavior, but he feared saying too much in front of Franklin.

"I never explained . . ." Tess looked at Ian and back at Franklin.

How could Ian possibly be upset? He'd barely shared an intimate moment with her. But he wanted to pry Franklin away from her and have him leave the property at once. He knew better. It wasn't his place.

"So, you came all the way from New York City to fetch Tess?"

Ian didn't take his eyes off her. He wanted to see her reaction to his question. Why did she come west if she was engaged? He could plainly see she was hiding something.

"Yes, sir," Franklin said. "I plan to wed her and take her back to the city where she can live in a proper, beautiful home. A home she deserves." Franklin looked at the cabin and winced. "Nothing like this."

Tess kept her eyes on the man. "Franklin, I don't—"

"Shh," he said, placing his finger over her lips.

She allowed him to keep his finger on her mouth for a moment before pulling her head back.

"No need to fuss over it. You don't belong here." Franklin pointed again to the cabin. "This is no place for a woman."

"But, it's different—"

"Darling, I must insist. I can't bear to see you stay here. It's terribly worse than I imagined." He leaned forward and kissed her on the forehead.

Tess smiled at his touch, but there was reservation in her look. Was it a smile of relief or dread?

Franklin seemed to be a gentleman with good manners, and a calm disposition. He just cared about Tess. Why did Ian want to drag her away and keep her far from him? He had no money, no home, and nothing at all to offer her. Franklin's clothing looked as though it was bought at one of the fanciest stores around. And he traveled all the way to Colorado Territory to take a woman home, to boot. It was obvious money was no issue.

What he would give to shake Tess and tell her to speak up, and let him know she wanted to stay. But, maybe she didn't. Maybe now that her father was gone, she wanted to go home.

"Oh, my, I almost forgot to tell you. I have a traveling companion." A smile widened across his face.

"A companion?" Tess crinkled her forehead.

"It's a surprise," Franklin said.

"Oh, I'm sure I will love to meet this surprise," she said, cringing on the inside, hoping she would not be alarmed.

"I needed a riding companion, and they wanted to make sure our plans went smoothly."

Tess truly hoped it wasn't his daughter, Missy. The young girl could make the most satisfied person angry with one smug look. She was hoping to perhaps be surprised by one of his sons, if she must.

Even the thought of her grandmother arriving with Franklin made her stomach knot. But, Tess knew better than to believe that her grandmother would travel to such a heathen place, or so she would say. The woman wouldn't be caught dead traveling by stagecoach.

"I'm meant to stay in the city, with the cultured people," her grandmother would say, when her grandfather suggested outings to the country. Her condescending behavior made it easier to leave New York City. Tess was quite tired of the cultured people.

"You will be delighted," he said putting his arm on Tess again.

Ian wanted to smack it off.

"Where's this surprise?" Tess questioned. If only Franklin would tell her, so she might be able to brace herself before the traveling companion was revealed.

"In town, resting. I told them they didn't need to come all the way out to the ranch. I hope you'll be able to contain your excitement when you see them."

"Me, too," Tess said, blinking slowly.

* * *

Tess tried to get ahold of her racing thoughts. The weight of Franklin's affections weighed heavily on her. Her insides were like a tumultuous tornado, stirring everything up.

Her emotions still ran high after meeting with the Indian men. It was beginning to be unclear if her heart was still pounding from the fear of the encounter, or because Franklin had shown up unannounced.

She tried to have a Christian attitude about Franklin's daughter, Missy, but she couldn't stand the young lady. Tess had known her most of her life and Missy had never once said a nice word to her. The last thing she wanted to do was become her stepmother.

Missy spent most of her time in New York City trying to sabotage the relationship between her father and Tess. At the time, Tess agonized over how to handle her soon-to-be stepdaughter. But when she called off the relationship, she was relieved she wouldn't have to bear the weight of that responsibility. Sure, God called her to be loving and kind to all, but she wondered on occasion if Missy was the exception.

She knew one thing for sure, she was thrilled her grandmother didn't come west. That might have been the end for Tess. It pained her to think that she never wanted to lay eyes on the woman again, but she didn't. Of course her grandmother wanted to get rid of her. She couldn't stand Tess.

Oh, how she missed her grandfather. He always knew how to deal with the crotchety old woman.

Tess looked at Ian. His face seemed distressed. Was he jealous of Franklin? Perhaps he feels freed from his offer to take care of her until Luke arrived. She hadn't even had the chance to tell him that Luke died and wouldn't be coming. Confusion wrapped tighter

67

around her, and her heart sank at the idea that he might leave the ranch.

She would tell him, in due time.

As she watched Ian, she focused on his face. Moments earlier, when he held her in his arms, she wanted desperately to feel his kiss. Was it part of God's plan to bring Franklin back into her life, keeping her from Ian? For once, she felt as though she could differentiate between loyalty and love. And what she was starting to feel for Ian wasn't loyalty.

"You look deep in thought, Darling," Franklin said, pulling Tess out of her thoughts.

Tess couldn't help but appreciate him. He'd done so much for her and her grandmother since her grandfather's death. But she didn't like the idea that he rushed back into her life and now called her darling. It was like he was laying claim to her, in front of Ian. *Is this how men think?*

"Just surprised," she said, forcing a smile. "I never expected to see you here."

Franklin walked up in front of her again and placed his hands on her shoulders. He looked down at her and said, "I have to admit, my heart was torn in two the morning of our wedding."

Tess wanted to look away, but he deserved more. She nodded. Her feelings went out to him. Even without love, it was hard enough for her to walk away from him. He was a good man. But that was it. She didn't love him.

"After you left, it didn't take long for me to decide I would come west, swoop you up into my arms, and take you home."

"I wanted a chance to know my father. But . . ." Tess looked down.

"I am so sorry about your loss. I know what your father meant to you, and how much you wanted this. But, now that he is gone, I want you to come home with me and be my wife."

"Francine is coming. I must stay for her. I have to make this work out here."

Franklin lifted her chin. He stared into her eyes, "I know that you will come to love me. I'm older, I know that, but I can take care of you. You will want for nothing."

She peered at Ian out of the corner of her eye, still standing nearby, and back at Franklin. Her heart ached for Ian. But, she couldn't fully trust him. How would she know he wasn't after her land? Could she walk away from all of this?

"I've some business to attend to in town," Franklin said. "I will send a carriage for you later. I would like to share a meal with you tonight. Then I can reveal the mystery guest." A smile widened across his face.

Tess just hoped she could withstand another surprise. This one brought her world into an upheaval.

***

The carriage arrived on time, just as Franklin said. She stepped out on the front porch as the driver climbed down from his station.

"You look mighty fine tonight," Ian said, coming around the corner and startling her.

"Oh, I didn't realize you were outside," Tess said, tugging at the end of her white gloves.

"Thought I might ride into town with you. Make sure you get there without a hitch."

"I am sure I won't need an escort."

"That actually wasn't an option. I'll be coming with you. I'm sure ol' Franklin won't mind me riding with you. After the Indians passin' through this mornin', you might need a little extra lookin' after. When you get into town, I'll see you to Franklin's and go visit Thomas and Catherine for a spell."

Tess nodded. She would appreciate the escort. "I'm sure they would love to see you."

Ian waved the driver back up to the top of the carriage and extended his hand for Tess. She slid her gloved hand into his and climbed inside. Ian followed and sat down across from her.

Ian tapped on the side of the carriage and it lurched forward, tilting back and forth.

"About earlier today," Tess said. "I should've explained—"

"No need to go explainin'. I've got it pretty well figured out."

"I want to," Tess said. "My grandfather died and left me alone with my grandmother. She wanted me out of her house. She's—she's always had a dislike for me. Franklin seemed to be the only way out... at the time." Tess looked down at the ground.

"Maybe she was angry your grandfather had passed."

69

"No, she's treated me with contempt all of my life. I've never understood it." She pinched her lips together. "When Franklin offered his hand in marriage, she saw it as a way to get rid of me. And fast."

"Did you know him very well?"

"I've known him all my life. He was a parishioner in my grandfather's congregation. He's a good man. Honest, upstanding. He's a loving man. He would make a fine, loyal husband."

"If it's such a fine match, why did you leave and come west?"

He crossed his arms, and if she wasn't mistaken, looked quite interested in her answer.

No one had asked her that question. She realized at that moment, she'd never said those words aloud to anyone. "I received the letter from my father the morning of the ceremony. I decided then I would come west and have a meaningful relationship with him. But, when I told Franklin of my plans, I expected to feel some heartbreak."

"And?" Ian asked.

She creased her eyebrows. "I felt relief. I've harbored the secret in my heart all this time. I want a man to love me with passion, not loyalty. I want to love a man because he stirs my soul."

"Maybe one day—"

"Oh, my. I've said too much. I apologize. A woman shouldn't be speaking in such ways." Tess felt a warmth travel through her body. She'd never felt it around anyone but Ian. She knew better than to tell a man of her innermost thoughts, especially a man she barely knew.

"Shouldn't you tell what's on your heart, rather than tell people what you think they should hear?"

"It's inappropriate. I won't speak of it again."

He laughed.

"What's so funny, Mr. Bidwell?" Tess' voice grew stern.

"You gals seem to keep all those feelings pinned up like a corset—"

"Mr. Bidwell! Don't speak of such things. You don't know me well enough to talk of those matters."

"Oh, I know you well enough to know you're scared." One eyebrow poked up on his forehead.

70

"If you know me so well, then tell me what I am so afraid of." She crossed her hands and placed them in her lap. She was ready to hear what he had to say.

"You're scared of everything around you. The ranch, Franklin, your grandmother… me."

"That's preposterous. I've never."

"Never what?"

"I've never had someone talk to me in such a way."

"I don't mean to hurt you Tess, but it's obvious you're going to let Franklin make your decisions for you."

"How do you know? You've seen him for all of five minutes."

"That's all the time I needed to see you giving in way too easy." She figured he drew out his words to make his point.

"I must be polite. He's come all the way west to court me. I doubt you'd ever do that for a woman."

Ian leaned forward in his seat. Tess pushed her back against the seat behind her, realizing she had nowhere to go.

He stared at her for a moment, making her face heat up. His blue eyes seemed to see right through her.

His voice grew quiet. "You don't know what I'd do for a woman I love, do you?"

The carriage stopped and rocked. Ian opened the door and disappeared. Tess realized at that moment she was holding her breath. She let it out and felt paralyzed. Ian had something over her. She knew what it was, she just wasn't sure she was ready for it.

"Ya comin' or what?" Ian hollered from outside.

She took a deep breath and leaned forward to climb down from the carriage. Ian stuck his hand out for her. She stared at him for a second and refused his hand before getting out of the carriage. She stood on the ground and pulled at her dress, straightening it.

Tess looked up at the woman standing nearby and felt the blood drain from her face. "Grandmother?"

Chapter Nine

Ian couldn't get Tess out of his mind. Would she go back with Franklin? He had more power and money to woo her than Ian would ever have. He had nothing. Only a past he couldn't change.

She'd be better off with Franklin. He'd be able to take care of her financially. Besides, she wouldn't have to worry about Barrington or Indians if she returned home. She was far too refined to live out west. He had to stifle his feelings for her, especially before they grew any stronger than they already were. He'd never felt such a pull on his heart as he did with Tess.

"Ian!" Catherine said, opening the door of their home. "Come in. Sit down."

Ian walked through the door and sat down at the table. He'd never realized until now how good it felt to come to town to visit friends and not head straight to the saloon.

"How's Tess?" Thomas said, walking in to the room.

"A suitor from New York has come to town." Ian wrapped his cool hands around the cup of coffee Catherine set in front of him.

She stopped as soon as she set it down and looked at Thomas.

"Will she return with him?" Catherine asked.

"Possibly. He wants her as his wife."

"Perhaps that's what she needs." Thomas said, sitting down at the table, across from Ian.

Ian nodded, but deep down, he was hoping Tess would need him.

***

Tess pulled off her gloves and laid them on the table by the door.

"This is quite a lovely place, Franklin," she said, looking around at the massive structure.

"I have it rented for a while. At least until I can get you to return," he said, smiling at her.

Tess moved closer to her grandmother and leaned in to show some sign of affection. Her grandmother fanned her hand against her back a couple of times and pushed her away.

"What are you doing here?"

"Eliza wanted to come with me," Franklin interjected. "She thought the trip would allow her the opportunity to see her son again and bring you back with us."

Tess looked at her grandmother and back at Franklin. "Does she know?"

Franklin nodded. "I told her the news of your father after I returned from the ranch."

"It's a pity," she said. "I do wish he could've made something of himself. I should have known it would never happen."

"Grandmother, he's your son." Tess struggled to understand her lack of compassion toward her only child.

She ignored Tess' comments and walked in to the parlor. Her grandmother sat down and fidgeted with her dress, as if nothing monumental had happened in her life. Tess wasn't sure she'd ever understand that woman and her indifference.

"Your meal is ready, sir," one of the servants said.

Franklin helped Eliza from her chair and crossed the room to escort Tess to the table.

He held his elbow out to his side. Tess slipped her hand into the crook of his arm and followed him to the table.

Not much time had passed since she departed New York City. The china looked ravishing against the pristine tablecloth. But somehow, in the short time since she arrived in Denver City, she learned to enjoy her quiet meals at the rickety old table in the center of her father's small cabin. Even though it had only been a few.

She knew she should be enjoying someone fetching her tea, serving her food, and placing her napkin in her lap, but the lure of the simplicity of the cabin was becoming strong.

While they ate, Franklin and her grandmother talked of things at home. Many of the parishioners were hoping for her return with Franklin and her grandmother.

All the while they were talking, Tess couldn't get her mind off her conversation with Ian on the way to town. He talked to her with such audacity. It was improper for such a conversation to be held, but she couldn't help but want to continue their discussion.

She'd never bared her deepest thoughts for another like she did today. Her mind struggled to stay in the conversation at hand, and continued to return to Ian. No one had stirred her soul in such a way.

Once again, she reminded herself that she needed to control her emotions. She had to be wise in her decisions and Ian was not a refined, wealthy man like Franklin. But nothing in her wanted wealth. She wanted someone to love her with a passion so stirring that it was undeniable.

Although Franklin served on the church board, she saw more of a Godly spirit in Ian. His heart longed to talk about God and do things that were pleasing to him. So it appeared.

She might have a stirring for Ian, but she was letting her feelings get in the way of reality. He worked for a mean, vindictive man. For all she knew, his words were a way to sweet-talk her into giving up the land. *Be cautious*, she chided herself.

Tess looked at Franklin. He was secure, loving, and cared for her. What more did she need? Love was something only the fortunate were able to find and keep. Not her.

* * *

The sun beat down on Tess and Ian as they rode into town the next day. She hoped it would stay out long enough to pick up Francine and Lizzie at the station, but gray clouds loomed in the wide-open sky.

"You seem upset. Everything okay?" Ian asked her, riding up next to her on Slater. Anxiety gripped her and she wavered on how to tell Francine about the death of their father. Would she stay? Tess feared the worst.

"I'm just nervous to see Francine. It's been a while." Tess had yet to tell Ian about her husband, Luke. Not only had time escaped her, but words as well. Tess always feared the worst.

"She'll be happy to see you. You're sisters. What could go wrong?"

If he only knew.

74

"I need to do a few things in town. Go on home when you're ready. I'll be close behind you," Ian added.

Tess nodded, trying to get past the fear to leave his side.

As they neared town, Tess could see the stagecoach sitting in front of the station in the distance. Tess drew in a few deep breaths, hoping to slow down her heartbeat.

She pulled the wagon next to the station, stepped down, and hitched up the horse. Flutters filled her stomach as Tess walked up the stairs and opened the station door. She looked across the station room and her eyes met Francine's.

Her shoes clicked across the empty room as she made her way to her sister.

"Francine, I can't believe it's you." She leaned in to hug her sister and felt a large bump against her belly. "Can it be? Another one on the way?"

"I am due in just a few months," Francine said.

Tess wanted to stand and stare at her older sister. A flood of emotions rushed in on her, but she held back the tears.

"Who's the beautiful little thing hiding behind you?" Tess said, smiling at Lizzie, now standing behind her mother.

Tess knelt down and peeked around her sister. "Who's that back there?" She teased. She leaned around and tickled Lizzie on her side.

Her eyelids fluttered, knowing their father should be there with her greeting his very first grandchild. Tess couldn't help but wonder how Francine would take the news. Lizzie would never know her grandfather.

"Are you my Aunt Tessie?" Lizzie said, moving her mother's dress out of the way long enough for Tess to get a glimpse of the little girl.

"I am. I can't believe I finally get to meet you," Tess said, gently pulling her by the arm and hugging her. Tess bit her lip to keep from crying. Her family was falling apart before they even had a chance become a union. She wanted to scream the truth, get it out. She'd find the right moment, if there ever was one.

"Ma'am? Where do you want your trunk?" The stationmaster interrupted. He stood waiting at the door.

"The wagon right out front," Tess said, pointing outside.

Lizzie walked forward and leaned against Tess' lap. "Pa is talking to Jesus."

"I know. He is probably talking to him about you." Tess knew Luke was complete in heaven, but as long as Lizzie lived on this earth, her life would be missing her father, and now her grandfather.

"Do you really think he's talking about me? To Jesus?" A smile grew wide across her face, and her cheeks reddened.

Tess nodded.

"Mama, Pa is talking about me." Her voice grew high.

Francine's hand went up to her mouth, stifling a cry. She sat down on the bench and lowered her head.

"Francine, I am so sorry about Luke." Tess wrapped her arm around her sister. She had to tell her about their father. She was sure the pain of losing Luke was unbearable. Tess opened her mouth to say something, but nothing came out.

"He said he didn't feel good, wanted to rest. The next moment, he was on the ground… gone."

Tess felt the weight of the world fall on her. Telling Francine about their father would be harder than she imagined. How could she put it off any longer?

"I am so sorry you lost Luke. He was such a good man, always a good husband. I know you loved him with all your heart."

Francine nodded.

Tess told Francine of Franklin and their grandmother's arrival in town, while riding back out to the ranch. She assumed Francine would want to travel back into town after freshening up to see their grandmother and introduce her to her first great-grandchild. The news of their grandmother in town seemed to give Francine a small dose of comfort.

When they arrived at the cabin, Francine stepped down from the wagon and took Lizzie by the hand. The young girl leapt from the wagon one step at a time until her feet hit the ground. She took off running around the side of the house.

"Don't go too far," Francine yelled.

"She's okay. There's nothing out there that can hurt her. Besides, she needs to run off some energy."

"Let's go inside," Tess said. "We need to talk." Her heart pounded against her chest.

"Sounds serious," Francine added, with a tail of laughter.

The two walked inside the cabin and left the door open, to keep an eye on Lizzie, still outside playing.

"Francine," Tess stepped close to her sister. "It's Pa."

"What do you mean?" She smiled, but her eyes filled with fear.

"He's gone," Tess said.

"Gone?" Francine asked. "That's just like him. I should've known this would happen." Her voice raised in anger. "When's he coming back?"

Tess looked down at the floor and back at Francine. Her eyes filled with tears. "No, he's dead, Francine."

"This can't be." Francine's voice trailed to a whisper at the news. She turned and faced the open door. Outside, Lizzie played. A butterfly flittered across the front porch. Lizzie ran up the steps and chased it back down, giggling.

"Francine?" Tess watched the back of her sister. Her silence permeated the room. She stepped around the side of Francine to gauge her emotions.

Francine stared straight ahead. "Why didn't you tell me?"

"I didn't know how to tell you," Tess reached out to touch her sister's shoulder.

"He's dead?" Anger crinkled her face.

"Yes," Tess answered, letting the tears flow.

"Why didn't you let me know?" Her voice darkened into a growl.

"How?"

"I might have stayed in Atchison."

"How can you say that, Francine?" The comment angered Tess. "I'm your family."

"We're barely family, Tess." Francine's words stabbed like daggers.

"We're sisters." Tess turned her back. Anger raged inside of her. "I thought you were coming out here to be a part of this family. Sisters are family."

"Admit it, Tess, you never wanted a sister around."

For years Tess dreamt of becoming best friends with Francine. She wanted nothing more than to be a part of her sister's life. Not just a part, but consistently in her life.

77

"I would have sent a telegram if I had known where you were," Tess said. Her eyebrows creased together. "I didn't know of his death until I arrived."

Francine's eyes never left the door. Her lips pressed together and she breathed in a deep breath.

"How did he die?" She said, almost whispering.

"I don't know."

"Should've stayed in Boston. Maybe Luke would be alive."

"I'm so sorry, Francine," Tess said, trying to stifle her tears. "All I can say is I'm sorry."

"What do we do now?"

Tess had pondered the question for days.

"I was hoping you and Lu—you might have some savings. We can make it until the spring and sell off the cattle."

"I don't have any money," she said, laughing sardonically. "It was stolen. I barely retrieved our luggage from a hotel, and spent the remainder of my hidden money on food before arriving here.

As her chin quivered, Tess forced herself to look away.

Francine paused for a moment. "The undertaker took my wedding band as payment for Luke's burial. I had to bury my husband in a plain, rectangle pine box. I barely gave him a decent burial."

Tess wanted to go to her sister, wrap her arms around her, and take away her pain. There was nothing she could do but wait. Wait for her sister to heal. No matter how angry Francine became, Tess vowed to stay by her sister's side.

"I'd best tell Lizzie. She's looked forward to meeting Pa."

Tess wanted to give the two space, time to talk. She grabbed a match on top of the stove and struck it against the metal. She lit the burner and replaced the lid. She placed the kettle on top of the stove and waited for the whistle to sound.

As Tess lifted two cups from the shelf, she heard the snap of the reins. Tess ran to the door to see Francine race by in the wagon. She whipped the reins again, causing Lady to bolt forward.

Lizzie stopped playing and ran to Tess' side. "Where's Mama going?"

"I don't know, honey." Tess stood helpless as she watched her sister ride off.

"The rocks," Tess said, recalling the rocky drive. She'd hit one the first time she drove through the wagon wheel ruts. If Francine hit the larger rock at the speed she was traveling, it would surely flip the wagon.

Chapter Ten

Tess watched Francine race down the road, moving faster and faster, fearing for her sister's life.

The movement of the wagon became smaller, but she could still hear the wheels turning fast, moving behind the horse.

Tess stood helpless, wanting to run after Francine, but knowing she would never catch her.

"She'll be back." Tess made a promise to Lizzie she wasn't sure she would be able to keep. Would Francine come back?

"Mama . . ." Tears streamed down Lizzie's face. "I want Mama."

Tess lifted her up into her arms and held her tightly. She couldn't offer her any thing more than sympathy.

Tess turned to carry Lizzie into the house, knowing the young girl must be exhausted.

A shattering crack echoed across the field.

Without putting Lizzie down, she ran toward her sister, her heart pounding against her chest.

Lord, let me find her alive.

Tess followed the wagon wheel ruts, snaking back and forth through the weeds and pinions. Lizzie grew heavier. She hoisted her onto her hip and kept running. Her hip ached from the weight of the young girl, pressing against her bone.

Lizzie leaned into her chest and wrapped her small arms around Tess as tightly as she could.

"Francine?" Her voice grew shrill. The sound of her own feet pounding against the dirt grew louder in her own ears. "Francine?" she yelled again, swallowing her cries.

Tess gasped when she saw one of the wagon wheels sticking up in the air, still spinning.

As she neared the wheel, the spinning slowed. The wagon was now fractured and turned on its side. One of the wheels dug deeply into the earth.

Tess set Lizzie on the ground and ran to the side of the wagon, searching for Francine. Pieces of her bonnet lay ripped on the ground next to the bench, which was mangled and splintered.

The horse lay sideways on the ground, still tied to the wagon. He lifted his head and whinnied. Tess dropped to the ground, searching still for her sister.

Francine's leg was pinned underneath the corner of the wagon.

"Can you hear me, Sis?"

Please God, let her respond.

Francine lay unconscious. Tess backed out of the cramped spot and stood up next to the side. She slid her hands underneath the side of the wagon and tried to lift it. As she struggled to lift it, one of the boards ripped off, sending Tess sprawling backward.

As she threw the board to the side, splinters dug into the palm of her hand. Back on her feet, Tess grabbed the board and pushed it underneath the side of the wagon. She put all her weight on the board, hoping the wagon would move upright. Nothing.

"Lord, I need you right now," Tess yelled out.

"Tess?" As if from above, Ian's voice soothed her in her panic.

He flipped his leg over Slater and dropped to the ground.

"Francine's under the wagon. Her legs are pinned," she said, struggling to press down on the board again.

"Is Lady alive?" He yelled.

"Yes, she tried to get up a minute ago, but the wagon has her held down."

"Grab her reins, and try to pull her up. I'll help push the wagon," Ian said, pointing toward the front of the wagon. "Move Lady to her left, away from Francine."

"Lizzie, stay out of the way, honey," Tess said. She picked up the little girl and moved her far from the trap.

Tess ran to the front and pulled the reins beneath Lady's bridle. "C'mon, girl. Get up! Get up!"

Lady bounced a couple of times, lifted her head and shoulders, and tried to stand. She fell back down again.

"C'mon, Lady. You can do this." Tess pulled again at the reins, this time digging her heels into the ground as she tugged. "Lord, give us strength."

"Haw!" Ian yelled from behind the wagon.

Lady rolled onto her legs and stood up, lifting the wagon. Tess moved her to the left and out of the way. Ian pushed the back of the wagon until it was clear of Francine.

Tess knelt down and laid her head on Francine's chest. Her heart was beating strong. "She's alive. But her legs, they look broken."

"Let's get her in the wagon, so we can get her to town," Ian said, lifting her into the bed of the vehicle.

Tess realized Lizzie's tears were becoming more intense. She picked up the little girl and lifted her into her arms.

"We're gonna get help for your Mama." Tess slipped her foot onto the step, climbed up into the wagon, and sat down on the seat. She pulled the reins into her hands and gave the horse a slap with the leather straps.

"Mama. Mama," Lizzie said, stretching her arms out toward her mother. Tess tugged at Lizzie with her free arm, keeping her from climbing into the back of the wagon and onto her mother.

Lady's muscles bulged as she pulled, but the wagon was cemented to the ground.

"Ian," Tess said, "Check the wheel on the other side."

"It's broken. We'll have to do something else. That'll never get us to town."

"What are we going to do?" Tess could hear the panic in her own voice.

"I'm going to have to take her into town on my horse."

"But her legs," Tess said.

"If we don't get her to town, she'll die."

"Of course," Tess said.

"Help me get her up."

Tess followed Ian to the bed of the wagon. He lifted Francine and walked her to his horse. He put her across the saddle. Ian gripped his leg and moaned.

"Are you okay? Can you get her to town?"

"Yeah. We'll make it."

As he flipped his leg over the saddle, he pulled her back into his arms.

"Ian," Tess said, "Be careful. She's with child."

He nodded.

"We'll unhitch the horse from the wagon and meet you at the doctor," Tess said.

He rode ahead. All that he left behind was a cloud of dust.

Her hands moved at a frantic pace, trying to unhitch the horse. "Come on. Let's go follow Mama," Tess said to Lizzie, holding out her arms for the little girl to come. Lizzie fell into her arms.

Tess grabbed the horn with one hand and lifted herself and Lizzie onto the saddle. She pulled at the reins and Lady raced them toward town. Tess held on tightly to Lizzie. She wanted to wrap the girl up in her arms and tell her nothing more could harm her. But she now knew that might be a lie.

"Will Mama go see Jesus?" Lizzie asked Tess, her voice cracking.

"We will pray that Jesus lets her stay with us a lot longer," Tess said. Her eyes stung, burning with tears. Tess truly hoped the Lord would give Francine and her unborn child more time on this earth. Lizzie didn't deserve to lose both of her parents.

***

Ian rode up to the infirmary and pulled on Slater's reins, slowing to a halt. His thighs burned as he slid off his horse, still holding Francine in his arms. Thunder rumbled across the sky. Dark clouds rolled overhead. He hoped Tess and the young child would be okay riding in the open.

He hoisted Francine more securely in his arms and walked up the stairs to the door of the infirmary. Ian pushed on the door with his foot, knocking it open, and walked through.

The pain in his old wound flared again, stealing his breath. He limped and gritted his teeth, hoping his leg wouldn't give out from under him.

"I need help," he yelled, hoping the doctor was close.

A nurse darted from around the front counter and raced to his side. "Let's get her in the examining room."

The nurse led Ian down a darkened corridor and into the last room. "Set her down here."

Ian placed Francine on her side, on a bed in the middle of the room. He reached down to straighten her legs.

"Don't touch her," the nurse quipped. She reached out and squeezed his hand to stop him and pointed to Francine's leg. "Look, her bone is visibly broken. You might make it worse."

Ian glanced down at her leg, snapped in two places. He'd seen plenty of blood in his day, but seeing the bones turned his stomach. He'd be surprised if she lived through this wound.

"Stay with her while I run get the doctor."

The nurse left the room and Ian reached inside his pocked to pull out a handkerchief to wipe the blood from his hands. He cleaned them off as best as he could and sat down in the chair against the wall. If he couldn't do anything for her, he'd pray.

Ian bent his head down, pressing his hands into his forehead. *Lord, I ain't much on words, but Tess needs her sister, and that little girl needs her Mama. I know just how much she needs her Mama. Keep her from dyin' and give her back her legs for walkin'. Thank ya Lord. Amen.*

Just as he finished, the doctor came into the room, with the nurse following behind.

The doctor hovered over Francine, lifted both of her eyelids, and checked for signs of life. His fingers rested on her neck. "She has a strong pulse."

"Will she live?"

"Don't know. What happened to this woman?" The doctor continued combing over her entire body. Her arms were scraped and bloodied from the fall.

"She was trapped under a wagon."

"For how long?"

"I don't know. Her sister found her. I came upon the scene." Ian felt useless. How could he help her?

The doctor pulled her skirt up above her knees. Ian turned and faced the wall, giving Francine privacy.

"Her legs are broken. I don't know if the blood flow was stopped long enough. We might have to amputate."

"Amputate?" Ian never even considered the possibility.

"We have to do surgery. Right now."

"She's with child," Ian said, turning around to face the doctor. He choked before taking a deep breath. If Ed Porter were

84

alive, he would be devastated that one of his daughters was breathing in death.

The doctor stopped and felt around her abdomen. "I don't know if we can save the child, but we might be able to save her."

Ian knew how excruciating it would be to share the devastating news with Tess. Thunder cracked again and rain pellets hit the roof. Tess and Lizzie were riding in the storm. He wondered if they would make it safely.

"I'll need your help getting her ready," the doctor said, motioning Ian around the other side of the table.

Ian nodded and followed his orders.

"When I give you the word, I want you to lift her middle section and turn her on her back," he said. His hands were in a frenzy, directing Ian and the nurse. "Sarah, I want you to hold her legs as steady as possible. We don't want her in worse condition."

The three worked together and managed to get Francine on her back.

The doctor stopped and looked at Ian. "Son, the only thing you can do now is pray."

Ian backed out of the room and stood listening just outside of the door. The sound of tearing fabric sounded in the background.

Tess. Ian walked down the hallway, opened the door, and walked out on the porch. He hoped she would be right behind him, but she and the young girl were nowhere in sight.

Rain hit the ground with force, turning the dry, dusty streets into mud. The awning kept him dry as he watched for the two. Sheets of rain blanketed the small city, making it almost impossible to see.

Chapter Eleven

Tess leaned over Lizzie, trying to shield the young girl from the biting cold rain. Her small body shook in the chilly air. Tess slid her arm tighter around her waist and hoped the warmth of her own body would give Lizzie some heat. Almost hailing, the pellets felt like small needles against her skin.

Tess struggled to see just feet in front of her. She relied on the horse to guide their way into town.

A lightning bolt shot across the sky and the wind howled in her ears, pinching the edges with pain.

A small house on the edge of town came into view. A glorious laugh popped out when she recognized the preacher's house. She led the horse toward the house and climbed off.

"I'm cold," Lizzie said, her teeth chattering.

"We're going to get you warm by the fire." Tess carried Lizzie to the door and pounded on it with her fist.

Thomas opened the door. "Tess! Come in out of the rain," he said, waving her in. "Let's get you two dried off."

"Take the girl first. She's freezing. Her teeth have chattered since the rain started."

Catherine disappeared from the room and appeared again, this time with a blanket. She spread it over her lap and stuck her hands out in front of her. "Give the child to me."

Tess placed Lizzie in Catherine's lap. She threw the blanket over the child and rubbed it against her wet, matted curls.

"Thomas, build a fire," Catherine said.

A cry erupted from Lizzie. "It's gonna be okay," Tess said, hoping she was right.

"I want Mama."

Tess bit her bottom lip, trying to keep from bursting into tears. She hoped her sister would live to hold Lizzie and give her the comfort only a mother could give.

"My sister's at the infirmary. I have to find Ian or he'll go out in the rain searching for us."

Thomas placed several logs in the hearth and lit the fire. "It should warm up in here in a few minutes."

"Let Thomas fetch Ian," Catherine said.

"I want to see how my sister is doing. I need to know if she's… alive." She whispered, keeping the possibility of her death a secret from Lizzie.

"I'll go," Thomas said. "I'll tell Ian you are safe. It will give you a chance to change into something dry. I'll be back shortly with a report of her condition."

Tess nodded reluctantly.

Thomas grabbed his coat and lifted the handle on the door. The wind blew it open, slamming it against the wall. Sprinkles of rain blew in the house. He stepped outside and pulled the door shut.

Tess looked at Catherine and hoped the news she would receive would be promising.

***

Ian continued to scan the horizon for Tess and Lizzie. He paced the front porch of the infirmary. He had to go find them. He knew this land, even shrouded in rain.

Thunder boomed overhead and a flash of light illuminated the street. At that moment, he noticed a man running in his direction.

"Ian," he faintly heard, over the loud downpour of rain. The man bounded up the steps and lowered his jacket that he held on top of his head.

"Thomas," Ian said, "what're you doin' here?"

"It's Tess," he said. Before he spoke, he drew in several deeps breaths.

"Is she okay?" He grabbed his friend's shoulders.

He nodded before speaking. "She's fine. That's why I'm here. Her and the young girl made it to our house. They are warming by the fire."

Ian wanted to leap for joy. *Thank you, Lord.*

"How's her sister?" Thomas questioned.

"The doctor's workin' on her now," he said, looking toward the ground. "It ain't lookin' good."

"I'm so sorry. Tess has been through so much pain and trial already."

"Explain to me how the Lord can let this happen," Ian asked. He had read through some of the Bible, but couldn't understand how the God of the universe could let so many bad things happen to a good person.

"It's hard to imagine what she is going through right now. God doesn't promise that things will be easy here on earth. In fact, He tells us in the Bible that while we are here, we will experience pain and loss. That doesn't mean He doesn't have compassion on His children."

Ian could understand loss. When his mother died, his heart never fully healed. It wasn't until he came to know Jesus that he learned to read the Bible and lean on God. The pain didn't seem to have the same stronghold as it did before. It wasn't gone, but surely lessened.

"God does promise us that He will stay by our side and carry us through the storm. When it feels like the waters will rise too high, He will lift us up out of the pit," Thomas said. He shook as thunder cracked across the sky. "Even in these storms, I'm reminded of His power."

"Doesn't He have the power to stop all these bad things from happening?"

"Sure, He's God. But this world is broken. Precious people are ripped from our lives. God gave us the promise of salvation in sending His Son to save us from the brokenness. He's given us a reason to praise Him through the storm. His Son died so that one day, when we meet Jesus in heaven, we will be able to live whole."

Ian thought about his past. His sins were enough to embarrass a gambling hall girl. When he made the decision to follow Christ, the weight of a life spent digging for meaning lifted.

"My Ma told me about Jesus as a youngin'," Ian said. "I didn't listen. Didn't figure I needed Him, especially after she died. I spent a lot of years searching for something, but it was never there. Guess He waited patiently for me. Didn't see Him there, but looking back, I know He was."

"I'm sure your Ma put in a good word for ya," Thomas said. He looked at Ian and smiled.

"I want her to have a son she'd be proud of," he said, crossing his arms and looking down at his feet.

"I think she can already say that," Thomas said, reaching over and placing his hand on Ian's shoulder.

***

"You look like a wet mop," Eliza Porter said, staring at her granddaughter Tess. "I'm surprised Franklin wants anything to do with the likes of you. Can you not clean up before presenting yourself in public?" Her eyes traveled the length of Tess' body.

"I'm not here to impress Franklin." Tess paused for a moment, once again recalling the reason she'd wanted to leave New York City. Her grandmother made the decision easy for her. "I came to tell you that Francine is in the infirmary. She's—"

Eliza flew into a panic. Her voice rose high. "Where? Where is she?"

Franklin came into the room. "Tess? You look afright! Is everything well?" He walked over to her.

At least he knew how to show compassion.

"Francine. She's gravely hurt. When I told her about my father, she rode off in the wagon. It hit a rock and flipped over onto her."

"This is all your fault," Eliza yelled. The wrinkles around her eyes grew tighter as she moved closer to Tess. "If the two of you hadn't decided to come west and move in with your philandering father, none of this would be happening."

A twinge of guilt raced through Tess. Maybe she was right. But she couldn't plan the future. She had no idea this would happen.

"Leave the poor girl alone," Franklin said. "Her sister is in her worries as well." Tess glanced at him and a slight smile grew across her face. There was no mistaking his caring heart. "Leonard, get the carriage for us, please."

His servant followed orders and opened the front door. Rain continued to pour down, worsening the mud on the street out front.

Leonard walked back in the front door, now drenched from the rain. "Sir, the carriage is ready to take you." He stood with his hand on the doorknob. "Sir?"

Tess glanced at Leonard and back at Franklin. "Franklin? Are you all right?"

His eyes moved slowly toward Tess. She walked in front of him and placed her hands on his arms.

"Franklin? Can you hear me?" He stared at her as his jaw opened.

His body went limp and he fell to the floor.

Chapter Twelve

The door to the infirmary opened and the nurse stepped out. Ian stood up, took his hat off, and held it in front of his chest.

"How's she doin'?" He crinkled the brim of his hat in his hands, waiting for an answer.

The nurse, Sarah, shook her head. "Doctor's still working on her. It's not good. Her legs are badly broken."

"And the baby?" Ian looked at Thomas and back at Sarah.

"I don't know. We'll be lucky to save the woman." Sarah shook her head, turned to go back inside, and closed the door behind her.

"I best tell Tess," Thomas said. "Why don't you come back to the house and get some dry clothes and a bite to eat?"

"I'll stay here. 'Sides, I'm not too hungry. I want Tess to be able to stay warm and comfortable. She needs to know someone is up here watching out for her sister."

"I'll tell her," Thomas said before running back into the rain.

Ian wanted to hold Tess, tell her everything would be okay. If only he knew it would be.

***

Tess leaned over Franklin as he lay on the floor unconscious. "Franklin?" Tess tugged on his arm and tried to roll him over, but his weight was almost too much.

Leonard dropped to his knees, grabbed Franklin's arm, and pulled him onto his back without much effort.

"We must get him to the settee," Tess said.

"Leonard, can you lift him, or at least pull him to the other room?"

"I believe I can. I can at least try, Miss." He stood up and walked around Franklin. Tess lifted his head and Leonard slid his

91

hands underneath his arms. He raised Franklin up enough to pull him toward the parlor.

"Grandmother," Tess yelled as she walked around and held one of his feet. "Grab Franklin's other foot and help."

"I'd never do such a—"

"If you don't grab his foot, he may not get better, and you'll be stuck living in Denver City."

Eliza dropped her parasol and moved quickly toward Franklin. She slid the palm of her hand under his other foot. The three of them moved Franklin into the parlor and hoisted him up onto the settee.

"I'll run get the doctor," Tess said. "Grandmother, stay by his side and make sure he doesn't fall off."

"Miss, take my coat. You will catch a fright if you keep running through the rain," Leonard said.

Tess lifted the coat and draped the large thing over her body. The weight pulled at her shoulders. She flew from the parlor and ran out the front door, grabbing her grandmother's parasol as she went by. Raindrops pounded all around her as she ran out in to the street. The thickness of the mud made it hard to lift her feet to move faster. Tension built in her shoulders, bit by bit.

Lord, please let Franklin live. He's a good man.

Tess felt her heart ache for the man who had been so generous and kind to her in the past year. So many times on the trip west, she praised God for not entering into a binding relationship with him, only because she did not love him. But now, his arrival to fetch her may cause his death. How could it be anything but her fault?

Tess grabbed a handful of her skirt and lifted the already-muddied hem up off the ground. Her feet moved a bit faster beneath her. The streets were barren. Most people were inside their homes, out of the rain.

As she neared the doctor's office, she could see Ian in the distance, sitting on the front porch. His elbows rested on his knees and his head hung low.

"Tess," he said as she approached. He stood up and waited on the porch. "What are you doing here? Where did you come from?" He looked around her.

"I went to tell my grandmother about Francine." Tess stopped for a moment to catch her breath. Her chest pained with a lack of oxygen in her lungs, and she took several deep breaths.

"Slow down a little," Ian said. "It's all right." He placed his hand on the side of her arm.

"Something is wrong with Franklin." Tess continued to try to pull more air into her lungs with deep breaths.

Ian's forehead grew tight. "Is he... is he all right?"

"It appears to be the same symptoms my grandfather had just before he died."

Ian's eyebrows pressed together and he shook his head back and forth with a look of question.

"Stroke," Tess said.

"The doctor is with Francine. I don't know if he can help you."

"I have to try." Tess opened the door to the infirmary and walked through the door, slopping a trail of filthy mud and water behind her. Ian stayed mere steps behind her.

"They are in the last room on the left."

Tess knew she must hurry. She didn't want Franklin to suffer the same fate as her grandfather—death.

Tess spotted the room at the end of the hallway. A sliver of light shone underneath the door. Tess tapped on the door, partially open, and pushed ever so gently against it.

A gasp of air flew into Tess as she saw her sister lying on the operating table. Her belly, rounded with child, protruded. Tess wondered how the baby inside of her fared. Would it live? Would Francine live?

"Miss? I am performing a surgery. What do you want?" His voice stirred with anger.

"I'm so sorry, doctor. That is my sister—"

"Please wait outside until I am done. I will tell you of her condition then."

"I know, but my friend, Franklin, needs help." Tess felt her stomach rumble and the tension tightening in her shoulders. She couldn't bear to see her sister lying on the table, not knowing if she would see her beautiful face again. A hand rested on her shoulder, and Tess felt a peace shuffle through her. She knew it was Ian's hand lending her comfort.

Before she looked down at the floor, the doctor looked up from his surgery and glanced at Tess. "What are his symptoms?"

"His jaw went limp. Lameness took over and he slumped to the floor. Just before he fell, his words became slurred."

"Stroke," she heard him faintly say.

"Sir?"

"He needs to be blood let." The doctor cleared his throat.

Tess felt woozy just thinking of the idea of cutting someone to let their blood flow.

"Are you capable of it?"

She paused and swallowed hard. The lump in her throat did not go down with ease. "Yes." Tess had to muscle the word off her tongue.

"It must be done immediately. Go now."

Tess whirled around and faced Ian. "Pray for me."

He nodded. "Let me help you."

"No, I would rather you stay here for Francine." Tess moved around him and ran toward the door. She had no time to waste. She had to save his life.

***

Tess threw open the front door of Franklin's house and stepped into the foyer. "Grandmother?"

Still in her coat, Eliza stepped from around the corner and into the foyer. "What did the doctor say?"

"We must let his blood."

At the mention of the action, Eliza's face turned white. Her eyes rolled back in her head and she started to drop.

Leonard rounded the corner just in time to catch the old woman and lay her down on the floor.

Tess couldn't help the laugh that bubbled out of her. "She never could handle anything like this. Course, I'm not sure I'm any better." Tess reached up and felt water on her forehead. At this point, she didn't know if it was rain or sweat.

Leonard stood over Eliza. "What should we do with her?"

"Take her in the other room and let her rest on the settee opposite Franklin. It'll be a little more padded than this hard floor. We don't want her waking up angry that we left her on a wet floor."

Tess knew her grandmother well. The most minuscule slight would for certain anger her, especially if it involved Tess.

Leonard slid his hands under her legs and her back and lifted Eliza with ease and placed her on the settee.

Tess knelt down next to Franklin. She lowered her ear to see if he was still breathing. His breath warmed her ear and she sighed.

"Leonard," Tess said, turning and looking at the tall, lanky man. "We need a large bowl, a wet towel, and a pitcher of water."

He nodded and left the room. What would she do without Franklin's faithful servant?

"Oh! And we need a sharp, clean razor!" She yelled to him. Her stomach turned at the mention of the razor. She glanced back at her grandmother and wondered if she herself might end up fainting and have to be put on the floor in the middle of the two patients. "Poor Leonard, he has no idea what he's dealing with," she whispered under her breath.

The clanging of pots could be heard throughout the house. Tess was grateful for Leonard's fast movements.

"Franklin, I must take off your jacket and your shirt." Tess felt uncomfortable unbuttoning the buttons, but knew that his life depended on her fast and necessary decisions.

Tess stood to her feet and pulled the shirt open, popping buttons in every direction. *I didn't ask the doctor where to let out the blood.* Queasiness oozed across her.

"Lord, give me guidance," Tess said aloud. Instead of trying to pull his arm out of his sleeve, she started a tear at the edge of his cuffs and ripped the material all the way up to his shoulder.

Leonard returned to the room with the necessities for the procedure.

"Miss, do you need a cold rag?"

"Do I look that awful?" Tess figured she looked frightful. Her clothes were still sopping wet from the rain. She glanced back at the floor, stained with mud. "I'll probably catch a death of a cold."

Leonard handed Tess the razor.

Tess drew in a deep breath and exhaled. She uncurled Franklin's fingers, exposing his palm. The razor sat in the bowl on the floor. She lifted it in between her fingers and moved it toward his exposed palm, trying to steady her grip.

The razor pressed against his skin, leaving an impression. Tess glanced up at his motionless face, and back down at his hand. Crimson red blood began to flow into the bowl beneath.

95

Leonard knelt down beside her. "You're doing a fine job, Miss."

"I'm having a hard time steadying my hand."

"You are giving him another chance at life."

"I appreciate your encouragement, Leonard. You've been quite a help. I just hope Franklin survives this."

"He's a fine employer." He looked at her and nodded.

Tess looked down at the blood dripping from his hand into the bowl. "How long have you worked for him?"

"Fifteen years, I believe."

The two sat on the floor next to Franklin, watching him.

"He's a dear man." Tess smiled as she studied the features on his face.

"His heart was broken when you left, if you don't mind my saying." Leonard pressed the clean, wet rag into the bowl of water and wrung it out.

Tess lowered her head. "I know." Her heart ached each time she thought of their parting back in New York City. It pained her to tell him she was leaving him. She knew he would always treat her well and take care of her.

Tess took the rag from Leonard and laid it across the wound. She slid her hand underneath Franklin's and curled his fingers around the rag, hoping to stop the bleeding.

"Can you take this bowl and dispose of it?" Tess asked, hoping not to have to touch it. It was a wonder she hadn't passed out alongside her grandmother.

"Yes." He stood to his feet and lifted the bowl, carrying it with all gentility.

"Thank you, Leonard," Tess said, smiling up at the man.

Tess tore a piece of Franklin's shirt and wrapped it around his hand to stop the blood flow, with the wet rag still inside.

Eliza was still unconscious on the other settee. Tess rinsed her hands in one bowl of water and dipped a clean rag into the other bowl of untouched water. She wrung out a great deal of the water and folded the rag small enough to set it on her grandmother's forehead.

Her eyes fluttered open. "Where am I?"

The high tone in her voice went straight through Tess. It brought back a rush of memories she'd rather not deal with. She took a deep breath and exhaled before speaking.

"You're in the parlor. You fainted."

"How is Franklin?" She turned her head to look across the room.

"We are praying he will be fine, Grandmother."

Eliza started to sit up, but Tess pressed her hands against her shoulders, pushing her back down. "Stay here for a bit. Let your body rest. We don't want you fainting again."

Amazingly, she complied. Although Tess wasn't fond of the woman, she didn't want to see her hurt.

"This is all your fault." Her voice changed to a stern quip.

"How so?" Tess wasn't sure she wanted to hear her explanation, but was curious enough to listen.

"If you hadn't turned him down back home, none of us would be here. He wanted to come get you and bring you back."

"Why did you come? You didn't have to be here to bring me back home. We both know you don't care one way or another what happens to me." Tess stood up and put her hands on her hips. She figured now was as good a time as any to get things out in the open, where they should have been years ago.

"Why would you say such a thing?"

"Grandmother, you've treated me horribly since I was a child. Francine enjoyed so much more, including your loving attention."

She scrunched her face and sat straight up. "That's because your grandfather decided you were more important than anything else around that house."

"Are you jealous of the relationship we had? Is that what this is all about?" Tess curled her upper lip in disgust.

"Mercy sakes, no. I wasn't a bit jealous—"

"You were jealous of me, because he didn't give you as much attention. Isn't that true?"

"Child, you have always been exasperating. You must have inherited that trait from your father." She swung her hand up in the air, as if to flit her thoughts through the air.

"You never said why you came out west." Tess stood over her, staring down.

"To get you to come back to New York."

Tess wanted to scream. No one could get her angry faster than her grandmother. No one.

"There's more to it than that," Tess said. "I'll figure out your reason for being here. Mark my words."

Chapter Thirteen

Tess lifted Lizzie into her lap. The young girl fought to keep her eyes open, calling for her Mama several times. She finally gave in to sleep, and Tess was happy. She knew the little girl needed it.

It felt good to be in dry clothing and sitting in front of the fire. Leonard was truly a blessing. He took over Franklin's care so Tess could see to Lizzie.

More than once Tess prayed God would spare her sister and Franklin's lives. With the loss of her father, she had a taste of the pain Francine was going through after losing Luke. She didn't want Lizzie to lose her mother, too.

Thomas came through the front door. He stood in the doorway, drenched, with rain pouring off his clothing. A puddle grew underneath his feet.

"What's the latest report?" Catherine said.

"She is still in surgery," Thomas said quietly.

"And the baby?" Tess asked.

He shook his head back and forth. "They won't know for a while."

Tess' hand went up to her mouth to stifle her cry. No point in waking Lizzie. She didn't need to be awake to worry about her Mama.

"Tess, it's in the Lord's hands. We are praying and He is by her side now."

She pinched her lips together, nodded her head, and forced a smile.

"Ian is watching over her while you tend to Lizzie. He won't leave her side."

Something deep down gave Tess the comfort that she could truly trust Ian. He was a man of his word. She wanted to be at her sister's side, but she knew Lizzie needed her and that Ian would do everything he could to make sure Francine would be taken care of.

Catherine busied herself with a basket of food and dry clothing for Ian.

"Thomas, don't you catch a cold running out in the storm," Catherine said. She handed the basket to Thomas and kissed him.

"Thomas?" Tess said.

He stopped at the door and turned to face her.

"Please tell Ian . . ." She paused. Tess wanted to go to him, thank him for taking care of her family, but she knew at the moment it was impossible. "Tell him . . ."

"I know," Thomas nodded and smiled. "He knows. too."

He left the house and Tess stood up with Lizzie. She lifted her in her arms and the little girl's head dropped onto her shoulder.

"Let's put her in the bed for now. Maybe she can get some sleep," Catherine said.

Tess followed Catherine to the bedroom. Gently she laid Lizzie on the bed and covered her with the blanket. Her blonde curls fell across the pillow.

"She looks just like her Mama," Tess said, letting the tears flow.

"How is Franklin?" Catherine asked.

"When I left, he was stable. There's nothing more we could do. We have to let the doctor see him when he is finished with Francine. For now, Leonard will tend to him."

"This town needs more than one doctor."

Tess nodded. "I'll see to him later. I wanted to make sure Lizzie had a familiar face to look at for a while. Poor girl lost her father. I just pray her mother survives."

***

As the rain let up, Tess decided to walk to the infirmary. Patches of sunshine poked through the clouds. Steam rose from the mud-caked streets as the sun dried up the rain.

Tess spotted Ian on the porch of the infirmary. Thankfulness filled her heart at the sight.

"Have you heard anything?" she said, walking up the stairs. "Nothing."

Tess sighed and turned to watch the setting sun.

"It doesn't look good, Tess," Ian said.

100

She nodded. Tess didn't get a chance to even spend a day with her sister before the accident. She would give anything to go back and start the day fresh.

"I waited to tell her about my father until we arrived at the cabin. Maybe I should have told her while we were at the station," she said, crossing her arms on her chest.

"You can't blame yourself for what happened."

"She was distraught." Tess paused for a moment. "I didn't tell you. Her husband died in Atchison."

"That's why she ran?"

"The news of my father was too much for her," Tess said. "What will I do without my sister?" It seemed as though all of her options were dwindling before her eyes.

Now Franklin might not survive. Maybe her only option was to return to New York City as his wife. Would her agreement to marry him strengthen him?

The infirmary door opened and Sarah walked out on the porch. Her dress was covered in blood. "Sir, the doctor would like to see you."

"Tess is her sister," Ian said, pointing to her.

"Follow me," Sarah said, walking back inside the building.

Tess followed her down the long hallway, growing dark in the evening hours. Sarah stopped and lit the candle in the wall sconce, brightening the hallway, and then led her into a room.

"Have a seat here. As soon as the doctor cleans up, he will be in here to talk to you."

"Is she. . ?" Tess had to know.

"I'll let him explain," Sarah said. She touched Tess on the shoulder and walked out of the room.

Her heart pounded against her chest. Tess wanted nothing more than to build a relationship with her sister.

Silence filled the room. Footsteps echoed through the hallway and Tess wanted to hold the moment. She didn't want to know if her sister was dead. Tess wanted her here.

She lowered her head and closed her eyes. Tess drew in a deep breath and tried to keep the tears from flowing.

The footsteps stopped and she waited for the door to open.

"Doctor, come quick," Sarah yelled. He turned and ran to the end of the hallway. Tess stood up and opened the door of the doctor's office, fearing the worst.

Was she dead?

***

Ian knew the direness of the situation. However, he couldn't help but think about Tess' words when she spoke to the doctor about Franklin. He'd spent the past day worrying about her returning to a man who had more to offer Tess in one year than he could in a lifetime.

Friend. Ian figured he was silly, dwelling on one word. When she approached the doctor about Franklin's condition, she hadn't said, "fiancé." Would she stay in Denver City, in spite of Franklin's trip west to marry her and take her back home?

His heart longed for Tess more each day. He could no longer fight the way he felt.

"You look deep in thought," Thomas said, arriving this time with a basket. He held it out in front of him.

"What's this?" Ian asked as he reached out to grab it. He lifted the small piece of material covering the top.

"Catherine put it together. She wanted you to have a bite to eat."

A warmth spread through Ian. Not only had they taken him in when he left his uncle's ranch, they continued to show kindness at every turn.

"She shouldn't have gone to the trouble," Ian said.

"She wanted to. She didn't like the idea that you were up here hungry." Thomas sat down on the chair next to him.

"I've been in much worse conditions than this." Rain or shine, just living at his uncle's was far worse. He'd never been around such kind people as Thomas and Catherine. He couldn't recall the last time someone gave without expectation of return.

"Tell her I'm much obliged," Ian said.

***

The sun disappeared behind the mountains and the infirmary grew dark. Tess leaned against the wall, waiting for the doctor to return. His quick exit left her tormenting herself with questions about Francine.

Footsteps reverberated across the floor, pounding back and forth. Were they in a race to save her sister's life?

"Did you meet with the doctor?" Ian said, as Tess walked out on the front porch.

"No," Tess said. "I was waiting for him in his office and the nurse called for him. Now, I don't know if Francine is dead or alive." Her hands went up to cover her mouth. "Lizzie needs her mother."

"The young child?"

Tess nodded. "She can't lose her mother. Lizzie's so young. She needs Francine."

The creak of steps across the wooden floor caught Tess' attention. She returned inside just as the doctor appeared.

Sweat covered the doctor's face. Red stains tarnished his white coat. *Francine's blood.*

"How is she?" She took a deep breath, preparing herself for the worst news.

Ian stood by her side. She was grateful for his help. If he hadn't shown up when he did, Francine would likely be dead. With the broken wagon wheel, Tess would not have been able to take both Francine and Lizzie into town on her horse.

Having Ian by her side was a comfort. She was coming to rely on his help. She glanced at his face, which was focused on the doctor.

"Your sister is a strong woman," the doctor said. "She's still alive."

A sigh escaped Tess. "Thank you."

"Don't get too comfortable with my words. She is still teetering on the edge of death. She lost a lot of blood and both of her legs are broken in several places."

Tess knew the situation was dire, but her insides wanted to jump for joy.

"If," the doctor stressed, "if she lives, she may never walk again."

"What about the baby?" Tess asked.

The doctor laughed. "Your family has a will to live. The baby has a very strong heartbeat. I cannot tell you if the baby sustained any injuries, but time will tell."

"Can I see her?"

"You may. But she is still very unstable," he said. "Follow me."

Tess stayed behind the doctor as the two walked into the other room. The room was dimly lit, providing enough light to see, but making the environment conducive to rest.

Tess walked over to the bed and sat down in the chair. Francine's body was tattered and bruised. The doctor had stitched up a gash on her face and set her legs to keep them from moving.

"Lord, let my sister live. Give her the strength to go on without Luke and Pa," Tess whispered. "She needs you more now than ever."

Tess thought about when they were younger. They talked about their father arriving, days before he was due in town. The excitement would build and when he arrived, neither girl would let him out of their sight. So much had changed since their youth.

When Francine married and left for Boston, Tess spent many nights crying for her older sister. So many times she prayed Francine and Luke would move back to New York City and she could have the relationship with her sister she had dreamed of for so long.

Francine moaned and turned her head. Her eyelids fluttered and Tess held her breath. She would stay by her side no matter the outcome.

Tess reached up and touched her sister's hand. She would give anything to tell her she'd be up and walking in no time. But, would she live to walk?

Chapter Fourteen

The doctor leaned down and placed his brass stethoscope on Franklin's chest. Once he listened to his heart, he unwound the makeshift bandage from his hand and surveyed the cut Tess made.

He looked up at Tess without an expression. Had her inexperienced incision made matters worse for Franklin? If she caused an infection because of her lack of expertise in the matter, she wouldn't be able to live with herself.

"Looks like you might have a future as a nurse, Miss Porter."

A weight of fear rolled off of her. "I'm not so sure. I didn't think I'd be able to keep my hand still long enough to do what was needed." She held her hands in front of her and clasped them together.

"I'll bleed him again while I am here," he said. "You'll have to do it a few more times over the next couple of days."

Tess feared cutting him the first time and she didn't want to have to do it again. But, she knew this might be the only thing that would save his life.

"I do believe it was a stroke. Your fast action will most likely allow him to have full use of his body, after some healing time, Miss Porter."

Tess smiled. She wanted Franklin to go home to New York City feeling perfectly normal.

"Leonard," Tess said. "Can you go get the doctor the items he will need for Franklin?"

"Yes, Miss." He scurried out of the room.

"Grandmother, I believe you'll have to leave for this procedure. We don't want you fainting again."

A snide smile popped up on Eliza's face. "When Leonard returns, I will have him take me to see Francine. I'll sit with her a while."

Tess figured that would be best. Her grandmother loved Francine dearly and she knew the woman would be good for Francine's spirits. If she couldn't be by her side, she would rest easier knowing someone who loved her could hold her hand.

"I'd like to meet my granddaughter. I'll have Leonard take me to her while I am out."

"Why don't you walk with me to Thomas and Catherine's, where Lizzie is staying? It's a cool day."

"Walk?" Eliza's exasperation made the answer obvious.

Tess thought about Catherine and Thomas and all of the help they offered. They had no connection to her family, yet they gave freely. She hadn't worried a bit about Lizzie. The young child had taken to Catherine as if she were her own. Tess knew she was in good, safe hands.

She just hoped Francine would wake up soon and be able to thank them herself.

***

Ian awoke to a loud stomp on the wooden front porch of the infirmary. He jerked his head forward and stood up out of the chair, almost toppling forward.

"Young man," an older woman said. Her voice was stern. "I don't believe sleeping right here is a wise choice."

"Pardon?" He'd fallen into a deep sleep. Ian rubbed his eyes. "What're you talkin' about?" He recognized her from several nights prior when he dropped Tess off at Franklin's home.

"Paupers don't belong in front of the infirmary. They belong somewhere else in this god-forsaken town. Who knows where it might be, but it's obvious to me that is where you belong."

"Ma'am, I ain't a pauper. I'm waitin' on Tess to return. I promised to keep an eye on her sister." It was plain to see she didn't remember him.

She waved her hand in front of her like she was shooing a fly. "No need for you now. I will be sitting with her. You may leave your… your post."

Ian stood still. He wasn't about to take orders from her.

"You obviously didn't hear a word I said. You may leave. Tess shouldn't be fraternizing with the likes of someone like you anyway. I don't believe her fiancé would tolerate another man looking out for her."

There was that word again. *Fiancé*. Ian could feel his heart pumping faster. It was times like this he had to call on the Lord to keep his temper from flaring up. He could see this woman could anger the mud right off a pig.

"I can't imagine what made Tess want to come to this place." She waved her hand again. This time she swung it wide, and Ian figured she was trying to include the whole town. "I don't tolerate men like you back home, but it appears the West is quite a different place."

"Yes, 'tis." A crooked smile crept wide across his face and he knew that would get right under her skin.

Eliza let out a loud sigh. She looked at Ian and down at the doorknob on the front of door of the infirmary.

The smile stayed on his face.

"Well, aren't you going to open this door for me?"

"Like ya said, it's different here." He leaned forward and whispered, "More progressive." Ian sat down in the chair and lifted his legs to rest them on the banister in front of him.

Eliza grabbed the knob and jerked the door open. After she closed the door, her feet pounded against the floor inside, echoing down the hallway. If anything would wake up Francine, he figured it could be that woman. No wonder Tess left New York City in a hurry.

***

"I do believe Franklin is waking up a bit," the doctor said. "Franklin? Can you hear me?"

Franklin's eyes opened and he looked slowly around the room. His head turned toward the doctor.

"Might want to say something to him. He'd probably like to hear your voice."

Tess walked closer to Franklin. She touched his hand and said, "Franklin. Can you hear me?"

The lids on his eyes closed and he smiled. "Yes." The word slipped out a bit slurred.

"Ask him his name," the doctor said.

"Do you know your name?" Tess blinked back the tears. She hated to see him in this condition.

"Frraankliin . . ."

"The stroke has affected him. But with some extra exercise, he'll be closer to normal in no time."

Tess wanted to believe the doctor, but after the loss of her grandfather to a stroke, she'd have to wait and see for herself.

The doctor wrapped the new cut on Franklin's arm. "Can you sit up?"

Franklin nodded and lifted his head. The doctor slipped his hand underneath Franklin's arm and helped him into a sitting position.

"I want you to mash up his food. Keep it simple and watch him at all times. He might choke a little on the food at first."

Tess nodded and took the doctor's instructions.

"I must get back to your sister." He stood up and closed his bag.

"Doctor?"

He looked at Tess.

"Will she live?"

"I wish I could tell you. She's in dire condition right now. If she has a will to live, it will give her a better chance of coming out of this."

Tess nodded. She knew her sister's life was in God's hands.

The doctor left and Tess prepared some food while Franklin rested in the parlor.

When she returned, she pulled a small table up next to Franklin and set the food down. She dipped her spoon into some soup and lifted it to Franklin's mouth. He swallowed the first bite without any trouble.

"See there, not so bad. You'll be back to normal in a short time." Tess smiled, but her eyes began to water. Nothing could be worse than seeing Franklin, a tall, stout man, sitting almost useless. She'd help him get back on his feet. It was the least she could do.

He reached his hand up and touched her arm. "I... I'm sorry."

A bubble of laughter blurted out of Tess. "You have nothing to be sorry about. I don't mind taking care of you."

"I… love… you." He took another bite and Tess rested the spoon in the bowl while he finished chewing.

She wanted so badly to reply, to make him feel better, but her heart wouldn't let her.

***

The fall winds blew against the cabin, causing it to creak. Pieces of metal roof scraped and twisted together.

Tess wrapped a shawl around her arms, lit the stove, and slid the teakettle over the burner. She hadn't had a chance to think about her encounter with the bank teller several days prior. His words ricocheted through her mind, trying to make sense. Her thoughts passed between disbelief and anger. Did she have a brother? Could it be? Her father did have a penchant for women in his younger days. But, why wouldn't he tell them about a brother if it were true?

Tess looked over at Lizzie, who was still sleeping on the bed. She'd wait until Francine was better before taking the little girl to see her. She didn't want her to see the wounds Francine had sustained. The young girl already had enough questions about the day her mother ran and wrecked the wagon.

Tess poured hot, steaming water over some loose tea and set the teapot back on the stove. She sat down at the table and pulled her Bible closer.

Howls of wind pressed against the cabin. A loud crash banged against the side of the cabin, waking Lizzie from her slumber. Tess bumped her tea, spilling the contents on the table.

Lizzie woke up and slid off the side of the bed on her stomach. She stood rubbing her eyes. "Where's Mama?"

"She's resting. Come sit with me and we'll warm in front of the fire."

Lizzie walked toward Tess and tripped on one of the uneven floorboards, knocking it to the side. Tess ran to her side and picked her up, comforting the girl.

As Tess moved the floorboard back into the open hole, light flickered off a metal box. She set Lizzie down in a chair and peered into the hole.

Tess set a lantern at the edge of the opening, trying to see within. Could it be papers? Perhaps the deed to the ranch?

Tess nervously stuck her hand down into the hole. A rattle buzzed near her arm and she screamed, jerking her arm back out.

"There must be a rattlesnake under the house." Tess stood up and kicked the board back into place, over the hole. She would have to figure out a way to get the box out from under the house, without getting bit by the snake.

She considered asking Ian to get the box out from under the house, but she certainly didn't know him—or trust him—well enough to allow him to see the box. His uncle might have him on a mission to find the papers, and she didn't want to lead him right to them, if they were in fact in the box.

The sun set over the mountains and Tess put Lizzie back to bed. Tess ran her hands through Lizzie's curls and pulled the blanket up over her shoulders.

Tess peeked out the window, scanning the front yard for Ian. She didn't want him to see her outside looking for a stick and question her motives.

Once she saw he wasn't around, she looked around for a long stick and came inside. She lined up several lamps along the edge of the hole where she would be reaching in.

"Maybe if I'm afraid of fire, you will be, too," Tess said to the snake. Tess stood several feet from the opening and lifted the wood board with the stick. The corner flipped up and she pushed the wood piece out of the way.

The lights shone brightly down into the hole, and she could see the black metal box. As she stepped closer, the rattle sounded and she gasped. Tess lunged backward, tripping over her dress. The snake's head rose up and leaned against the wood. He slithered between the cracks and up onto the floor. Tess froze. The stick was more than a few feet away. How would she fend it off?

Tess stood up slowly and moved along the wall for what seemed like an eternity toward the front door. As she turned the knob, the wind caught the door, slung it open, and slammed it against the wall with a loud thump. The snake drew up and hissed. Its tail wiggled, rattling Tess to her core.

The cold wind whipped through the room. One of the lamps flickered and blew out.

The snake slithered toward the stove and stopped along the wall. She picked up one of the other lanterns, still lit, and moved it several feet behind the snake, hoping to push it toward the door. The snake stayed immobile, only jutting its tongue out now and again.

Tess wasn't about to let a small creature get the best of her. She didn't come all the way west, lose her father and possibly her sister, just to die from a snakebite. She wanted to bang some pots together, and scare the snake out the door, but she was afraid of waking Lizzie. She didn't want the poor child to be scared to death, or worse, jump off the bed only to be snake bitten.

She couldn't possibly holler for Ian at this point. He would see the opening and the box.

The snake slithered toward the door and Tess' insides burned with fear. Her heart beat frantically against her chest.

For a brief moment, the snake stopped at the doorway. It turned and curled its way across the room toward the bed. Tess caught her breath in her throat and panicked. Lizzie slept soundly in the bed, inches from the snake.

"Dear God, protect Lizzie," Tess whispered. The snake curled its wiry body around the leg of a caned chair sitting near the bed, attempting to get to the warmth under the covers, moving ever-so-close to her precious niece.

Tess' fingers fumbled for the knob on the lamp. Her hands shook against it as she turned it up, illuminating the entire room. The snake lifted its head up, pressing its body up and onto the chair.

Tess inched across the room, tiptoeing and trying not to startle the snake. Able to make it back over to the stick, Tess picked it up as she kept her eyes on the creature. She moved closer to the hearth and tore at her hem, ripping a large section of her dress off. She wrapped the cloth on the end of the stick and stuck the tip in the fire, lighting up the material like a torch.

She moved back across the room toward the snake. Lizzie turned in her bed, startling the snake. Its head snapped toward the unaware girl. Tess lunged at the bed and swung the fire at the snake. It retreated backward and slithered off the bed and back onto the floor.

Tess followed the snake, swinging the fire close enough to move it toward the door. Sweat now dripped from her brow and her clothes clung to her body. She bit her lip and held her breath.

Tess continued pressing the fiery torch in the serpent's direction, moving it toward the open door until it finally slithered out the door. She slammed the door, and exhaled.

The burning material dropped to the floor in bulky, black ashes. Tess returned to the fireplace and nudged the end of the stick in the fire, knocking off the remainder of the ash. She pulled the charred stick out and rested it against the wall. Somehow knowing she had a fairly useful weapon in the room gave her a sense of relief.

Tess looked over at Lizzie, still sleeping in her bed. She smiled and sat down at the table. Her legs shook and she placed her hands against them, trying to settle them down. She never dreamed she would have to fight off snakes and fend for herself when she planned to come west. So many times in the past week, she wished for her father to be by her side. Fending off a snake was one more reason.

Tess peered again at the hole in the floor. Her father must've hidden the box under the floor. She knew the contents had to be of great value. Tess took a deep breath and got up from the chair. Before reaching in, she again surveyed the cool, dark hole for snakes. When she could see none were below the house, she leaned in and lifted the metal box out and set it on the table.

Tess pulled her hair back, twisted it into a knot, and tied it up. She pursed her lips and blew off the dust settled on top of the box before fiddling with the clasp. The hinges on the box squeaked as it opened.

Several letters were inside, faded and yellow. She recognized his handwriting on the front of the envelopes. Tess lifted out one yellowed letter addressed to her. Her father went so far as to buy a stamp for the postage, but never mailed the letter.

What could the letter contain that was important enough to remain inside of a box, under the floor, and not be mailed?

She flipped it over, finding it sealed. She broke the seal, pulled the letter out, and unfolded the page.

Tess furrowed her brow as she began to read.

"Dear Tess,

"I must write to you and tell you something I have been hiding all these years. You must know it will change your life forever. Cecelia, the woman you knew as your mother, is not the woman who bore you."

Tess set the letter down on the table and took a deep breath. She fought back tears building in her eyes. How can this be? Dare she read on? She looked toward the fire and back at the letter. She lifted it again and continued reading.

"I was married to Cecelia, but the whiskey and gambling pulled me away from home too many times. I am not proud of my sinning ways. While in Boston, I met another woman who made me feel alive. It was a feeling I'd never felt before. Her name is Mary Sikes. I dared not divorce Cecelia and leave her alone. She deserved much more than I could ever give her. Her untimely death when you were a child was most likely caused by me."

A rush of emotions flooded through Tess. Anger seethed deep inside of her. How could he lie to her all these years? Who else knew of this? Isolation pressed in on her. She set the letter down on the table and stood up. Tess paced the room, not knowing what to believe.

The truth of her mother was almost more than she could bear. What else had he lied about?

Tess sat back down and picked up the letter. She wanted desperately to ignore it, but she had to read on. What more pain could he cause?

"Mary was not welcome in your grandmother's house. I am not proud to say she was a woman of prostitution. When she was carrying you, she left the gambling halls and I created a small home for the both of you. She died from scarlet fever when you were but one year old. I tried everything I could to save her. I took you home and your grandmother eventually raised you. From the day I left you in her arms, she treated me with contempt. Her own son.

I am sorry for the lies. I love you as much today as I did the day you were born. Your mother treasured you until the day she died.

Love, Pa."

Tess set the letter back down on the table and took a deep breath. She wanted to scream. Her father was right. Nothing would ever be the same. Did he know the impact it would have on her life? To make matters worse, he wasn't there to confront.

Her mother a prostitute? How could she go on, knowing her mother was a woman of the night? Knowing Cecelia wasn't her mother was like losing her all over again.

Her heart broke for Cecelia, and what she must've gone through when he left. Was he right? Did her own presence drive

Cecelia to death? Questions filled her mind, and she knew they would never be answered.

A rage filled within. There was nothing that could be done.

She lifted the lid on the box once more and moved the other letters to the side. A golden locket sat at the bottom, tarnished with years.

Tess nudged her fingernail in the locket, popping it open. What she saw next made her heart skip a beat. The locket held a picture of her father on one side and a picture of a woman on the other. Her identical. It had to be her mother.

Chapter Fifteen

How could Tess' father let her live her entire life without knowing who her real mother was? What good did it do now to tell her that she was born of a prostitute? Her insides churned and she pushed the hot tea away.

Tess stared at the picture of what had to be her mother, in the locket. It was like looking into a mirror. Her eyes, cheeks, even lips were exactly the same. Everything Tess held dear came crashing down around her.

How did Cecelia, the mother she always knew, feel about this woman? Tess gasped. Is Mary the reason Cecelia died? Her death was always somewhat of a mystery. Tess always believed she was sick. Did she take too many pills because of Mary, forcing her sickness and ultimate death?

Although so many things were explained in that letter, more questions loomed in her mind. How could her real mother be a prostitute? Her father rarely came home. Now she knew the reason.

Tess crinkled the letter in her hand and stood up. She dropped the letter back on the table and paced across the room. As Tess walked past the mirror, she stopped. How could this be? Tess stared at her face, the face of the woman in the locket. Someone she knew nothing about.

For years, her grandfather lied to her, telling her she looked and acted like Cecelia. All to protect her from a life of shame?

But still, shame flowed in and settled on Tess. Did anyone else know about her real mother? She walked back to the table. Tess picked up the letter, and wadded it up tightly. She set her sights on the fire. If she burned the letter now, no one would ever know. No one could know.

Tess looked at Lizzie, sleeping soundly. She needed her mother, Francine. She didn't need to be raised by the child of a prostitute.

She set the letter back down in the box, and placed it under the floorboard, where it belonged. Tess moved the wooden board over the hole and pressed down hard on it, hoping no one would ever see it.

***

Francine blinked a few times while trying to adjust her eyes to the light filtering into the room through the window. She looked over next to the bed. A woman in a white dress stood next to her.

"Oh, your sister will be pleased to know you finally woke up," Sarah said. "You're in the infirmary."

"My legs hurt somethin' awful." She turned her head and peered down toward the bottom of the bed. A cry erupted and Sarah sat down in the chair next to Francine's bed.

"You've broken both your legs in several places. You need to stay put."

"My baby?" Francine said, trying to swallow the pain. The lump in her throat felt like a ball trying to work its way down.

"The baby still has a strong heartbeat." Sarah rested her hand on Francine's shoulder.

"What happened?"

"You took quite a spill. Your sister said you fell off a wagon. You were trapped underneath."

Francine closed her eyes. The accident roared into view in her mind. She kissed her daughter on the head and climbed in the wagon. Her heartbeat sped up thinking, about the horse running in front of her, jerking the wagon along.

She hit the reins against the horse several times, causing the wagon to drive faster. The back of the wagon slid in the ruts, knocking her around in the seat. When the wagon hit a rock, it was the last thing she remembered.

"I don't want to die," Francine said. Tears flowed down her cheeks. "How could I do this to Lizzie?"

"The Lord has plans for you. He wants you here. Sometimes we think we know best. We get angry or scared and we run. It's in our running that we miss out on God's plan and we get hurt," Sarah said. "He only wants what's best for you."

116

"It doesn't feel that way." Francine reached up and dried the tears from her face. Each time she thought of Luke, she wanted to turn it all around. She just wanted him back. And now her father was gone, too.

"I've racked my brain with thoughts of what I could have done differently the day my husband died," Francine said.

"I didn't know your husband died."

Francine nodded.

"You can't change what happened."

"I know that," Francine said, her voice cracking. "But what if?"

"You can't spend your life wondering. You have to move forward, as hard as it is. You have the will to live. I've seen many people come through here and pass away. Your daughter needs you. Let her be your reason to get better."

Francine took a deep breath and choked. Her hands grabbed at her neck. She tried to breathe in, but her throat closed, making it impossible to get air.

"Doctor!" Sarah yelled. "Come quick!"

Francine struggled again to breathe. She wanted to kick her legs, but they were trapped. She struggled to move.

The doctor came into the room and leaned over Francine. A light flashed in her eyes just before the darkness overcame her.

***

"I want you to carry a revolver," Ian said, walking around to the back of the house.

A knot formed in her stomach at the thought of having a weapon by her side. Deep down, she hoped nothing would bring her to the point of having to use a gun, but she knew reality dictated she protect her life from Henry Barrington, his men, and snakes.

"You need to know how to shoot it." Ian lifted one of the two revolvers from his holster and held it out in front of Tess. The light glimmered off the barrel.

Tess held it in her hand and was surprised at the weight. "I don't know if I can do this." The West was wild, but Tess never believed she'd see it firsthand.

"I set up a target across the field. You can get some practice before we head to town." Ian pointed to a small can in the distance, sitting atop a fencepost. "The better you get, the farther we'll move it."

Tess nodded. She gripped the handle and held it up.

Ian walked up close to Tess and placed his hands on the revolver still in her grip. A marathon of butterflies flew through her at his touch.

"Are you paying attention?" Ian asked, taking the revolver back.

"Yes... Yes." His close presence made her take an extra breath.

"All you gotta do is pull back on the hammer and pop open the cylinder to see if it's loaded. Here, you try." Ian pushed the cylinder back in place and handed the revolver to Tess.

She pulled the hammer back halfway until it clicked. It was harder than she thought. Tess pressed the print of her other thumb against the cylinder and tried to push it open. "It's not working."

"Push harder. Like a man." A smile grew wide across his face and Tess knew his humor had kicked in again.

She smiled in return and shoved her thumb once more against the cylinder, this time popping it open.

Ian reached in his saddlebag and pulled out a few combustible cartridges, holding them in the palm of his hand. "Keep it full. If you miss the first time, you still have five shots before reloading."

"I hope it never comes to that." Tess didn't want to imagine a situation where she had to pull the trigger once, let alone five more times.

"You're out west. There's plenty of animals that will threaten your life, not just people. Count on it." The smile on his face was replaced with a stoic look of concern and the seriousness of the situation gave her alarm. Would she truly have to use the revolver on someone?

Ian showed Tess how to load each cartridge one-by-one, into each chamber.

"Your hands are shaking," Ian said, as he seated the cartridges with the loading lever.

"I've just never used a gun before now." Tess watched his hands move with speed. It was obvious he'd done this many times.

Ian placed percussion caps on before closing the cylinder.

She feared having this type of power, although it could save her life.

"See that can I set out?" He again pointed in the direction of the fence.

"Yes. I see it."

He walked around behind her. "Lift your arm up, pull the hammer, aim, and shoot."

Tess pulled up her arm straight out in front of her and pulled back on the hammer. Ian's warm breath floated against her ear as he moved in close to help her aim. He wrapped his left arm around her waist and pulled her close. With his right hand, he held her arm to help her aim. She pulled the trigger faster than she planned, firing the gun. The blast echoed through her ears.

"Where'd you shoot? You didn't even get close." Ian laughed out loud as he moved away from Tess. "You need lots of practice."

Tess wasn't about to tell him that his presence made her knees weak, causing her to miss.

"Let me try again," Tess said. "This time, you stand over there." Tess waved her hand in his direction.

Again, she lifted her arm out in front of her, drew the hammer back, squinted one eye shut, and pulled the trigger. This time the crack of the bullet shot the can clean off the fencepost high into the sky.

"Woo hoo!" Ian yelled. "You might have a knack for this after all."

Tess felt a sigh of relief wash over her. At least she could aim.

"Let's just see if that was luck. Keep that revolver pointed down and I'll run out and set up a few more cans."

Tess waited while he set up some more targets along the fenceposts. Each can was further than the last.

When Ian returned he said, "Let's see what you've got."

Tess took aim and shot the first can off the post. In her mind she kept count of the bullets. If she had to shoot at something planning to kill her, she wanted to make sure she knew when she needed to reload.

"Good job." Ian seemed to revel in the game. "Try the next one out."

Tess followed directions and shot the next three cans off the posts, one after another.

"Guess I don't need to teach you nothin'. You're a natural." Ian laughed again and shook his head.

"I've got cartridges for the bullets in the lean-to. I'll give 'em to you and I want you to keep some extra with you, and keep the rest in the house."

"I can't say I want to carry a gun with me, but I have to admit that was sort of fun."

Tess enjoyed his closeness, much more than learning this new sport.

***

Ian tightened the reins on the horses and waited for Tess to come outside and join him. Although he knew she was going into town to take care of Franklin, he enjoyed the ride, talking with her.

Ian felt a peace wash over him. Something inside of him believed she had the determination to run the ranch and survive the winter.

His insides churned when he thought of her brother. How could he tell her he knew about her brother? He couldn't break a promise to Tess' father and tell her, even with Ed gone.

Tess and Lizzie came through the door of the cabin and walked down the stairs. Ian put his hands around Lizzie's waist and hoisted her into the wagon. Before he could make it around to the other side of the wagon, Tess climbed up and sat down.

Silence filled the air the first few minutes of the ride into Denver City.

"What was my Pa like before he died?" Tess asked.

He rode for a moment, thinking about how to answer her question. "I don't want to lie to ya, Tess. Before your Pa got sick, he spent a lot of time in the saloons," Ian said, adjusting his hat on his head. "When he got sick with fever, he ended up in the infirmary. I went down to check on him a couple of times. Each time I left, I was just sure he wasn't gonna make it outta there alive."

Her smooth forehead crinkled together into wrinkles. "I never knew he was sick."

"Sometimes a man faces death and starts to do some thinkin'." They rode a few paces without talking. "Preacher Thomas was makin' his usual rounds, visiting some of the folks in the infirmary. He sat down and talked with your Pa."

Tess smiled and Ian's heart could've melted right out of his shirt.

"Your Pa later told me that he let Jesus take over his life. Didn't think he could live life drinking and bein' a sinner any more. 'Course I didn't believe him. I had to see it for myself." Ian's smile broadened across his face and he looked over at Tess. He knew she needed to hear the good things about her father. She probably spent most of her life hearing only negative things about the man.

"One evening I saw him riding his horse down to the saloon. I followed him, 'cause I knew he'd slipped up. Figured God couldn't get ahold of him, he was too much of a sinner. I stood outside for a few minutes waitin' to see what he was gonna do." Ian laughed loud and slapped his leg. "He was in there sharin' Jesus with all the folks in the saloon. That was the first time in my life I was glad somebody proved me wrong. Your Pa was a changed man."

"And how did you come to know Jesus?" Tess said.

He looked over at her. Some of her hair had fallen out of the bun and it draped across her shoulders. Her face was turning a light tan from the sun and her lips were as pink as a flower.

Tess looked up and Ian turned away quickly.

"After watchin' your pa." He paused for a moment. "He never wavered in his decision. I saw how he had a desire to read his Bible and learn about the God that worked miracles and gave people hope. I saw change in a person I had never seen before."

Ian lost hope when his ma died years ago. He wanted nothing to do with the God that took his ma away. He wasn't angry at the Almighty, he just figured it was mutual distrust between him and God. Seeing Ed change from a drunk to a man with the intention of following God, no matter the cost, was enough to convince Ian he needed to try out Jesus.

"That's about the time your Pa started talkin' about sending for you and your sister. He told me one night he wanted to give your family a chance. His sickness wore him down quite a bit, so I'd come out and check in on him on occasion. We'd sit and read the Bible and ask each other questions. It was like two blind men walking in a snow storm, tryin' to find the way," he chuckled. "But we learned a lot."

Ian glanced over at Tess wiping a tear from her cheek. "It might not 'a' seemed like it at times, but your pa loved his kids." For a moment, Ian thought he'd let out the secret about her brother. His panic turned to calm when he realized she would only think of her and Francine, not a brother.

"Why didn't he show it?" she asked. "All those years I waited for him to come home and be the father he was supposed to be."

"He made some bad choices puttin' alcohol first. It jails a man. Ruins you."

Tess nodded.

"He got pretty dern excited when you all decided to come west." Ian looked ahead at Denver City coming into his sights.

"I just wish he were alive so I could have this same conversation with him." Tess sighed.

Ian wished he could take the pain away. There wasn't a day that passed when he didn't think about his ma. She was taken too soon, and there wasn't a thing he could do about it. Somehow, learning to trust God always made it a little easier.

***

Catherine pulled the curtains back, letting the sunlight shine in, spilling onto the floor. Tess was grateful she was able to leave Lizzie at her house throughout the day. It was apparent Catherine enjoyed having the young girl around. The two played on the floor and sang songs.

Catherine jerked back and threw her hand on her belly.

"What is it? Are you okay?" Tess asked, stepping close to Catherine.

"I'm having pain in my belly and my back." A tear rolled down her cheek. "My stomach knots at the thought of losing another baby." She ran her hand across the growing bump. She whispered, "I pray constantly that the little one inside would grow to be healthy."

Thomas walked into the room and Catherine looked at Tess and held her finger up to her lips. "I'll be out making my rounds." He kissed her on the forehead and walked out the door.

"I've haven't told him about the pain," Catherine said. "His heart still aches from the child we lost. It took him months to get over it. I don't know how much he can go through again. I don't want to worry him."

122

"Don't go through this alone, Catherine," Tess said. "He's your husband. I know he can help you get through this."

She drew in a deep breath. "The pain seems to be subsiding a bit."

Catherine sat down in a rocking chair and lifted a needle from a pincushion on the table next to her. She lifted two quilting squares and began to sew.

"I try to control my negative thoughts, but at times like this it becomes a strained task," Catherine said. "My emotions ransack my heart each time I think about the baby I lost." She paused for a moment before speaking again. "Never seeing the child's face again tears me up at times. When the child was stillborn, I tried to memorize every detail of her face. Her tiny nose, her fingers and toes, and her tiny wisps of hair." Tears fell from her face. "But, then some days, I can't remember what she looked like, and it makes it so much harder."

Tess sat down next to her and slid her arm across her shoulders and embraced her in a hug.

"I know the baby is in heaven, but I continue to have the sense that something is missing. I'll have to wait until I get there to hold that child in my arms again."

"I know it seems impossible, but the Lord will get you through this. He will. He promised to be at your side through the most difficult moments in our lives," Tess said. "I'm having to remind myself of that right now. Each day is a challenge. Adding my grandmother to the troubles doesn't help any. It's times like this I really have to pray for patience and guidance."

"Will you return with Franklin?" Catherine asked.

"I don't know. I feel as though everything is a tumbled mess. I can't afford to pay Ian, my sister is in the infirmary, and Franklin needs my help."

Chapter Sixteen

Francine rustled in her bed and opened her eyes. She blinked, trying to clear her eyes from the fog that seemed to be covering them.

She looked around the room. "Grandmother?!"

"You're finally awake," Eliza said, as she covered her mouth with her hand. "We've been so worried about your state." Eliza leaned in close and tapped Francine on the shoulder a couple of times.

"Where's Lizzie?" She lifted her head to look around the room. The muscles in her neck tightened and she laid her head back down on the pillow.

"Settle down now. She's taken care of. Not to worry."

Francine felt a wave of relief wash over her. But a dull pain ached in her legs. She ran her hand across her belly. The reality of her situation hit her again. What had she done?

"Where am I?"

"You're still in this wretched town."

"What town?"

Her grandmother laughed. "Denver City, of course."

"What are you doing here? I mean, you're so far from home." Francine winced from the pain in her legs.

"I came out with Franklin to get Tess and bring her back home."

"Bring her home?"

"Didn't she tell you she was engaged to him?"

Francine moved her head from side-to-side, but in usual fashion, her grandmother didn't wait for a response.

"When she got the letter from your father to come west, she broke off the engagement with him—the morning of the ceremony, no less—and left. He decided to come after her. Now that your father is, well… you know, there's no reason for her to stay."

"I can't believe he's gone." A tear ran down the side of her cheek. Francine didn't remember anything after hitting the rock while racing away in the wagon, but she did remember Tess telling her about their father's death. It all came rushing in at once.

Francine felt the cries come rumbling up. She wished again for sleep. Nothing could take away the physical and emotional pain she was feeling.

"There, there, child. No need to fret." Her grandmother rubbed her shoulder. "I'm so sorry about Luke, my dear. I wish I could take it all away for you. I understand your grief."

Francine wondered if she really did understand her grief. Francine truly loved Luke with all her heart. The marriage between her grandparents was arranged and although they stayed married until her grandfather's death, there were many times she questioned their love for each other.

"Where's Tess?" Francine wiped the tears from her face with the back of her hand.

"She's tending to Franklin. It seems he's had some bad luck of his own. He's had a stroke." Eliza pulled at the tips of the gloves on her hands and slid them off, laying them across her lap. "He's unable to walk or feed himself at this point."

Francine couldn't believe all she was hearing. Her father and Luke gone, now Franklin with a stroke.

"It's a wonder the man is still alive. I thought he'd go like your grandfather. The more I come sit with you, the more responsibility she will feel toward the man. Hopefully it will lead to kindred spirits and she'll make the choice to go home with him."

Francine knew it was useless to argue with her grandmother. The woman would set her sights on something and not stop until she got her way. She assumed it would be the same with Tess. Eventually, Tess would see her grandmother's way and go back home to New York City.

***

"What do you say we talk about your father's ranch, Isaiah?" Henry Barrington said, walking up to the young man.

"What about it?" He ran the brush over his horse's back once more and set it down on the bench inside the barn.

"I'm betting you've got hold of some papers that could help me out a lot." He moved his hand down on his waist, just above his revolver.

Isaiah figured he was trying to make a point. "Don't know nothing 'bout no papers."

Three of Barrington's hired men walked around the corner and stood next to Barrington. Isaiah felt a rush of panic well up inside. He slid his hand back on the horse, petting the animal, and slinking his hand toward the reins. He'd jump on and ride if the men tried to round him up again.

"I think you know a lot more than what you're letting on," Barrington said. "Don't you, boys?"

The small band of men smiled and nodded their heads.

"You owe me, boy."

"I don't owe you nothin'."

"I took you in when no one else wanted you. Namely, your father. He didn't care a whit about you. Those sisters of yours don't care about you, either."

"You don't know nothin' about them. Nothin'." Isaiah gripped the reins tighter hoping none of the men would see him shaking.

"I want that land, and I don't really care how I have to go about getting it. Do you get my meaning?"

Isaiah stared at the man. He wasn't about to give in easily.

"So, where's the papers?" Barrington moved a little closer.

"I told you. I ain't got 'em. You'll have to find 'em yourself."

"Boys, I think Isaiah here's trying to outwit us."

They laughed and Isaiah could feel the hairs on his arms and the back of his neck prickle up against his clothing.

Isaiah gripped the reins and threw his foot in the saddle, and rode away. The horse took off before he even had his leg over the saddle.

"Boys, don't let him get away!" Barrington yelled.

Isaiah got a clean head start. He rode hard toward his father's land. He knew a few places he could hide out—if he'd make it in time. He looked over his shoulder and saw the men gaining on him.

***

Ian's horse trotted toward the cabin. The cattle were all accounted for and eating in the higher meadows. The stream was getting lower and he hoped the coming snow would create enough runoff when it melted. They wouldn't have to worry about moving them to a new pasture.

As he approached the house, a horse, without a rider, came into view. Ian instinctively reached around and felt for his revolver. He pulled it out and flipped the cylinder open, checking to see if the gun was loaded. Full. Ian wondered if there would ever be a day he didn't have to rely on his gun.

He neared the house and slid off his horse. He hid behind the large animal and walked it slowly toward the cabin, his hand on his gun, ready to draw.

A cough emerged from the silence as Ian closed in on the intruder.

"Help... " a man said, barely audible. He coughed some more.

"Who's there?"

"Ian?" A man's voice gargled and coughed again.

He rounded the corner and saw Isaiah lying next to his horse on the ground, in front of the cabin.

Ian released the trigger on the revolver and secured it in his holster. He ran to Isaiah.

"What happened? You're covered in blood!"

He pulled on Isaiah's arm and flipped him on his back. He groaned as he turned over.

"Who did this to you?" Ian's voice grew stern. He'd seen enough fighting to last a lifetime.

"Barrington's men—I"

"I told you to stay away from them. They're nothin' but trouble." Ian lifted Isaiah up and sat him against the porch steps.

"I had nowhere else to go." Isaiah looked up at Ian.

He could tell the young man was trying his best to keep from crying.

"If you're not gonna tell Tess and Francine who you are, why don't you get outta town and find a place to live where you can make an honest livin'? This life ain't for you."

"Nobody decent'll hire me."

"You'd be surprised at how many nice folks are out there, just waitin' to help." Catherine and Thomas came to mind. They'd helped Ian more in the past few months than anyone ever had.

"Let's get you out back by the well and get you cleaned up." Ian hoisted Isaiah up and threw his arm across his shoulder to help walk him to the back of the house. Isaiah didn't make too much noise when he walked, so he figured he at least didn't have any broken bones. Only broken pride.

Ian dropped the bucket into the water, drew it back up, and set it on the edge. He dipped his handkerchief into the water and soaked it through. He wrung it out over some of his cuts, getting most of the wounds cleaned up.

"Why are you here helpin' Tess?" Isaiah asked, still coughing.

"She needs it."

"There's more to it than that."

"Your Pa was a good man. 'Sides, when I met your sister, she seemed different."

"You love her?" Isaiah said, eyeing him.

Ian laughed out loud. "You gettin' protective of your sis?"

"No, just wonderin' what makes her so special."

"She has a strong spirit. Reminds me of my Ma. Fragile, but not afraid to take a go at life." Ian rinsed out his rag and shoved it in his back pocket. He'd dry it out later.

"I don't know where to go," Isaiah said with reservation.

"You got any money?" Ian asked.

"No. They took everything I had."

"What were they after?"

"The deed to the ranch."

"You got it?" Ian wanted the truth up front.

"No. Never had it."

"Why should I believe you? You've lied to me before," Ian said.

"You don't have to believe me. But, I ain't got nothin' to hide—"

"You got lots to hide." Something inside Ian wanted to give Isaiah a chance. No one had ever given him an opportunity to do the right thing. Maybe trusting him a little would give him a reason to go straight, talk to his sisters, and make something with his life. "Why

128

don't you stay in the lean-to with me for a few days. At least 'til ya figure out where you need to go."

"What about Tess? Won't she know?"

Ian felt dishonest going behind her back and letting him stay at the cabin, but he couldn't very well tell her that she had a brother staying with them after the promise he made to her father. This one small lie seemed less harmful than the admission of family, and a disloyalty to a man that led him to his saving grace. Besides, he couldn't turn a hurting man away.

"Keep your horse in the barn. She won't go out there. You can help me check on the cattle, do some chores. She'll be in town all day taking care of a man."

"What man?"

"He's from back New York City. He said he was her fiancé—"

"Fiancé?" Isaiah's voice rose a pitch. "What're you chasin' after her for if she's made a promise to another man?"

"First off, I ain't chasin' her. It's sort of a help to your Pa. Second, she said she broke it off."

"Seems sort of fishy to me. My Pa's gone, you don't owe him nothin'. And if she broke it off, how come she's there with him, and not here with you?"

Ian knew the answer. She never promised herself to him. They had one brief encounter that didn't amount to much, he wasn't about to kid himself into believing that she cared for him any more than she cared for another.

Knowing she was taking care of Franklin ate at him a little. But, it also served to show him that she had a selfless heart. She did it because she cared and he had no one else to help him. Except her grandmother, and she didn't appear to be much help—more of a hindrance.

"Tess' grandmother is in town."

Isaiah was looking down at his torn shirt and jerked his head up at the comment. "I s'pose she'd be my grandma too, then?"

Ian nodded. "Gotta say, though, she's not the nicest lady I've ever met. Full of spit'n fire."

"Sounds like she passed it on to me." A look of wonder, mixed with fear, crossed Isaiah's face.

"Wish I knew more about who and where I came from. I didn't know much 'bout my Ma's side. They were all dead and gone. She'd tell me stuff 'bout 'em at times. But, my Pa is who I want to know about. He left us when I was a baby. He came back now and again. But, I didn't never forgive him for that." Isaiah's eyebrows crinkled up. He turned away and sniffed.

Ian knew tears were coming. He'd let him talk, get his anger out. He understood, his own Ma had to raise him alone.

"She had a hard time gettin' money. There were times she had to… sell… herself—iffen you know what I mean—just to make a little money to feed me. She'd sit up and cry at night. I'd pretend I was sleepin', but I heard every cry. I didn't want her to worry that I wouldn't love her." He stood up from the edge of the well and raised his hand. "I did love her, ya know."

Ian nodded his head. "I know ya did. You can't fault her for doin' what she had to do."

"No, but I can sure blame my Pa for not bein' there for her. When I got that letter from him a while back, I came to get money from him. But sometimes, it felt like I was talkin' to a mirror. We were so alike. I'd never had that. I liked it. But, my anger got the best of me every time. I just couldn't get past him hurtin' Ma like that. He owed me. Now, Tess and Francine owe me."

"Isaiah, they don't owe you. He did them wrong, too. But, when he called you all out here, he wanted to make things right. He just didn't get a chance." Ian regretted it for the lot of them. He wondered several times why the good Lord took their father before they all had a chance to be a family, once and for all.

"You keep outta sight. Stay in the lean-to until we leave each mornin'," Ian said.

Isaiah nodded.

"Let's get you somethin' to eat." Ian just hoped he was doing the right thing.

Chapter Seventeen

Tess walked through the front door of the infirmary and down the hallway to visit her sister. She tapped her finger against the door and opened it. Francine's eyes were closed. She sat down in the chair next to her sister and watched her for a few minutes.

Francine opened her eyes and smiled. "Tess, I'm so glad you're here."

Tess slid her hand into Francine's and smiled back at her sister. "It's I who is glad you're here. I thought we lost you."

Francine stared up at the ceiling. "Tess, I'm so sorry for the other day. I… I couldn't handle the pain of losing another person. We came out here because of Pa. I never considered that he might be gone when we arrived."

"I'm here. Don't you care anything about that?" Tess felt a nauseating warmth travel across her body. She wasn't sure she wanted to hear the answer.

"I thought this would be a new chance to get to know Pa, and let Lizzie grow up with a grandfather that really cared about her." Francine turned her head and looked at the wall on the other side of the room.

Tess fiddled with the knob on the lantern, sitting on the bedside table, making the room brighter. She wanted to see her sister's face as they talked. Did Francine even want Tess around?

"Francine, you're all I have left. I don't want to lose you, too." Tess hoped her sister would respond in kind.

"I've been lying here thinking about all this, Tess. We need to give up this dream of living on a ranch as a wonderful family. It will never work."

"Why don't you give it a chance?" How could Francine decide to leave without giving it a try?

"We can't run a ranch by ourselves," Francine laughed, and winced a moment later from the pain.

"I have someone to help us. We don't have to do it alone. He knew Pa and wants us to run this ranch."

"How do you plan to pay him? Neither one of us has any money. Can we even buy food to survive on for the winter?" She turned her head in the direction of Tess and pressed her lips together.

"I've thought about this. We can get credit at the general store. We'll pay them back, in the spring, when we sell the cattle."

"What if something happens? What if we can't sell the cattle? I don't think your friend will be too willing to help then."

"Lizzie and I might go back to New York City with Grandmother. I can't live out here like this." Francine turned her head and Tess knew the conversation was over.

She sat for a few minutes praying that Francine would say something else or change her mind. Her silence hurt worse than anything she could say.

Tess walked down the stairs and outside. Her body ached from worry. Maybe if she walked, things would clear up in her mind and she could work out the soreness.

Now that her father was gone, she wanted nothing more than to have Francine stay. But she couldn't talk her into something she wasn't willing to do. She would have to pray that her sister would change her mind.

"Lady, what do you think you're doin' down here in this part of town?" A haggard voice called out, startling Tess.

She glanced up and looked at her surroundings. Rotten wood benches and broken chairs sat crumpled on the porch of one of the buildings. The sign at the top said "Saloon."

"I... I'm sorry. I didn't mean to come here."

The woman belted out a laugh so hard it could have hit Tess on the face if she were any closer. "I don't think you need any of my services."

The top of her dress was unbuttoned, letting almost everything loose. The bottom was torn and frayed. A cigarette dangled from the edge of her lip. Her hair was pulled back with a small frayed ribbon.

Tess wanted to stare, but knew it wouldn't be proper.

"You look mighty scared," the woman said. She took several steps closer to Tess.

Tess took a deep breath and smelled her foul breath.

"Look at me," she demanded. Her voice grew lower and more stern, startling Tess.

Tess glanced at the woman out of the corner of her eye.

"Can't ya look at me? Am I too dirty for a pretty girl like you to even look upon?" She took a drag off her cigarette and blew smoke in Tess' face. "I used to be like you. Real pretty. My hair stayed brushed and my teeth were white as snow. You think you're better than me. You're not. You are me."

Tess pressed her lips together and turned to walk away.

"I'll always be here, rotting away. Your turn is coming up."

She has to be drunk.

Tess ran around the corner and her breathing intensified. She stopped and leaned against the brick wall of a building to catch her breath.

Was her own mother so harsh and disrespectful? So disgusting? Tess looked down at herself. She felt filthy after talking to the woman. She wanted to burn the letter from her father and forget she ever knew her mother was a prostitute. She was nothing, and if anyone ever found out, she would be cast out of church and society.

Ian's face came to mind. He wouldn't possibly help a woman who was born of a prostitute. He could never know.

Tess walked to the edge of the building and peered around the corner. The woman who offended her stood against the rail post on the porch of the saloon. Her blouse was still open and inviting the darkest of men. The woman yelled out as several men walked by her.

Tess wanted to go to her and shake her. Let her know that she was filthy and degrading.

She couldn't help wondering if her mother stood outside of a run-down building yelling at the men that passed down the street. Did she call to her father and lure him in? Her stomach knotted at the thought.

How did her mother end up in such a place? What led her to become a woman of the night? Tears flowed down Tess' cheeks like a flooding river.

***

133

Tess watched Ian allow Lizzie to hold the reins on Slater. The little girl loved riding in front of Ian. She giggled every time the horse galloped.

Tess couldn't refuse to fall in love with Lizzie in the short time she'd been staying with her.

As she looked around at her surroundings, Tess felt a sense of peace wash over her. An early snow fell on the tips of the mountains in the distance. She knew it wouldn't be long before snow fell in the low country.

For a moment, Tess felt more complete than she had since she arrived. The beauty of the Rockies that surrounded her felt like home.

A shot rang out in the distance, echoing across the foothills. Tess' horse jumped at the sound, and she felt a surge of fear pump through her bloodstream. She tugged on the reins to settle her horse down and looked over at Ian.

He glanced at Tess and back toward the cabin. "Barrington."

"Are you sure?" she asked.

Ian flipped the reins on his horse and trotted over to Tess. He lifted Lizzie from his lap and set her in front of Tess. Tess slid her arm around Lizzie's waist.

"Stay back a bit. I want to get closer and have a look." Ian lifted his revolver out of his holster and cocked it, ready for anything.

He rode off in the distance and Tess lagged behind. As much as she hated to, Tess leaned down and reached inside of her saddlebag to make sure her gun was near. She pulled it from the bag, checked to see if it was loaded, and slid it back down out of sight.

Tess watched Ian grow smaller in the distance. Another shot rang out. Her feet itched to tap the side of Lady and run after Ian, but she didn't want to jeopardize Lizzie's safety. She trusted that Ian could handle the situation. She nudged the horse forward and kept heading toward home.

As she neared the cabin, she spotted Ian riding back. The trembling in her body subsided at the sight of him.

"You've got two dead steers out in the pond," he said, still out of breath.

"Who would shoot the cattle?"

134

"I don't doubt that Barrington sent one of his men to do the dirty work. I didn't see anyone, but they most likely shot the cows and rode over the crest of the hill and disappeared fast. He thinks the more pain and financial distress he causes you, the quicker you'll run out of town and not return."

Ian lifted his leg over Slater and dropped on both feet to the ground. He came over to Tess and took Lizzie from the saddle. Tess swung her leg over and felt two hands around her waist. As she came down, she almost fell forward into his arms. He placed her on the ground and her face was only inches from his.

They stared at each other for a brief moment before Lizzie pulled at Tess's dress, interrupting the two.

"How can he get away with that?" Tess said, lifting Lizzie into her arms.

"He's got more people stuffed in his pocket to do his deeds. Money will buy you a lot of people you think are friends. It will buy you ignorant people to do your biddin'."

Tess still couldn't help but wonder if Ian was getting paid to stay at the ranch and try to work his way into her heart, ultimately getting her to sell the ranch to Barrington. "Can't we go to the sheriff?

"He's in his pocket, too."

That made sense. He'd been no help when she went into town and told him about the men following her. She wondered if there would ever be a way to get out from under Barrington.

Ian pulled his bag off his horse, threw it in the lean-to, and disappeared in the barn.

Tess put Lizzie down and let her run around in the grassy area.

When Ian came back out with a rope, he attached it to his saddle and got back on his horse.

"Are you riding out there again?" She asked, looking up at him.

"We have no choice. Those steers'll rot in that water and none of the other cattle will drink out of it. I need to get them out." Slater must have sensed the urgency. He turned a full circle and lifted his head up and down a few times. "Stay here and take the girl inside," his voice grew stern. "I'm not sure how safe it is out there."

The wind picked up, blowing Tess' hair. She hated to think what might happen if Ian were gone and someone came.

"Make sure your gun is loaded," he said. "You might need it."

"I just don't know if I can shoot a man." She shook her head.

"You might not have a choice. It's you and Lizzie . . . or them."

Tess loathed the idea of having to use a gun. But she didn't want anything to happen to Lizzie. She'd never forgive herself if Lizzie got hurt and Tess hadn't done all she could in her power to protect the little girl.

***

Ian hoped he could get the cattle out of the pond before the sun crested over the mountains and darkness fell around him. As soon as the sun dipped behind the mountains, the temperatures dropped enough to sting.

The rest of the cattle were spread out, grazing in the field. It didn't take him long to get the two steers out of the water and taken care of. That was more money Tess would have to go without. His anger seethed at Barrington. Even Ian couldn't understand how a man could be so cold and evil.

A sliver of the sun still shone above the mountain peaks. Ian rode out a little farther to check on the rest of the herd. It looked like only two had been killed. He worried that they might try to take out a few at a time before the sale in the spring. A man with a gun and a sneaky way about him could get rid of quite a few in the herd without ever being seen.

He rode back to the cabin as darkness fell. The long day began to wear on him. His leg ached in the cooler temperatures. He wondered how his leg would do in the coming months. Would he be able to keep up the pace needed to run the ranch? Ian knew Tess would be up to the challenge. He just hoped she'd stay to find out.

After he put his horse in the barn, Ian strode over to the cabin, savoring the moment he never thought he'd have. He could see her through the window, cooking something. She let her hair flow down her back. Tess smiled at Lizzie and lifted her arms up, playing with the young girl.

A feeling of home filtered through him. His mother's face flashed in front of him for a split second. He hadn't felt at home

136

since he was a child. The feeling almost overtook him. A part of him feared letting the emotion in, knowing it might not last forever, even though he wanted it to.

Chapter Eighteen

Mismatched teacups were lined along the top of a wooden shelf, along with a can of tea. Tess opened the top and held it up to her nose, taking in the comforts of home. The teakettle whistled and she pulled it off the black stovetop and poured a stream of hot water into the cup.

A brown ledger sat underneath the sugar canister on the table. Tess blew the dust off the top and opened it, thumbing through the pages while studying the information written in what had to be her father's handwriting. Dates were listed in the left column and amounts of money on the right. Levi's Mercantile was scrolled in ink at the top of the page. Numbers grew larger with each page she turned. According to the ledger, her father owed a tremendous amount of money.

It started with fencing materials, food, and a few household items. The amounts were large. Money she couldn't pay back—not until the spring. She feared she would barely be able to pay his bills, let alone Ian. How would they have money for the following winter?

Tess decided to keep the information from Ian—for now. After all, he was only helping on the ranch. If he was working for his uncle, it would be information he could pass on, and she wasn't about to give out details. It was up to her to decide how to manage the finances and keep things going. Tess decided she would talk to the storeowner down at Levi's and try to secure more credit when they went into town tomorrow to see Francine and Franklin.

So many times over the past few days Ian had shown a considerable amount of character and honesty. How could he still be working for his uncle? She knew deep down her feelings toward him were becoming serious. Her heart never ached for a man like it did for Ian.

Each time she thought of him, guilt flooded her over Franklin. She couldn't possibly turn him down a second time, especially after he traveled all the way from New York City for her hand in marriage.

Tess wanted to marry for love, and for the first time in her life, a man stole her heart. She smiled at the thought of Ian. She would have to see if he truly was the man he claimed to be.

***

"Can I get another blanket?" Ian asked Tess before turning in for the night.

"Sure, it must be getting colder out there," Tess responded.

He nodded. It felt wrong to be hiding Isaiah in the lean-to, but he felt he had no choice. If he let the young man go into town, he'd end up in the wrong place, perhaps getting himself into more trouble. He didn't want to bother Thomas and Catherine again—he didn't want to take advantage of their generosity by adding another hardship to their lives.

Maybe the Lord would understand his promise to Ed to keep her brother a secret.

Tess walked outside with a folded blanket in her hands. "I'll give you mine. It's warmer in the cabin. We've got the fire inside, so we don't need as many covers."

"Much obliged." He stood in the doorway for a moment, staring at Tess. He could look at her all night.

"Did you need something else?" A delicate smile graced her face.

"No. No." He shook his head. "'Night."

"Good night." He heard the door close gently behind him.

Ian slung the other blanket over a makeshift bed in the lean-to for Isaiah.

"Get comfortable. This is home for now."

"You know, Barrington's quarters were a lot fancier, but I'd rather be here. I don't have to sleep with one eye open all the time."

Ian nodded. He knew from experience what Isaiah meant. He'd spent most of his life dodging others. When he stayed with Catherine and Thomas, just after quitting his uncle's ranch, he slept better than he'd slept in his entire life.

His entire life could be packed into one satchel, now sitting on the dirt floor. He lifted his small Bible out of the top of the bag and set it on the side table Tess brought out for him.

The book had become a treasure in the short time since he'd left Barrington's, thanks to the help and guidance of the local preacher, Thomas, and Tess's father Ed. He missed his time with Ed. He'd grown to love him like a father. A father he never had.

"What're you readin'?" Isaiah asked.

"The Bible." He held it up for Isaiah to see.

"I never learnt to read. Always wished I could. Ma said there ain't nothin' worth readin' to go to all that trouble learnin'," Isaiah said. "I always disagreed with her on that one."

"Want me to read to you some?"

Isaiah remained silent for a moment and stared straight ahead. "I'd like to hear 'bout that Isaiah fellow. Ma said that's who I was named for."

Ian opened the Bible to a passage in Isaiah. "We can start reading from the beginning."

Isaiah leaned back on his bed and pulled the covers up to his chest.

Ian looked down at him and wondered how he ended up in such a mess with Barrington. Isaiah wasn't a bad person. He seemed to have a good heart.

Ian read for a while until he noticed that Isaiah had fallen asleep.

Something inside of Ian felt nothing short of comfort in his surroundings. He had wanted to be close to Tess. He had wanted to protect her for the sake of Ed, but never planned on falling for her.

Barrington had run a few people out of town, broken and poor. The minute he saw his horse on Tess' ranch when she first arrived, it spelled trouble. That man wanted her land and Ian knew Barrington would do whatever necessary to get it.

Ian despised working for Barrington. He was evil to the core. He knew Barrington would stop at nothing to see Tess run out of town, or worse... dead.

Ian hoped Barrington would leave Tess alone. He didn't figure anyone would listen though. At least not the sheriff.

The moment he first saw Tess when she walked through the church doors played over in his mind. His breath was knocked clean out of him. He couldn't take his eyes off of her. She was beautiful. His heart broke for her, knowing she would miss her father terribly. Just as much as he missed his own mother. Ian turned the knob on the lamp and closed his eyes, getting some needed slumber.

***

Sitting in church would be a welcome way to start the day. Tess buttoned her dress and slid her gloves onto her hands, out of habit. But just as soon as she put them on, she grabbed the fingertips and pulled them back off, setting them down on the table. White gloves had no place out west. Her fingers caressed the monogram at the edge, a reminder of what used to be.

She crossed the room, her dress hem picking up dust along the floor, to the small wood-rimmed mirror on the wall. Tess lifted some of her hair out of the way, studying the cut on her head. It had healed quite a bit. Tess put a bonnet on her head and tied the strings below her chin.

She could hear Ian outside hitching up the wagon. Thankfully he'd been able to pull it out of the mud and fix the wheel since Francine's accident.

Lizzie sat on the edge of the bed, swinging her legs, dressed and ready to go to church. She'd asked for her Ma more than once, and Tess tried to comfort her as much as possible when she cried for her. She knew it wasn't the same as Francine, but she could at least help her through this time.

"C'mon, let's get goin'." Tess held out her hand and they walked out front together.

Tess and Lizzie climbed up into the seat, hoping to make it to town in time for church.

Ian climbed into the seat next to them. His arm rubbed against her and a jolt of electricity ran through her. She looked at him and turned away before he saw her.

He snapped the reins and the horses lunged forward. The ride to town was a little more than a mile. The mountains soared to the sky in the west, capped with snow, and the prairie stretched out east as far as her eyes could see.

What she would give to sit next to her father on the ride to town. She'd cried so much her eyes ached. The weight of responsibility pressed down on her like a bag of sand across her

141

shoulders. Would she be able to keep the ranch? She had to carry on her father's dream. If not, his life would be in vain.

So many questions invaded her mind. Would she be able to find the man who claimed he was her brother and get the papers back that were rightfully hers? How long would she have to fight Henry Barrington?

A chilly breeze blew across her face as she neared town. Although it was only late August, Tess was surprised to see some of the leaves beginning to already turn yellow and red. The Aspen trees glittered like flecks of gold in the wind against the white trunks.

Ian pulled the wagon to a halt next to the little church where she last saw her father. Going back to the cabin seemed like less emotional strain, but she had to face her circumstances. What better place than a church where she knew the fellowship will strengthen her?

***

Tess climbed down from the wagon and walked inside the sanctuary.

"I was hoping you would come today," Catherine said. A grin grew across her face and she looped her hand in the crook of Tess' arm. "Let me introduce you to some of the folks here."

"This here is Mrs. Barstall. Her husband was a Fifty-niner," Catherine said.

Tess stretched out her hand to the older woman, who reciprocated with a firm handshake and a loud voice.

"I always tell people you better get involved once ya get to town." She slapped Tess on the arm, jarring her into paying attention. "No time to get settled, just nosey your way in and take over. That's what I did. My husband may have lived and died on the Cherry Creek River, but as fer as I'm concerned, I'm doin' all the livin' on his diggin's." She laughed so loud Tess thought her cackle would shake the sanctuary.

"I'll do my best to remember that advice," Tess smiled, wishing she had half the enthusiasm.

"You're gonna join us at the quiltin' bee, ain't ya?" She nudged her with her elbow. "That's where all the gossip comes out." Before Tess could answer Mrs. Barstall snorted and walked away.

"She's a bit feisty," Catherine said. "But I've always found her to be correct in her assumptions. She has a passion for the Lord

142

that I've never seen before. She must've had a rough childhood, she says her mama and daddy died when she was a young girl. Had to make it on her own."

"I like her. She's different," Tess said. "By the way, what are the Fifty-niners?"

"A group of men that came to the area seeking gold in 1859. A few found some flakes, but most lost out and moved on." Catherine's voice hushed to a whisper. "Mrs. Barstall's husband found a lode so big, they figured even their grandkids would never have to work. She gets involved in everything around here—politically and socially. Doesn't hurt a person to have her on their side."

Tess could see Mrs. Barstall needed quite a bit of refining; however, it didn't seem to bother the lady. She seemed as content as anyone else.

Catherine continued to introduce Tess to people in the congregation.

"I hope I can remember some of their names." Tess laughed.

"Believe me, you'll learn their names soon enough. There are a few here that are determined you remember more than that." Catherine smiled and winked.

Her husband, Thomas, cleared his throat up at the pulpit. Catherine took her seat in the front pew, and the rest of the congregation followed.

A small, crudely-made piano, covered in dust, sat at the front of the church. The songs were sung a cappella and she wondered if anyone knew how to play the instrument.

She missed hearing the sound of the piano at home. It would feel good to hear the chords played once again.

As the singing ended, Tess glanced in the back of the sanctuary, her eyes landing on Ian. Her heart fluttered. Something about his presence gave her peace of mind. She liked knowing he sat just a few pews away.

It warmed Tess' heart, knowing Catherine stayed by her side during the service. Although her heart did ache for her father, knowing he used to sit in the same pews. But she felt connected and comfortable around Catherine. Almost as though they were life-long friends.

Tess hoped Francine would recover soon and be able to come to church. It pained her when she thought about the possibility of her sister never being able to walk again. She didn't want that to be the reason Francine stayed in Denver City. She wanted her to stay because they were sisters and she loved her.

***

"Grandmother, I noticed you weren't in church today," Tess said, handing her coat to Leonard, standing in the foyer of Franklin's rented house.

"Lord knows those people need to be churched more than I do."

"No one is exempt from sin," Tess said, knowing that would get a rise out of her grandmother. She smiled at Leonard when her grandmother turned and walked into the other room.

"Franklin, you're up!" Tess said. "Have you walked at all today?"

"Once. Leonard took me on a swing around the house. I don't have to lean on him as much. Maybe the two of us could walk together."

"That would be nice." Tess stepped up to his side and let him slip his hand through the crook of her arm for balance.

"Let's go outside and get some fresh air," he said.

A chill was in the air as they walked around the grounds of the two-story house. "Tess, I want to ask you something."

She looked down. Franklin stopped her. He slowly lifted his hands to her shoulders and turned her toward him. "Tess, I want to get down on my knees to ask you something." He laughed. "But I'd never get up."

She giggled with him.

"I know that you walked away from our ceremony. I believed it was because you had to complete this part of your life. I want you to come back home and we can become man and wife."

Her insides churned. Tess knew the question would come, but she didn't want to have the conversation.

"I am so sorry that your father is gone and that you will never have the kind of relationship with him that you desired. But, I want you to come back with me," Franklin said.

Tess knew he would. She knew the truth in his words.

"You don't belong out here."

144

"I always believed New York City was home," Tess said. "But now, I feel different. There's something about this place. I don't know if it's the lay of the land, or the open freedom it holds." *Or Ian Bidwell.*

"Marry me, Tess. Be my wife. I will always treat you kindly and take good care of you."

She knew his comment was true. But, everything was so uncertain. The ranch, her sister, Franklin's health, Ian. "I will consider your request. But, I need time to consider it."

A smile grew across his face. "I will wait for you, Tess. As long as it takes."

That's what she was afraid of. She didn't want him to wait for her.

Franklin stuck his hand through her arm again and the two circled the house and returned inside to the warmth.

"What did you say to him?" Her grandmother asked as she walked into another room to prepare some food for Franklin.

"I don't believe that's any of your business." Tess didn't appreciate her tone.

"It is my business. I came all the way out here to make sure you were on the next stagecoach out of this horrid place." She gripped the side of Tess' arm and squeezed.

Tess jerked her arm free. Suddenly, the truth of her grandmother's behavior hit her. Her lips grew tight. "I know now why you've always despised me."

"What are you talking about?"

"You humiliated me in front of other church members back home, you were jealous of my relationship with grandfather, and you treated Francine with more respect than you've ever offered me."

"That's preposterous." Her grandmother crossed her arms.

Tess looked around the room before speaking, to make sure no one could hear her words. "You know who my mother is, don't you?" she whispered through gritted teeth.

Eliza turned and stared at Tess. She paused for a moment before speaking, almost as if she were not going to speak at all. "She was a . . . a woman of the night. She was the reason your father turned from this family."

"She was a human being, despite her occupation." Tess tried to convince herself as she made the statement.

145

"You look just like her." Eliza wrinkled her face until her eyes were only small slits.

Tess drew her head back and opened her mouth. "How well did you know her?"

"Well enough to know she ruined our family. She almost cost your grandfather his job as the preacher."

"How?"

"If someone were to find out his only son took a prostitute in his bed, he'd be removed from the pulpit in an instant."

"Why did you keep me all those years if you despised who I am?"

"Your grandfather made me. If it were up to me, I would have left you—" Eliza silenced herself.

"Left me where, grandmother?" Tess moved closer. Her heart pounded hard against her chest. Did she want the answer?

"Left you in the orphanage." She stood up straight, proving her proud attitude, even at the expense of a young child's life.

"You left me in an orphanage?" A cry erupted from Tess. Her own grandmother tried to pawn her off.

"When your mother died, your father brought you to the house. I wasn't about to take in her… her baby."

"But, I'm your son's daughter. Doesn't that mean anything to you?"

"Too bad your grandfather isn't here for you to thank. He talked Cecelia into keeping you as her own child. If it weren't for the two of them, you'd be long gone."

"How can you be so cold toward your own flesh and blood?"

"I know who belongs in the house of God, and it's certainly wasn't your mother, and I'm still hard-pressed to let you in the door."

For the first time in her life, Tess felt condemned. She wanted to scream at her grandmother, tell her she belonged there just like everyone else, but she couldn't.

Tess' heart sank. In that moment, she realized that she, too, believed the same as her grandmother. Many times over the years, people entered her grandfather's church and she judged them. She didn't believe they belonged there, never realizing, until now, that her own beliefs mirrored those of her grandmother's. Tess wasn't sure she could stomach that fact.

"Nothing to say?" Her grandmother snipped.

Tess walked from the kitchen and brought the food to Franklin. She had a lot to think about.

Chapter Nineteen

The sun inched its way across the sky, arching toward the mountains in the west. She told Ian she would meet him before supper, so they could ride back to the cabin together.

Anger had built up inside of her, not only after the conversation she'd had with her grandmother, but for allowing herself to be so judgmental all these years. How could she let her own sin cloud her beliefs?

Tess slid her shawl around her and set her chin. She would return to Larimer Street in search of the woman she saw several nights prior.

A chill in the early evening air bit at Tess. So many words raced through her mind. What would she say to her? Would the woman even talk to her? Tess had been so rude and condescending toward the prostitute.

As she approached the saloon, Tess scanned the small crowd for the woman. Groups of men huddled around the saloon. Cigarettes dangled from their lips. Curse words flew freely. She wanted to run the other way, return to Franklin's, to the safety of his home.

But she couldn't. Tess couldn't recall a time she'd had this much desire to speak with another person. She wasn't sure what the woman would say. She didn't even know what would come out of her own mouth.

A man brushed against her bumping her shawl off her shoulders. "How 'bout a little peek at what you've got in store." He winked and laughed a disgusting, belly-aching laugh.

"I'm not—how dare you." Tess pulled the shawl back up across her shoulders. Words were not enough to tell this man she wasn't what he thought she was. Thoughts of the woman who birthed her continued to race back into her mind. Her mother must've recoiled at the simple touch of a man about to use her. What brought her mother to this point? Why did her father love her?

Tess entered the saloon where she saw the woman the other day. A smoky haze filled the large hall. Smells of body odor and stale tobacco smoke stung her senses.

She scanned the room for the woman but couldn't find her. The urge to turn and run overwhelmed Tess. She didn't belong in that place. But what woman did?

"Back again, eh?" A scratchy voice from behind caught her attention and she turned around to find the woman she was looking for.

"I... I was looking for you." Tess knew her words would have to come from the Lord.

"Me?" Her lip curled up and she pulled her head back.

Her breath reeked of alcohol. The potent smell almost knocked Tess backwards. She tried to hide the repulsion creeping up in her throat.

"I just came on the stagecoach. I—"

"That's a might truth. Not too many gals that look like you come walkin' over to these parts. Twice!" She laughed and Tess caught sight of more skin than she ever cared to see. A part of her wanted to pull the shawl off her own body and drape it across the woman.

"I came to ask you to sit in church with me one Sunday." Tess realized the words were out of her mouth before she had any time to think about them. Would this congregation allow a prostitute into their fold? Would Tess be ridiculed for inviting her?

"Church? Honey, you must have fever. Look 'round. I make men happy for a livin'. And it ain't by cookin' their supper or holdin' open the hymnal for 'em."

Tess nodded. "I know."

"Then what crazy notion made you come down here to try and drag me to a place where I'll never be wanted? 'Sides, God's house might just go up in flames if I step foot inside."

Tess could imagine how the woman would feel. She'd most likely broken every one of the Ten Commandments. More than once.

"You're worth so much more than this," Tess said.

"Worth more? I ain't worth nothin'. We'll except what I'm paid. Why do you think I'm here? Nobody wants me. Sergio takes

149

good care of me." She pointed toward the bar. A dark, black-haired man stood behind it, pouring drinks.

"I'm sure Sergio is a fine man. But, you deserve more than to give yourself away… like this." Tess couldn't bring herself to say the words that no woman should ever have to utter.

"Honey, I 'preciate your concern, but you don't know nothin' 'bout a hard time. I need to make money and no one in this town's gonna hire me for anythin' better'n this. They don't want the likes of me hangin' 'round runnin' customers off."

"I hope you change your mind." Tess said. She wanted to take the woman away from all of this, but she barely had money to feed herself and Lizzie, let alone another mouth. Tess nodded, smiled, and turned to go.

The woman touched her shoulder, stopping Tess. "What's your name?"

"Tess. And you?"

"Matilda." She smiled. Several teeth were rotted and brown.

"In God's eyes, you are precious. His doors are always open, no matter what others might think." Tess had never spoken with such boldness.

"No one's ever cared 'bout me in such a way." Her demeanor changed in an instant from brash to that of an insecure.

"I'm glad we met, Matilda. I'll be at the white wooden church just a few blocks from here on Sunday." Tess smiled and leaned forward to embrace the woman in a hug.

Matilda's arms hung by her side for a moment. She brought them up and wrapped them around Tess, squeezing her.

"No time for conversation, Matilda!" A man yelled from across the room. "You got customers."

Tess' stomach turned at the thought. She wanted desperately to pull Matilda out of the saloon, but she knew it was impossible.

Nothing is impossible with God. Tess hoped Matilda would one day realize the same.

***

As Ian, Lizzie, and Tess rode back toward the cabin, gray clouds billowed across the sky.

"It's gonna start snowing in these parts pretty soon," Ian said.

A lightning bolt cracked across the sky and Lizzie screamed. Tess lifted her into her lap. Her tiny arms squeezed as far as they could go around Tess.

"Look," Tess said, pointing to the ranch in the distance. A single line of smoke rose to the sky, just above the house.

Ian snapped the reins and the horses moved a little faster, causing the wagon to bump up and down. As they neared the cabin, they could see bright orange flames licking the sky. The fire was in the barn, and had not spread to the house... yet.

"Take Lizzie in the house. She doesn't need to be near the smoke."

Ian jumped down off the wagon and ran to the well. Tess couldn't see how he would possibly be able to put the flames out with a few buckets of water.

She wanted to help but felt useless against the massive, growing blaze.

Tess got down from the wagon and stretched her arms out to pick up Lizzie. The young girl leapt into her arms and formed a tight grip around Tess' neck. Tess pried her arms off, and set her down on the floor once they got in the house, and lifted her chin to look in her eyes. "Stay here. Don't come outside, I don't want you to get hurt."

"Ok, Aunt Tess. Ok." Lizzie pushed a chair across the room to the window and crawled up. She stood on the tips of her toes to watch the fire.

Tess returned outside. She grabbed a handful of her skirt and ran around to the backside of the house. The heat from the massive fire intensified and burned against her skin, even from a distance.

Tess neared the horses, tugging at their reins, still attached to the wagon. Their eyes grew to large white saucers. Tess pulled at their reins. Her hands slipped as she tried to grip them. She reached again, filling up her fist with the leather, and turned them around.

"Be still, girl," Tess screamed, trying to be heard over the sound of the crackling fire. Once she managed to get them turned around, she led them to the front of the house, out of the line of fire and smoke. Tess unhooked them from the wagon. She hitched them around the post on the front of the house, hoping they would stay cooler on the front side, away from the fire.

She ran back in the house to check on Lizzie, who was still standing on the chair, staring out the window.

151

When she returned outside again, she sprinted to the well and hooked the bucket to the rope, and let it slide through her hands, burning the pink skin on her palms as it dropped, until it hit water. It seemed like an eternity waiting for the water to pour into the bucket.

Tess pulled the bucket back up to the surface, one tug at a time. The weight of the water was almost too heavy. She lifted her leg and propped her foot against the side of the well and jerked on the rope.

Ian ran to her side and grabbed the bucket. He limped back to the barn and threw the water on the fire.

Tess knew his attempts were futile. The barn was engulfed in flames. One thousand buckets wouldn't put out the fire.

Ian backed up and stood next to Tess. His face was black with soot.

"The lightning must've done the job."

Wood crackled and popped in the heat. Pieces of timber snapped and crumbled down inside the barn. A large section of the roof was destroyed and collapsed to the ground, shaking it beneath their feet as it hit the earth.

Ian grabbed Tess' hand and pulled her farther away from the barn as the walls tipped in and the entire structure fell in a heap of flames. Orange ashes fell around them like rain.

What would they do for a barn? The horses needed a place to rest at night, covered and out of the cold temperatures.

"We'll have to see about getting a barn built for winter," Ian said.

"We can't afford the wood," Tess said, as she watched the barn continue to burn, knowing they were helpless in the situation.

***

Ian stood outside Josiah's mercantile and stared at the sign above the store. The brand-new brick building was one of the nicer businesses in town. He could see Josiah through the window, restocking shelves.

In the yard, to the right of the store, fresh-cut pine was stacked high. Just what they needed.

Ian didn't want to ask for help from Josiah, but he knew the man would give him credit. No one else in town would give them credit with nothing to show for. Ian swallowed his pride, with a lump the size of Texas sliding down his throat, and went in the store.

The bell jangled on the door as he walked through. Ian didn't see Josiah and assumed he must've walked to the back of the store.

As Ian stood at the counter and waited for him to return to the front, he glanced at the thick black headlines on the newspaper. "Indian Attacks," was printed at the top of the page. Ian met several of the Arapaho camped outside of town. They were a friendly bunch. When he worked for his uncle, he came across several on the backside of his property. The men were returning from a hunt.

Ian talked with them, many of whom spoke English very well. He cringed knowing the White man moved onto their land and expected them to learn our language. But Ian understood westward expansion. Whether he wanted to see them moved farther and farther from their homeland or not, they would dwindle in numbers as the White man continued to move out and claim territory.

"Ian! What brings you in here?" Josiah slapped him on the back, jarring him forward.

"Wanted to talk to you—"

"Did ya see the paper?" Josiah tapped his finger hard against the newspaper.

Ian nodded, hoping they wouldn't get stuck on the subject.

"I told you 'bout them Injuns. They ain't nothin' but trouble. They're going up and down the prairie killin' folks. Somethin' needs to be done 'bout them."

Ian tried to keep his cool. Killing people for trying to protect their land made him quiver.

"Those men that killed all those injuns at Sand Creek last year had the right idea. Go in and wipe them all out. Then they can't breed."

"The government killed innocent women and children. They were trying to protect their land." Ian almost bit his tongue trying to make himself stop talking about it. He could rattle on about all the injustices the government ordered on those people.

"Look, Josiah, I came here to ask you something."

"'Course. What is it?" Josiah folded the paper over and left it on the counter. Ian was grateful they ended the conversation so fast.

"Our barn burnt down last night."

"Lightnin', wasn't it?"

Ian nodded. "Pretty sure. Didn't take long for it to burn the entire structure to the ground."

"We've got plenty of wood outside. You're gonna need quite a bit to build that again."

He was right. They would need to build the barn big enough to house his horse and Tess'. Plus, he'd like to be able to get the wagon in there on snowy nights. The wood weathered better if not sitting in the elements year-round.

"We've got a couple wagons, we can haul it out to the property. Might need to take a few trips, but we can get it out there."

"There's one more thing," Ian said. He wanted to forget the idea of owing Josiah money and walk out the door. He didn't want to be indebted to him. But, he knew he had no choice in the matter.

"Anything," Josiah said, staring at Ian.

"I need to put it all on credit."

"Let me look at my books." He pulled a brown ledger out from under the counter and set it up on top, flipping the pages. "I think we can do it. I wouldn't do it for anyone else."

"Much obliged." Ian said. He shook Josiah's hand and left the store. He walked out to the street. Ian made a commitment to Tess and he planned on keeping it, but the weight of chains fell across his shoulders, knowing he was now indebted to Josiah King.

***

Tess was glad to be able to return to town again. She liked the solitude of the ranch, and the wide-open space, but she loved to be around other people. Tess decided it was time to take Lizzie to see her mother. She wasn't sure how the young child would react, but she knew seeing her mother would be good for her and Francine's spirits.

They were surprised when she entered in the room and Francine was sitting up in her bed. The nurse said they would be getting her up more each day to work out the kinks. They didn't want her on her legs for quite some time. If she continued to heal well, they would get her a chair with wheels and let her sit by the window to get some fresh air.

"This room is stifling," Francine said. Tess could detect a bit of frustration in her sister's voice.

"It would be hard to see these walls all the time." Tess understood this had to be like a prison to Francine. Tess assumed being trapped in the room would force Francine to do nothing but

154

think about Luke, her father, and going back home. She could only pray her sister would be able to sort through it.

Lizzie wanted to crawl in her mother's lap, but the splints keeping her legs straight prevented it. The little girl talked the entire time they were visiting. She told her mother every detail about the ranch, including the fire.

"Tess, I think that proves we don't need to be out here. So many bad things keep happening."

"Pa wanted us here. It would have happened if he'd been here."

"We're not suited for the West. We are better off going to parties, chatting over tea, and quilting. We don't belong here. Don't you see?"

Tess couldn't refute the notion that everything worked against her since she arrived. Nothing seemed to go as planned, with the exception of Ian. Her entire body relaxed and felt secure when she thought of him. Her heart set to fluttering every time she got near him.

"We'll rebuild the barn, Francine. It will be better than ever."

"You were always the optimistic child. Grandmother could tell you that the city of New York burned to the ground and you'd be out raising money to rebuild it. I never could understand that about you."

Tess laughed. Her sister smiled and it was the first time they shared a moment she could be proud of. A part of Tess debated telling Francine about her birth mother and about the possibility of them having a brother. But, she didn't want to worry her sister. Not now. Not until she was better and more able to handle the news.

***

"What're you doin' here in town?" Ian asked Isaiah, standing near Josiah's store. "I was pretty relieved to find out you were gone when the barn burnt down."

"I'd followed you to town yesterday, to check on a few things. When I headed back, I saw the fire and I knew I couldn't return. Figured I'd stay here, outta the way."

"Where'd you stay last night?" Ian hoped he wouldn't get sucked back into Henry Barrington's charms, out of desperation.

155

"Had a small bit o' money, so I stayed at a hotel. Kinda nice. Hadn't had me a bath in quite a while." Isaiah smiled and Ian couldn't help but smile with him.

"You considered talkin' with Tess or Francine? Lettin' 'em know who you are?" Ian could see Isaiah's countenance turn from peaceful to constricted and angry.

"I don't see them wantin' anything to do with the likes of me." He shook his head back and forth. "Ain't nothin' but more pain gonna come from that meetin'."

"You don't know that. Tess is a loving woman. She wanted more than anything to get to know her father, although he spent his life dodging her. What makes you think she won't be interested in gettin' to know you?"

"It ain't never worked out 'fore now. Why would it change for the better? Besides, they're both gonna go back to New York City, what's it matter?"

"What makes you think Tess is going to go back?" He crinkled his forehead and stepped a little closer to Isaiah.

"You said it yourself, she's got a fiancé. He came all the way out here to get her. Why would she stay in Pa's rundown shack when she can have everything a woman wants?"

Isaiah rendered Ian speechless. He was right. Why would Tess stay here when she could go back home and never want for another thing? He had to quit kidding himself. She'd never have anything to do with him. He was a drifter. Even through he straightened his ways, Tess was refined and she would never want something to do with a man who had a deadly past. It was that simple.

Chapter Twenty

Levi's Mercantile matched many of the brick buildings throughout Denver City. She stared at the cream silk faille gown in the window, with red buttons adorning the front from the neck to the waist. The material looked like smooth silk, probably from New York City.

Her own clothes had taken quite a beating on the way out west. She'd worn them over and over, causing the material to fray a bit. When the men ransacked the cabin, they tore many of her gowns beyond repair. Maybe she could make a less elaborate dress from the remaining material.

At that point, Tess couldn't afford to buy material, let alone another dress. She opened the door of Levi's Mercantile and walked through. The bell at the top dangled against the door. Jars of pickles and knick-knacks lined the walls. Bags of flour, stacked up in rows, took up a portion of the walkway in the store. Tess maneuvered around them and walked to the counter.

She slipped her hand down in her satchel and pulled out the ledger.

"Can I help you?" A woman, dressed in a fine cotton faded-blue afternoon dress, approached her. Her hair was pulled back and knotted into a tight bun.

"I'd like to talk to the shop keeper about my father's bill." Tess laid the ledger on the glass countertop.

"Who is your father?" Her fingers tapped on the glass.

"Ed Porter. He was—"

"I know all about Ed Porter." A stern look crawled across her face. "He deserves everything he got comin' to him. He was nothin' more than a drunk."

Tess' eyebrows popped up and she cocked her head to the side. She was tired of hearing about her father and his escapades. He might have taken to the drink, but he wasn't here to defend himself. He couldn't have been that bad. He loved her and her sister enough to send for them.

"You plan to pay us back for what he owes on credit?" She jerked at the edges of her sleeves.

"That's just it. I need to talk to you about more store credit." Tess swallowed hard. She knew this woman wasn't about to negotiate.

"More store credit? You must be joking." Her scowl turned to a grin and back to a frown. "The last thing we are about to do is give you anything until the money he owes is paid back."

"I won't have any flour, or coffee, or basic necessities until I sell the cattle next spring." Tess choked back the tears. She could see she was getting nowhere with this woman.

"Come back when you can pay his bill." The woman turned and walked away from Tess before she could speak again.

The dry air parched her throat when she stepped outside. She grabbed the sideboard on the wagon and pulled herself up the step. Her foot caught on the hem of her dress and ripped a gaping hole.

She sat down hard on the buckboard and surveyed the tear. Crying wouldn't solve any problems, and eating eggs all winter long didn't sound appealing. She opened the ledger and scanned it again. The initials LK were etched throughout the book.

Could LK be the shopkeeper? She had to find out. Maybe he would give her a chance.

Tess grabbed a handful of her skirt and hopped down off the wagon. She opened the door to Levi's Mercantile and walked inside. This time, the bell clanged louder against the door.

"You're back?" The woman laughed. Her eyebrows crinkled together.

"Can you please tell me who LK might be?" Tess placed her ledger on the counter and stared at the woman. Her chin quivered, but Tess refused to take her eyes off the woman.

"That's Levi's… my husband's initials." She glanced at the ledger and back at Tess.

"I would like to speak to him," Tess said. The woman didn't move. "Right now, please." Her voice grew stern and she threw up a prayer, hoping this would work.

158

The woman disappeared from sight and moments later a tall, lanky man walked from the back room, ducking underneath the door frame. He walked up to the counter. "My wife said you wanted ta talk to me."

"My father, Ed Porter, must've dealt with you. Are these your initials?" Tess pointed to the ledger.

He nodded. "That's me, alright. He had store credit. I sure am sorry to hear about him passin'."

Her face relaxed and she paused for a moment. "Thank you."

The shopkeeper's wife walked up and stood next to him. Her eyes squinted into a narrow shape as she tried to stare down Tess.

"What can I do for ya?" He adjusted his apron.

"I understand that my father owes you a lot of money. I fully intend to make right on the loan." Tess cleared her throat. "But, I need you to continue with the store credit. See, I won't get paid until I sell the cattle next spring. As you know, that's a while from now."

"I'll make a deal with you, Miss Porter," he said. "I'll give you more store credit, and when you sell your stock next year, you put me on the top of your list to pay off."

"That's it?" Tess couldn't believe it was that easy. "I thought—"

"I liked your father. He was a good-hearted man. Didn't start out on the right foot around here, but he tried his best to make amends."

"But, your wife . . ." Tess looked at the woman still standing by his side.

"He called her plump once," he chuckled. "She's never liked him since."

His wife stormed away from the counter and disappeared behind the door.

"Thank you, Mister... ?"

"It's Klosterman, but you can call me Levi." As soon as the words left his mouth, a gasp came from the back room. He looked back in the direction his wife walked toward, smiled, and said, "She's a bit jealous at times, too."

Tess smiled and laughed.

"Get what ya need today, I know you got a little ride back home. I'll send Myrtle back out here to tally it up."

Thank you Lord. Tess couldn't believe her determination paid off.

***

"Well, I declare!" Tess heard a loud voice boom across the street as she walked out onto the porch of Levi's Mercantile.

She'd only heard that voice one time, but that was all it took for her to remember where it came from. Mrs. Barstall.

Tess smiled, helped Lizzie down from the wagon, and took her hand as they walked across the dusty street.

"Preacher's wife told me you had a sister hurt in there," she said, pointing back across the street to the infirmary.

"Doctor says she might never walk again."

"Don't you believe a word he says," she said, slapping Tess on the side of the arm. "We'll keep prayin' for that one and she'll be up in no time."

"She's got a strong will. I'm surprised if she would let God dictate how her life was going to turn out." Tess laughed at her own prediction. Her sister always was one to voice her opinion.

"I like you," Mrs. Barstall said. "Ya'll need to come on over to my house next week. I'm hostin' the quiltin' bee for the first time. I've decided to get all the fixin's for the meal at the end of the day. Fresh-baked bread, preserves, a bit of cake and some fresh squeezed lemonade. Although with this strange, cold weather we're havin,' I might ought to get somethin' hot to slip down the throat and warm us up a little."

"Sounds delightful." Tess thought it would be a great way to get to know more of the women in the church. "We'll be there."

***

Tess laughed out loud as she lifted up a pair of her father's pants in front of her. She laid them down on the bed and walked outside. "I'm not wearing those."

Ian looked up at Tess. "You can't very well ride out and check on cattle in a dress. Don't know too many women that ride around in a fancy get-up, unless you're ridin' side-saddle." Ian scratched his whiskers. "In fact, I don't think I've seen one woman ridin' side-saddle 'round these parts." He laughed. A crooked smile crept across his face as he stared at Tess.

She puckered her lips together and wanted to refuse, but she couldn't very well tell him to check on the cattle by himself. She had a job to do.

Tess returned inside and put on a shirt and pulled on the pants. She found one of her father's belts and pulled it through the loops. As she cinched it tight, she got to the last hole and buckled it.

As she pulled her boots onto her feet and started to lace them up, she heard Lizzie giggling outside. Tess walked to the window and watched Ian and the young girl play. He ran over and tickled Lizzie and she would turn and run the other way. Ian would then pretend to run and Lizzie would run up behind him, trying to reach up and tickle him.

He lifted her in his arms and threw her up in the air, to a loud roar of laughter.

Lizzie already loved Ian, Tess could tell. Ian was smitten with the little girl. Tess hadn't seen him smile that much since they met.

"She said she wanted to ride with me," Ian said, stopping and taking a breath. "If that's okay with you."

"Of course. I'm sure she misses her Pa greatly. That'll be good for her." They saddled up and started out for pasture.

***

"How did you hurt your leg?" Tess asked. Their horses walked together at the same pace toward the back of the property.

Ian knew the day would come when he would have to tell her about his past. He just didn't expect it would be this soon.

He looked up at the mountains, rising in the west. "I was... I got hit during..."

"The war?" Tess asked.

Ian shook his head. "I wish I could say that. I was in a saloon. I'd had a little too much whiskey fire in me." He studied her face as he told the story. "Made the bartender mad. He pulled out a pistol and took aim. Somebody knocked me down, and the bullet went right into my leg. If I'd stayed put, it woulda hit my head. I'd be six feet under."

"That's your story?" Tess said, followed by a few giggles.

Ian couldn't help but share in her laughter. "What's so funny about that?"

"I think I'd tell a story that you got hit in the war. Sounds a little nobler." A crooked smile grew across her face and she laughed out loud again.

"Miss Porter, I believe you're a bit feisty for such an innocent-lookin' thing."

Tess looked over at Ian and smiled. Not only did she accept his story, she laughed. He wanted to stop his horse, make his way over to Tess, and wrap her up in his arms, and never let her go. She carried a heart of forgiveness. How could he not love someone like her?

***

The sun rose in the east and Tess climbed out of her warm bed, knowing Ian would be ready to go out and check the fencelines early. She dressed and cooked a meal for him and Lizzie before helping saddle her horse.

Tess had learned so much about ranching in the short time since she arrived in Denver City. Although she wanted to nurse Franklin back to health and visit with her sister, she couldn't help her desire to ride the rugged landscape, especially with Ian by her side.

Yesterday, as they checked on cattle, Tess felt as though she'd come home. The mountains in the distance, the wild and unyielding nature of the land, and a man she could love for the rest of her life, were all in front of her. She felt safe and protected with him near her side.

It was evident Ian was a new Christian, but she loved his desire to learn more about the Bible and God's word. Several times in the past couple days he asked her questions about Joshua's courage when the Israelites prepared to attack Jericho.

She had to admit, there were times she didn't have answers, and became curious herself. Tess soaked up the love of learning about the Bible together. But all the while, Franklin continuously popped into her mind. She was grateful Leonard offered to take care of him today. She didn't mind helping the man who cared so much about her, but she had to admit, taking care of someone was exhausting.

Since Franklin offered his hand in marriage, Tess felt conflicted. She felt an obligation and a commitment to Franklin, but her heart continued to be drawn toward Ian and the Colorado Territory.

The foothills rolled at the base of the mountains. Tall green grass and scattered wildflowers blew delicately in the breeze. Ian, Tess, and Lizzie rode their horses deep in to the land.

So far, the fenceline appeared to be in good condition. Ian found a couple of spots that needed repairing, and stopped to fix the bristled wiring.

"Stay on your horse," Ian said, "this won't take but a minute to fix."

Tess reached forward and scratched Lady's neck. Instantly, something spooked her and she jumped. The horse backed up and started to rise up off her front legs. Ian stood up and grabbed the reins, calming the horse. He turned and scanned the horizon.

"Somebody's out there," Ian said, dropping his tools and watching in the distance for a moment before leaping onto his horse.

"Where? I don't see them."

He pointed down the fenceline to the cattle. One of the cows stood on the other side of the fence, off the property line.

Ian handed Lizzie to Tess, tagged his horse's side with his boots, and shot off toward the stray cow.

In the distance, Tess could see a man running toward his horse. Not comfortable enough to ride at a fast speed, Tess kept a distance between her and Ian as his horse sprinted toward the man. She could see Ian lifting his revolver from his holster as he neared the fence.

The man raced away as Ian drew closer. Ian stopped and waited at the fenceline. Tess caught up to Ian and watched the man ride off in the distance.

"What happened? Who was that?" Tess asked, waiting for his reply.

"I didn't get a good look at him," he said, out of breath. "I have a feeling it's one of Barrington's men. He hides them on his ranch and sends them out to do his dirty work."

"Why didn't you go after him?" Tess looked in the distance, now unable to spot the rider.

"He'll be back. I assure you. I don't want to get in the middle of a shooting match," Ian said, wiping his brow with a handkerchief.

"But, I thought cattle rustling was a hangin'—"

"It is. But if I ride over into Barrington's property, he'll shoot me for trespassing and that'll be the end of that."

"I don't understand. How can someone try to steal cattle, and then you can't even go after the man?"

"Things don't always work the way we want them to out here. You have to know your boundaries, Tess. Otherwise, you'll get yourself killed," he snapped.

Tess didn't mean to make Ian mad. She simply wanted to know the answer and couldn't understand why Ian didn't make more of an effort to catch the man. She kept quiet and rode back to the cabin in silence.

A rush of heat overwhelmed Tess as she thought about the possibility that Ian was still working for Barrington. Maybe he didn't kill the man simply because they still worked together.

Chapter Twenty-One

Tess was grateful Ian offered to bring her to town. She needed a break from ranching. Every inch of her legs ached from riding out to pasture to check on the cattle.

For several days, Tess had been excited about the quilting bee, and getting to know the local women. They rode to Mrs. Barstall's house at the north end of town, far off the road.

Tess tried to maintain her posture and keep her mouth from gaping open when they arrived at the mansion. Mrs. Barstall's home would probably take up an entire block in town. The structure was made of up red brick and white rock, accentuating the windows. Posts ran all the way around, holding up a porch on the second floor.

Aspen trees were planted all around the house, their leaves glittering in the wind like rows of gold. A widow's peak sat on top of the house with a black iron fence running around the top edges. She could imagine a person could see for miles from that perch.

Tess couldn't figure out how a person would ever need that much house. As far as she knew, the older woman didn't have any children and her husband was dead. What did she need with so much space?

Ian stopped the wagon and unloaded Lizzie. Mrs. Barstall was already out back greeting the women showing up for the quilting bee, and leading them in to her house.

Tess walked up to one of the women she saw in church on Sunday.

"I heard you were Ed Porter's daughter," one of the women said.

"Yes. My name is Tess." She pressed against her hair, up in a bun to make sure she still looked tidy.

"Erma Watfield," she said, extending her stiff hand. "Your father didn't attend our church long. Don't guess he was in church before that."

Tess didn't know how to respond to her comment. The words slid off her tongue with disdain. She knew what the woman was trying to imply. When Tess didn't respond to her accusation, she changed the subject.

"Mrs. Barstall's got more money than she knows what to do with."

"She's a nice lady. I've enjoyed her in the little time that I've talked with her.

"She's a troublemaker." The woman pursed her lips and tipped up her nose. "That's for certain."

Tess figured Erma must be here to see Mrs. Barstall's house and live off the generosity of the woman. Seemed a bit unfair.

"There's nothing wrong with having a lot of money," Tess said.

"It's all in how you earn it," she said. The woman popped open her parasol and sauntered away.

Tess wasn't sure what she meant. Didn't her husband find gold? The women out west weren't much different than some of the women she knew back home.

Tess scanned the yard for Ian and Lizzie. He said they would go to Thomas' after dropping her off at Mrs. Barstall's house.

Tess looked down the driveway, searching for Catherine, hoping she would arrive soon. She spotted their wagon coming up the road. Thomas was driving and Catherine sat next to him with a while parasol over her head, shading her. Happiness filled her heart at the opportunity to spend more time with her new friend. She felt as though she could share her deepest feelings and Catherine would love her all the more.

Tess wished Francine could be joining them. She figured her sister was tired of staying inside the room at the infirmary. Tess wondered if Francine would have accompanied her to the party, had Francine been well. She couldn't fret over whether or not her sister wanted to stay in Denver City. She would have to give her worries over the Lord and let Him work on her sister.

Tess waved at Catherine as the wagon drew closer. The wagon came to a halt, and she stepped out of the way. Thomas came around the side of the wagon and helped Catherine down. She took one step at a time getting down. Thomas held her sides as she descended.

Thomas was always kind and loving to his wife. Tess hoped one day she would be able to find a man who would take care of her, and care about every little detail of her life. Ian came to mind. She had never thought she would be attracted to a man with such a rugged past. Tess wanted so badly to know if he was truly who he said he was.

"Tess. I'm so glad you're here. Let me say goodbye to Thomas and I will be in, in just a moment."

Tess walked through the massive wooden front door. A staircase with pressed-tin tiles ran along the wall all the way up to the next floor. It was beautiful enough to be fit for a queen.

Candlelight flickered off the crystal chandelier hanging from the ceiling entryway that stretched all the way up to the second story. She hated to imagine who had the tedious job of lighting all those candles. She made quick measurement of the area and decided her cabin could most likely fit in the room with a little bit of space to spare.

A massive brown bear skin lay on the floor in front of a rather intricate, ornate piano in the parlor. It must've cost her a fortune to buy the instrument and have it shipped to Denver City. The fireplace was covered in smooth brick stones that matched the outside of the house. Not a detail was spared.

She heard the women chattering from the other room and stopped to admire a tintype taken of Mrs. Barstall and a man. Tess assumed it must be the late Mr. Barstall.

Mrs. Barstall was standing in the tintype with her foot resting on a small stool. Her dress was pulled, up exposing her leg all the way up to her thigh. It surprised Tess. She didn't expect Mrs. Barstall to openly display a something that showed so much of her body.

The tintype reminded Tess of the woman she ran into on the street the other day. She was not ashamed of allowing her bare body to be exposed to anyone passing by, namely men who would pay a sum of money to spend time with her. Tess shook at the idea. Each time the thought crept back into her mind about her mother's occupation, Tess pushed it back, desperately wanting to forget she ever knew.

Tess followed the sound of the women chattering in the other room. As she approached, she heard her father's name. Tess stopped long enough to listen.

"He was a drunk and nothin' more." The comment was told in a whisper, but Tess knew it came from Erma, the woman she met outside.

"I can't imagine that God would forgive his behavior. He frequented some of the saloons downtown. I can only imagine what kinds of horrid acts he was guilty of."

"Don't you know that God forgives all sins? None of you ladies is sinless. I know that much." Tess smiled when she realized Mrs. Barstall must've walked through another door and into the middle of their conversation. Several of the women gasped at her comment.

Tess couldn't believe what she was hearing. Mrs. Barstall didn't know Tess very well, yet she was sticking up for her father. The women sitting in the other room were shrewd and judgmental.

"I have a feeling half of you are here just to see what I have," Mrs. Barstall said.

Tess' eyes grew wide open. Catherine touched her arm. Tess turned her head and held her pointer finger up in front of her mouth. Catherine leaned in and listened to the conversation in the other room.

Not one word left the mouth of any of the ladies. Tess would have given anything to see the looks on their faces.

"Now, listen ya'll," Mrs. Barstall said, her voice growing back to a loud, higher pitched sound. "If you're not a sinner, you can go on out back and get yourself somethin' to eat, 'cause we sinners are gonna sit in here and have a right good time."

The room remained silent for a moment. One of the women stood up and sighed loudly. The swishing of skirts could be heard from someone rising and leaving the room. A moment later Erma walked in front of Tess and Catherine. Tess wanted to laugh out loud that the woman thought she was without sin. She had to muscle the smile off her face.

Tess looked at Catherine, struggling to keep laughter from bubbling out. Erma opened the front door and walked outside, closing the door gently behind her.

Tess and Catherine walked around the corner and joined the ladies at the quilting circle. Catherine sat down and pulled out her quilt square.

Tess moved across the room and put her hand on Mrs. Barstall's arm. "Thank you for sticking up for my father. No one around here seemed to care too much about him."

"Honey, I wasn't stickin' up for your father. I was stickin' up for me. I'm a sinner and I can't imagine where I'd be right now if not for God's good mercy on my soul."

Tess smiled. She wondered where she might be as well.

***

The sun peeked out over the horizon, warming the cool ground. Steam rose as the sun stretched across the sky, lighting up the day.

A group of teamsters rolled down the road, carrying loads of wood for the new barn. Tess told Ian she would provide plenty of water and sandwiches for the men who stayed to help. She'd busied herself all morning in the kitchen preparing fresh-baked bread. Thankfully Tess was able to find plenty of jam in the cellar. She hoped she wouldn't go through all the jars so they would have some left for the coming months. But she could live without the treat in exchange for help rebuilding the barn.

This was the first time Tess attended a barn-raising party. Quite a few of the local men from town were on hand to help. Tess set a table out in the back of the house with the few teacups she had and a pot of coffee. She had already made several pots before the midday.

Thomas came with Catherine. Tess appreciated her friend's consistent help with Lizzie. She wouldn't be able to wait on the men if watching Lizzie all the time. Catherine kept Lizzie occupied by playing and reading her stories.

Her heart swelled at the amount of help from the people she barely knew. If only Francine could see how much people cared in the community. People were friendly enough in the bigger cities, but no one seemed to stop long enough to help in the same fashion as they did on the frontier. If not for all the help, it would have taken

Ian and Tess more than a month to finish the barn. At this rate, the barn would be completed by nightfall.

***

The midday hour came and Tess got the sandwiches ready for the men to eat. They gathered around, sitting in different places in the yard, on stumps, and in the grass. Some sat on the stacked wood that was waiting to be used for the barn.

Josiah sat down next to Ian on the ground.

"I'm headin' to Fort Laramie tomorrow afternoon," Josiah said.

"That's quite a ride. What's up there?" Ian wondered what business Josiah had at the fort.

"Why don't you ride up there with me? It'd be like old times."

Ian wanted nothing to do with old times. He'd cussed, started fights, and had a temper that could flare up at a moment's notice. He didn't care to relive the past.

"I've got to help Tess on the ranch. I can't be goin' off."

"You might get you a few injuns." His words hissed out of his mouth. Josiah squinted his eyes and cocked a crooked smile.

"You're goin' up to get Indians?"

"I wanna be a part of settling the frontier. You can't settle the frontier with a bunch a wild injuns running around, can ya?" Josiah continued, "I plan to get me a fine lady one day and she don't want to live out here in the wild with crazed injuns."

"Have you ever tried to get to know one? They're good people." Ian figured it was pointless to try to explain things, but he tried nonetheless. "They're angry at the White man because we swooped in and stole their land."

"It wasn't their land. They didn't have no deed on it—"

"They didn't need deeds. They live off the land, they know who it belongs to."

"Why do you think all them tribes fight each other? It's over land. That's all their they're doin.' Fightin' to get their land. We just got more firepower and men, that's all. We're winnin'."

No one won when Indians died. "You're makin' a big mistake Josiah. You might get yourself killed."

"They've been killin' regular folks up and down the prairie. Scalpin' women and children."

170

"That's because the White man refuses to keep his part of the treaties," Ian said.

"White Kettle and his men had it comin' last year at Sand Creek."

"How do you figure?"

"They refused to do what the government wanted."

"Do you hear yourself, Josiah?" Ian felt his anger boiling. "How can you blame them? They wanted their land back. The army was asking them to give up more land. What was in it for them?"

"Their lives, if they had agreed."

Ian's hands balled up into fists. He hadn't wanted to hit a man since before he learned about Jesus and His merciful forgiveness. Before, he would have knocked Josiah clean out after a few words. Now, he took a deep breath and tried to calm his anger. It bubbled up more often than he liked.

"You don't get it, do you?" Ian said.

"There's nothin' to get. They don't listen, they lose their lives."

He'd seen far too many men kill Indians over a piece of bread, let alone land. Ian knew many men had grown immune to the feeling of remorse when it came to killing Indians. He knew there was no way to stop the land from being developed. But he didn't want to see so many lose their lives over it. "White Kettle and his men didn't stand a chance. They had no warning."

"They should've stood on guard."

Ian could feel his face heating up. He had to get away from Josiah. "I suggest you stay here and keep yourself from gettin' killed, Josiah."

"I'm headin' up tomorrow. You know where to find me if you change your mind."

Ian wouldn't change his mind if Josiah paid him. He never had a problem with the Indians. Why couldn't Josiah leave it alone? He made it hard to like him. Ian wanted to be thankful that Josiah saved his life. He even tried on several occasions to be friends with the man, but his moral choices were the opposite of everything he believed in, especially now that he made God the center of his life. He believed Indians were His creations, too. They were no different than the White man.

Ian looked over at Tess, who had been listening to their conversation. A smile of understanding crossed her face. There's no way she could have missed his remarks. Josiah had a tendency to be loud and opinionated.

Ian figured he'd have to live with Josiah staying a thorn in his side. Is this what Paul meant in the Bible? He always wondered if perhaps Paul had a true deformity or pain that continued throughout his life. Ian stopped to think what Paul might do in a situation similar to his own. The more he thought about it, the more he realized Paul would most likely love Josiah for who he was and pray that his ways would change. Ian just wondered how many Indians would be killed before he figured it out.

Chapter Twenty-Two

Tess walked toward Catherine's house, hoping her body aches would benefit from the short distance and work themselves out.

As she neared, she spotted the back of Catherine as she worked in the garden outside of the parsonage. The wildflowers were a myriad of colors and shapes.

"Looks like you won't be able to keep those flowers growing much longer in this cool air," Tess said.

"What a nice surprise," Catherine replied, her smile beaming. As she stood, Catherine bent forward and gripped her stomach. She screamed in pain and dropped back down to the ground.

Tess knelt down beside her, took off her shawl and placed it under her head. "What is it, Catherine?"

"I've been having more pain for several days. I thought it was part of the pregnancy, but this just doesn't seem right." Her face tightened and she pulled her legs into a fetal position.

"Take a deep breath and lets get you inside." Tess got behind Catherine and lifted her into a sitting position. She slid her hands underneath Catherine's arms and helped her up.

Catherine screamed again, loud enough to bring Thomas out of the church.

"Catherine, what is it?" He ran to her side, lifted her into his arms, and carried her into the house. Thomas placed her on the bed.

"It's that pain I've been having." She winced again and pulled up her legs. Her hands stayed on her belly.

"Let me get the doctor," Tess said. She glanced at Thomas before running from the parsonage.

Tess grabbed a handful of her skirt in both hands, lifted if off the ground, and ran toward the doctor's office. She bounded up the wooden stairs and through the door, searching for the doctor.

"Doctor? Doctor?" Tess' voice grew louder and more direct each time she called his name.

The doctor appeared from around the corner. "Yes? What is it?"

Tess filled her lungs with air and tried to speak. "It's Catherine, from the church." Her words came out choppy.

"Slow down, Miss Porter," the doctor said. "Take a breath."

Tess wanted him to understand, but she didn't want to take the time to regain her composure. She needed him to come with her, and fast.

"She's, there's something wrong with the baby she carries. Come quickly." Tess continued to draw large amounts of air into her lungs, but couldn't seem to recover from the run.

"Let me grab my bag," he said. The doctor disappeared to another room and returned within seconds. In his hand he held a black leather satchel. He nodded at Tess and the two ran out the door.

The parsonage was several blocks away, and Tess struggled to breathe, but she refused to slow down. She turned to see the older doctor just steps behind, trying to keep pace with her.

As she neared the parsonage, she spotted Thomas standing in the doorway. Her heart sank. Were they too late for Catherine and the baby?

Tess slowed as she reached the parsonage. Thomas stood in the doorway, tears streaming down his face.

"Are we too late?" Tess' voice choked on her words.

"No. But her pain is increasing." Thomas led the way into the room. Catherine's moans grew louder.

Tess moved aside as the doctor sat on the edge of the bed and began his examination. Thomas knelt down beside the bed and grabbed his wife's hand.

Catherine's pain increased at times and her crying intensified. Moments later, she would breathe more slowly and stop crying.

"She has a fever," the doctor said. "Thomas, may I see you in the other room?"

"Of course."

The two men left the room and Tess knelt down beside the bed. She placed her hand inside of Catherine's.

"This can't be happening again." Catherine's eyes looked dark and shallow. Her pain increased again and she closed her eyes.

"Hold on, Catherine. The pain will pass. Squeeze my hand." Catherine's grip grew stronger, pinching Tess' hand.

"I can't take this much longer." Tears streamed down Catherine's face.

Tess waited for her pain to pass. She dipped the cold rag in the bucket next to her, wrung out the water, and placed it on Catherine's forehead.

"I don't want to lose this baby," she said, taking deep breaths. Her cheeks grew larger with each breath.

"God will see you through it. You know there's nothing too big for Him."

"But I don't want to lose the child. I can't go without this baby." Her tears turned to sobs and Tess climbed up in the bed next to her friend and wrapped her arm around her.

The room fell silent and Tess heard Ian's voice in the other room. No doubt the men were apprising him of the situation.

Thomas returned and knelt down next to the bed.

"The doctor said that Catherine may lose the baby," he said, reaching up to wipe away a tear. "She is having contractions, and that is not good at such an early stage." He stopped and bit his lip. "God is in control and we will wait on Him to either give us this child, or take it back home with Him."

Tess marveled at his trust in God. She wondered if she, too, could have that kind of faith. When things got rocky, she found herself blaming God instead of trusting Him.

"The doctor said to let her sleep and rest. The bed rest will help keep the contractions from becoming too strong."

Tess nodded and sat up in the bed. She looked over to find Catherine asleep. She hoped she would be able to sleep for a long time and have relief from the pain.

Tess walked into the other room and found Ian sitting down with a cup of coffee. When she entered, he stood to his feet. The two shared a look and she walked around the table to talk with him.

"I am going to stay the night with Catherine. She needs a friend, along with her husband, to help when needed."

Ian nodded.

"Can you return tomorrow?"

175

"Yes, of course," Ian said. "Tess?"

Catherine's cries could be heard from the other room. Tess touched Ian on the arm and returned to the bedroom.

***

Ian rode back to the cabin with enough quiet to think. Lizzie laid her head down on his lap and fell asleep. His thoughts continually returned to Catherine and Thomas. Since their arrival in town, they had done so many things to help others in the community. He hated to see Catherine in so much pain.

Lord, I know it's gettin' late and you're probably doin' somethin', but I gotta ask ya to keep an extra eye out for Catherine. She's in a lot of pain and needs some extra help. If you can see fit to give her some rest from her pain, I'd be much obliged.

Ian had rather come to like praying. He did feel as though he were just having a conversation with God. It was easy and he trusted that God heard him, even as tiny as he was in the big world around him.

Other than Catherine's pain, he was grateful for the day's events. He thought about his latest readings in the Bible. Joshua was a man of God. He'd spent most of his life learning from Moses, the great leader. He recalled God's command to Joshua to attack the city of Jericho.

He imagined Joshua standing under a tree, trying to figure out what to do. Moses was dead, and all these Israelite people were running around with problems that needed solving. Ian was sure happy he didn't have to sort things out for a bunch of folks.

He admired Joshua and the man he became. He attacked the city of Jericho solely on trust. Joshua and the Israelites didn't wait until what they thought was the right moment; they listened to God and they moved forward in their march, shouting and blasting their horns as loud as they would blow.

Joshua trusted that God would bring destruction to the Canaanites and bring the city of Jericho to ruins. Ian had to admit that if God told him to destroy even Denver City with trumpets and marching, he'd have his doubts. Jericho, even with its solid rock walls, fell in shambles.

Could Ian trust God as much? Would he be able to leave his fate in God's hands? He wanted to trust, without needing a sign that God could handle his fears. Ian wanted to believe that nothing would happen to him, but the feel of Barrington's noose still clung hard to his throat, and it was a feeling he'd not soon forget.

Chapter Twenty-Three

Catherine dozed in and out of sleep after the sun went down. Sweat covered the bed, but Tess refused to wake her up, just to keep her dry.

"She seems to be sleeping a little longer each time," Tess said to Thomas, who was still pacing the floor after more than two hours.

"You need to eat," Tess said.

"I can't. My stomach is in knots," Thomas rubbed his forehead and walked the room again.

"You must. You need to eat in order to keep your strength. Catherine will need you in the coming days."

Thomas sat down at the table. Tess ladled some soup into a bowl and placed it in front of him.

"I suppose I might be able to eat a little bit. For her sake," Thomas said.

Catherine screamed and Tess knocked the soup off the table. She looked down at the mess on the floor, stepped over it, and ran back to Catherine's room.

"This baby is coming. It's too soon, but I know it's coming." She cried aloud.

"Catherine, we are here for you. Every step of the way," Thomas said. He looked at Tess and a tear rolled from his eye.

***

"Isaiah, what're you doin' here? I thought you were stayin' in town," Ian said.

Isaiah slid off his saddle and landed on the ground. "I saw you comin' back by yourself and figured it'd be safe to come on out and stay here again. I'm plumb out o' money."

Ian couldn't possibly turn him away now. He knew if he did, Isaiah would turn back around and go to Barrington for help. He didn't want to see the young man lost forever.

"Put your horse in the barn and stay outta sight. Tess should be back today."

Lizzie came running out from the house and ran up to Isaiah. "Who're you?"

"This is a friend," Ian answered. Although he was trying to protect Isaiah, and hoped he would get to know his sisters, the shadow of dishonesty weighed heavy on him. Especially now that Lizzie had met him. How would he ever explain this to Tess?

"What's your name?" She squinted her eyes in the sun as she looked up at the two men.

Isaiah got down on one knee. "My name is Isaiah."

"Izay?"

"I-zay-yah," he said again. "I figure it's not an easy name for such a little youngin'."

"I'm not a youngin'. I'm four." Lizzie held up three, then four fingers. "See?"

"I see. You're a right smart little thing."

A tear formed in Isaiah's eye. He stood up and walked away toward the barn.

"Where's he goin'?" Lizzie asked, after he abruptly walked away.

"He's got some chores to do," Ian said. He knew there was no way he could explain to her that Isaiah was her uncle and only wanted to get to know her.

Ian wondered if a day would come when the family would be as one. He could only pray.

***

Tess couldn't help but feel comfortable in Franklin's house. Leonard kept the fire stoked throughout the day and made sure tea came precisely at eleven o'clock and three o'clock. Lunch was prepared and delicious. A part of her felt guilty for eating so well, while Ian worked hard and had to put up with her mediocre cooking.

Although Tess was grateful that Leonard had sent home food on more than one occasion for Ian and Lizzie to eat.

"I'm glad you are able to feed yourself now, Franklin," Tess said. "I am sure it gives you more sense of freedom."

"'Tis true. Although I enjoyed our intimate moments together."

Tess smiled and lifted her teacup to her lips. She hoped he didn't bring up the proposal of marriage again. She wasn't ready to give an answer.

"Your friend Catherine, how is she faring?"

"The doctor says the child might live if she stays in the bed until the baby comes. She thought it would come last night, but the pain subsided and she seems to be doing much better today."

"I will keep her and her family in my prayers."

"Franklin, do you ever question why the Lord allowed this to happen to you?" Tess couldn't help but wonder why the Lord had allowed her father to die, her sister to sustain injuries, and Franklin to have a stroke.

"When my wife passed, I wanted to know why God took her at such a young age. She was a beautiful woman, filled with faith. I was angry for a long time."

"Did you ever overcome the feelings that came along with the anger?" Tess asked.

"I recall feeling angry that He took her and not some heathen off the street."

Tess nodded.

"But God made it evident that He cared as much about heathens as He did about my wife. I realized that if He could love them, so could I."

Tess appreciated his deep faith—yet another reason Franklin would make a good match. Why didn't her heart desire this man? He was everything she should desire in a loving husband.

But Tess' heart longed for Ian. How could her heart desire a man she didn't fully trust? Although he'd never given her a reason not to trust him. Yet.

**

Tess pulled the covers up to her neck. She felt the warmth of Lizzie's back against hers. The heads of the nails on the walls were white, and the windows were covered with a thin layer of ice.

She sat up and slipped her legs out from under the covers. Cold prickled her skin. As she stood, she tiptoed across the room to stoke the fire, which had almost burned out.

Tess placed a few logs in the fire and stuffed some kindling down below. She lit a match and held it under the wood until a small flame grew. The warmth rested against the front of her and began to travel across the room.

She felt sorry for Ian, still outside in the lean-to, most likely bundled up and still cold. He'd brought hay from the barn into the lean-to to keep some of the cold out and the warmth in.

Tess walked to the window and looked outside. Flakes of white, fluffy snow fell, covering the ground. A solid meadow of white was stretched as far as she could see. A single set of prints in the snow could be seen from the cabin. Had Ian already gone out to pasture? Why would he go out so early? She rubbed her arms and thanked the Lord she was inside.

Tess heard the door on the lean-to slam. She knew Ian would be coming in soon for breakfast. She promised to be ready by seven each morning so he could enter the house for breakfast. She hurried to dress and left Lizzie sleeping in the bed. She would let her sleep a bit longer.

Just as she finished dressing, Ian knocked on the door. She opened it and let him in.

"Feels good in here." He walked straight to the fire and rubbed his hands together.

"I slept a little longer than usual. Let me get some coffee started." Tess lit the oven and placed the kettle over the fire, heating the water. Fresh-brewed coffee would be delicious on a cold morning.

Tess looked over at Ian and caught him staring at her. She smiled and immediately her face warmed up. She looked again and as their eyes met, he turned away, looking back at the fire.

"Did you go out to pasture this morning?"

"No, why?" Ian asked. He grabbed a chair, turned it to face the fire, and sat down.

"Just wondering." Was he lying to her? She looked at him again. How did the prints get in the snow?

"I didn't expect it to snow so early on in the year," Ian said. "Probably means we'll have a nasty winter. I'm worried about the cattle."

Tess decided to drop the questioning for now. Fear rose up in her that he wasn't being fully honest with her. Was one of

Barrington's men there early in the morning? Was he keeping something a secret?

"Tess?" Ian asked. "You okay?"

She nodded. "Just thinking. Did it get cold enough last night to harm them?"

"No, but it will. Cattle have been known to freeze to death."

"Freeze to death?"

He nodded. "Seems strange, with them covered in a thick coat, but it's possible. If it stays cold, the snows won't melt and it will be harder for them get through the snow to eat the grass."

Tess had no idea there could be so many complications.

"I'll ride out today and check on the cattle. You and Lizzie need to stay in here where it's warm."

The kettle whistled and Tess poured the water through the filter and filled up Ian's cup. She set it on the table in front of him and poured herself a cup. She sat down across from him and sipped on the coffee. It was strong, but delicious. "Seems funny to be going to the Harvest Festival next week when it's snowing outside."

"That it does. But the sun could be out in a couple hours and most of the snow melted by dinner. You never know in these parts."

Tess laughed. She hoped her future would be full of laughter with this man.

***

"Francine," Tess said. "You're in a wheelchair." She walked over to her sister and wrapped her arms around her.

"Thank you. Dr. Stein and Sarah helped me in the chair. I've been looking out the window for quite a while."

"If you'd like, we can wheel her out to the front porch," Sarah said.

"It's much warmer now. The sun is out and the snow melted," Tess said. "Although it's a muddy mess out there."

Sarah pushed Francine outside on the porch. "The sun feels so good. It's been a while since I've smelled the fresh air."

"Francine, I need to ask you something."

"What is it?"

"Did Pa ever say anything to you about my mother?"

Francine laughed. "What do you mean? We talked about Mama on occasion. I always wished she had lived long enough to meet Lizzie. I wanted her to know my children so badly. I would give anything to have her around now."

"I don't think her death was from sickness."

"Of course it was. Grandmother said she was quite sick, couldn't get over a fever."

"I think she took her own life."

Francine laughed uncomfortably. "No, she didn't. Why would you say such a thing about your own mother?"

"She wasn't my mother." Tess didn't want to hurt her sister, but she needed to tell her the truth.

"Tess, you're not making any sense. What in heaven's name are you talking about?"

"Pa had an affair with a woman named Mary Sikes. It's because of her Mama died."

"What are you saying?"

"We don't share the same mother."

Francine's head snapped around and she looked at Tess. "That's ridiculous. Of course we share the same mother."

"We are sisters because Ed Porter was our father. But Mary Sikes was my mother."

"How can this be?" A look of confusion riddled her face.

"Francine, you know how Father was. He had other women. Often." Tess said, watching her sister stare straight ahead. Her eyes glazed over.

"It makes sense, Francine. Ask Grandmother. Look at the way she always treated me. She knew Cecelia was not my mother. She was angry with father and took it out on me."

Francine said, "I always disliked it when father left. But I pretended that he was off on a long voyage at sea," Francine said. "I would conjure up some romantic notion in my head just to keep from facing the truth of his whereabouts. My school friends all thought he was off on the high seas. I let them believe it. I didn't want anyone else to know that my father was out gallivanting around instead of taking care of his wife and children."

Tess understood. She had wanted to believe the same things, but she knew her father was gone with selfish intentions. "When I left home, Grandmother told me never to return. She was tired of raising someone else's child."

"But you were Father's."

"Yes, but she watched Cecelia take her own life because of Father's indiscretions. She didn't like the fact that Pa loved another woman."

A tear rolled down Francine's cheek.

"I'm not telling you this to hurt you. I am telling you so you know," Tess said.

Tess wanted to tell Francine about her mother's occupation, but she feared her sister might think of her in the same way her grandmother did.

"I remember a woman coming by the house when I was a little girl. She was with child. I do remember thinking how lovely she was. She entertained me in the sitting room. I can recall it because it was the only time Grandmother and Grandfather fought. It scared me. I'd never heard yelling like that before." Francine sat silently for a few minutes before speaking again. "It wasn't long after that you came along, and I never saw the woman again."

"She died a while after my birth."

"I'm so sorry, Tess," Francine said, and she reached her hand over and placed it on Tess'.

Tess feared adding too much sorrow to her sister's life. But she wanted her sister to know the truth about her mother before making the decision to return home. Tess wondered if she would ever be able to tell Francine the truth of her mother's profession.

***

"You hear about the Indian massacre?" Thomas said. He pulled a chair out at his kitchen table for Ian, and sat down in the one directly across from it.

"Ain't heard nothing about it." Ian crossed the room and sat down at the table with his friend.

"Josiah King got hurt in the raid."

Ian's elbows landed on the table and he placed his head in his hands. "Did he survive?"

"Newspaper said he took an arrow through his arm. They attacked a village of Arapaho, destroyed all their winter provisions, and took their horses. Something like five hundred head. I don't see how those people can survive the winter now. The ones that remain will die a slow death. They will have no choice but to go to the reservation. Will the Indian wars ever end?"

184

"Unfortunately, the way things are going, I think the only way that will happen is when the Indians are gone or all on reservations." Ian stood up and paced the room again. "There've been plenty of times I've wished death on a man. Six months ago I would've rejoiced at the idea that Josiah was on the verge of dying."

"And now?"

Ian stopped and turned to look at Thomas. "I'm not so sure. He's filled with hate toward the Indians. So much he wants to wipe them out. Never would have bothered me before. Since I found God, I know I should care more about Josiah, I'm just havin' a hard time doin' it."

"It's easy for me to love Catherine. But there are people in the congregation who make it hard to even like them, let alone have unconditional love for them," Thomas said. "The Bible tells us we are to love one another. It doesn't give exceptions, although I wish there were a few." Thomas laughed. "You're human, Ian. The first step is realizing that you are supposed to care."

"The man saved my life. He got me to a doc that could patch me back up. I owe him everything." He tapped his foot on the floor.

"Christ saved your life, too. He took our sin, so we wouldn't have to face eternal death. He's the only one you owe your life to. I am sure there are plenty of times Christ finds it hard to love me, but He does, in spite of my actions. Unconditionally. Give yourself time to grow. No one ever said it would be easy," Thomas said.

Ian's foot stopped tapping. He leaned his back against the chair. "Guess you're right. I've got some time before he comes back to town. Waitin' on him to return will give me a chance to pray about it."

"You'll find that when you pray for a man, your heart will begin to soften toward him. You'll see."

Ian walked outside. He moseyed over behind the parsonage. He stopped, crossed his arms, and stared at the mountains. Most of the foothills were still covered in snow, but the warm sun hovered over him.

Lord, you know how much I dislike Josiah. Give me strength to be loving and kind and find the good things in him. I pray that his hatred toward the Indians would be gone by the time he returns. Amen.

Chapter Twenty-Four

"You'll never be good enough for the likes of that preacher," Henry Barrington said. The church floorboards creaked beneath his feet.

His voice sent chills through Ian's body. It was like evil trying to squash the life out of a person. He turned around to face his uncle. "What do you want?"

"You're kidding yourself if you think you can turn from your old ways and sit in church with better folks. It's like you're a little boy all washed up for Sunday school, but that mud puddle is always calling out your name."

"You don't have any business over here with the preacher. Why don't you head back out of town and stay where you belong?"

"You belong to me, Ian. I own you. You'll never be able to get away from your past." The words slid off Barrington's tongue with ease. He was practiced in acting like a snake.

The sound of more footsteps sounded in Ian's ears. He lowered his hand and let his palm rest on his revolver, situated in his holster. "I don't want no trouble." Ian's blood started to boil. His face warmed up. He knew the feeling well. He hadn't fought anyone in a long time and didn't plan to start now. *Stay calm.*

"Boys, don't you miss ole Bidwell?"

A couple of laughs escaped from his men, and the sound scraped at the inside of Ian's soul.

"Why don't you come back to work? I know you miss that money falling out of your hands. You never wanted for anything."

"I don't need your money or your ways. I'm tired of bullyin' everyone off their land to help line your pockets. It didn't get me anything but trouble," Ian said.

"You didn't have any trouble. I made sure Sheriff Baker kept looking the other way."

"It ain't right, and you know it."

"So now you're too good to get what you want?" Barrington nodded at his men and they stepped a little closer to Ian.

"Don't move, boys," Ian said. He tightened his hand around the grip of the revolver. His thumb rested on the hammer. "Just cause I don't fight no more, doesn't mean I don't still know how. You know what I'm capable of."

"Ease off, boys. Ease off," Barrington said. "He'll come around to seeing our way of things again."

"Tess is here to stay and there's nothin' you can do to change that." Ian wanted to throw his fist, solve things the way he used to. It would only take a minute and all three men would be on the ground. But it wouldn't solve anything. It would only prove that he wasn't trusting God. He wasn't letting Him take care of Barrington. *'Vengeance is mine; I will repay,' saith the Lord.* Ian repeated the verse several times in his mind.

"You might not like her if she weren't such a pretty girl." Barrington's smile crept across his face.

"Don't you touch her again. I know you sent a couple of your men over there to scare her. She's different. You can't scare her off this land."

"Anything's possible. Ed Porter wasn't planning on leaving either, and look where he is now. It's a shame he fell."

Ian tightened his fist. *Keep it together.* "I better not find out you had somethin' to do with his death."

"His own son didn't seem to be too upset about it," Barrington said.

"Don't you dare bring Isaiah into this."

"Isaiah will learn to see things my way again," Barrington said.

"Not if I have anything to do with it." Ian kept his eyes on the three men still standing across from him.

"Keep on the lookout, Ian. We'll be seeing you." Barrington turned to walk away and his men followed. The conversation left Ian with a sour stomach. *Nothing good can come from that man.*

***

Tess wanted Catherine to come to the Harvest Festival, but she knew the baby would come too soon if she got out of bed.

Thomas was proving a good husband, doting on her and taking care of her while she stayed on bed rest.

Tess regretted that her finest dress was ruined after the men ransacked her house. She looked forward to wearing it for a special occasion. Instead, she sewed up one of her other dresses. This wasn't New York City and she didn't need too many frills for the festival.

Tess twisted her long hair up and pushed the comb in to hold it in place. She tied a bow into the top of Lizzie's hair. Her little ringlets refused to stay put.

Ian knocked on the cabin door, giving his signal it was time to leave for the party. Tess opened the door and walked outside.

His brown hair was combed back neatly and his face shaven. Her heart skipped a beat and she tried to look away, but she wanted to rest her eyes on him.

"You... you... I mean..." Ian stuttered. "You look beautiful."

Tess wanted to tell him to close his mouth, but figured it might spoil the compliment, so she let him stare for a minute.

"I got you something," Ian said, walking toward the wagon. "I wanted it to be a surprise." He lifted a large box with a dark green bow on top out of the back of the wagon, and handed it to Tess.

She walked back in the house and set the box on the table.

"Lemme see, lemme see," Lizzie shouted. Her little hands were frantically trying to open the box.

Tess gasped when she lifted the lid off the top of the box. A brand-new blue and white satin dress sat in the box. She lifted the thick, puffy dress from the package and held it up in front of her.

"How did you...?" Tess couldn't believe her eyes. No one had ever bought her such a magnificent gown.

"Just put it on. You deserve it after all you've been through," he said, standing in the doorway.

A warm tear rolled off her cheek and she wiped it away. "Thank you."

Tess and Ian kept their eyes on each other for a moment before looking down at Lizzie.

"You love her, don'tcha?" Lizzie said. She jumped up and down as she said the words and giggled.

Tess refused to look away. For a moment, she couldn't see herself being anywhere but here by his side.

Ian cleared his throat and Tess blinked several times. "I'll get Lizzie in the wagon. You change and meet us outside."

Ian lifted Lizzie up into his arms and walked outside, closing the door behind them.

A few minutes later, Tess emerged from the cabin. She stood on the porch and twirled around in her new dress.

"You will be the most beautiful woman at the festival," Ian said.

Tess wanted the moment to linger so she could cherish his words.

Ian stood next to the wagon with his hand outstretched. Tess walked down the stairs, cautious to keep her hem lifted out of the dirt. She put her hand in his. A warm sensation traveled up her arm and across her body. She lifted her leg up and almost tripped on her dress. Ian put his hand around her waist and Tess wanted to giggle, but held it in.

He walked around the other side and climbed in the wagon, snapped the reins, and they drove toward town.

Everyone was at the festival. Bales of hay were stationed along the entryway to the dance hall. Bright orange pumpkins were placed around the room, including next to the punch bowl.

Tess took her dance card and flipped it over to see if anyone had filled in a request. Franklin and Ian had both signed the card.

She creased her eyebrows and said, "When did you have time to fill out my card?"

"I raced in here when you were talking to some folks outside," Ian said, smiling at her.

"I don't know what to say." Her heart sped up at the idea of dancing with Ian.

"I reckon you can just say yes." He smiled and looked down at his feet.

"Yes," Tess whispered.

"Mighty fine you came tonight," Mrs. Barstall said. Her voice echoed across the room, although she stood only a couple feet from Tess and Ian.

"Mrs. Barstall. I'm so glad to see you here," Tess said.

"I don't miss a dance for nothin'."

Tess marveled at the colorful attire Mrs. Barstall wore. "Your dress is magnificent. Where did you find something so fine?"

"Right here in Denver City. Where else? We got some of the finest things from New York City."

Tess marveled at the detail and elegance of her gown. She must've paid a fortune for it.

"Look at you, honey." She pointed at Tess' dress.

"Ian bought this for me."

"He did, did he?" Mrs. Barstall bumped Tess with her elbow and winked. She knew exactly what the older woman was implying.

"Let me take that wee girl and get some punch," Mrs. Barstall said. "I'm sure your card is filled up. Don't make those boys wait."

"Franklin," Tess said, spotting the man several feet away. "I didn't think you'd come. But, I see you filled out some of the spots on my card."

"Indeed," he said. "I wouldn't miss a moment with you.

"You remember Ian." Tess pointed to him.

Franklin nodded and slowly stuck his hand out in front of him to shake Ian's.

"Glad to see you're up and movin'. You gave Tess quite a scare. You've recovered quickly."

"Yes, sir." Franklin leaned against a cane.

"Glad to hear it," Ian nodded.

The small band started to play and Ian turned to Tess. "I believe I have a dance to fulfill on your card."

Tess nodded and walked to the dance floor. "Excuse me, Franklin."

***

Ian was grateful Franklin was recovering from his stroke. However, he couldn't help but feel jealous of the man. He wanted to take Tess and have her all to himself. He knew it wasn't right to harbor jealous feelings in his heart, but he still feared that Tess might return to New York City and marry Franklin. Looking at her, Ian now knew he couldn't live without her.

He lifted her hand up and slid his arm around her waist as they walked onto the dance floor. He could feel her draw in a breath and hold it. He pulled her close and her cheek touched his. He could feel her warmth against him.

190

They moved to the music in slow motion. He wanted to stay close and never leave her side. Their feet moved around the dance floor as he held her tight with every twist and turn.

He pulled his head back and faced Tess. For a brief second, it felt as if they were the only two in the room dancing together. He slid his arm tighter around her waist and pulled her close.

The song ended and Tess took a step back. His heart raced against his chest. Her hand was still in his and he held it firmly, wanting the moment to last. The music started again, this time with an upbeat chorus. Ian pulled Tess close and laughed.

"Betcha didn't know I could dance." He swung her around and pulled her back, moving fast with the beat of the instruments.

Tess giggled. "I'm impressed. I thought you only knew how to ranch."

As the dance ended, Ian felt the tightness in his leg flare up. It hurt, but he danced through the pain, all to be in the arms of the woman he loved.

The music stopped and Ian and Tess walked off the dance floor.

"I believe my name is the next on your card," Franklin said.

Ian would turn her over to Franklin, but only for a short while. It was only fair Franklin would get the privilege to dance with Tess. He came from New York City, after all.

"She's a keeper," Mrs. Barstall said, walking up next to Ian.

"She'll probably head back to New York City with Franklin," he responded. It was his luck. He didn't deserve such a beautiful woman of God.

"Not if you put a stop to that. Tell her how you feel. I see the look in your eyes when you're with her. It's unmistakable."

Ian nodded. He knew her words were true. How could he convince Tess of his love? Would she be receptive and feel the same way?

He watched Franklin and Tess as they danced. She didn't seem to look at him the same way. He'd tell her. Tonight. It was decided.

***

Tess walked slowly with Franklin to the edge of the dance floor.

"I suppose I don't make a good dance partner." He lifted one hand up and held on to the cane with the other. "I suppose you don't want to dance with a crippled man."

"Franklin," Tess said, as she slipped her hand around his waist, "It's a privilege to dance with you."

Tess searched the room for Ian. As they turned, she spotted him on the other side. He lifted Lizzie up into his arms and began dancing with her. The young girl laughed as she wrapped her arms around Ian's neck.

Tess couldn't think of a more precious moment. She couldn't help but wonder what he would be like as a father. He'd so far provided shelter, safety, and love to the little girl. His heart seemed genuine. If only she knew his intentions. Was he truly a man after God's heart, or a man bent on making his uncle happy, saying whatever she wanted to hear in order to steal her land?

Ian turned and his eyes met hers. He smiled and her heart warmed. Tess smiled back at Ian, before remembering she was in the arms of another man. A good, decent, caring man.

"Much to my surprise, your grandmother was very intent on coming west," Franklin said. "She wanted to make sure you were coming back with me."

The idea again struck Tess as strange. Her grandmother was bent on getting rid of her before she came to her father's. What motive would she have to not only get her to return, but to come west to make sure it happened.

"How is the new preacher at my grandfather's church?" Tess asked.

"Your grandmother has given him quite a few tests."

Tess laughed. She knew the woman didn't let anyone into a position without some harassing. She always felt sorry for the people on the receiving end.

"What's so funny?" Ian said, walking up with Lizzie and joining their conversation.

"My grandmother. I will have to tell you all about it sometime," Tess said.

"Can you meet me outside in just a few minutes?" he asked.

"Of course," Tess said. "Is something wrong?" She crinkled her forehead.

"No, no. I just wanted to tell you something."

192

"Let me help Franklin for a moment and I will meet you outside."

"Ok." Ian took Lizzie and meandered over toward Mrs. Barstall.

"Would you like some punch?" Tess asked Franklin.

"That would be wonderful. Tess, my dear?"

She turned to face Franklin. "Yes?"

"I know you don't want to wait on a man, especially a man who wants to marry you. But I cherish your willingness to take care of me. Especially after all you've been through."

"I wouldn't have it any other way," Tess said, hoping he wouldn't bring up the conversation of marriage again. At least not at the Harvest Festival. "Have a seat and I will get you something."

She hurried off to get the punch for Franklin, mainly so he wouldn't ask her again about his marriage proposal, but she also longed to hear what Ian wanted to tell her. Would it be what she was hoping for?

***

Tess searched the room again for Ian. When she didn't see him, she assumed he must've gone back outside. As she walked toward the door, a man grabbed her hand and squeezed it tightly, pinching her fingers.

Tess tried to jerk away, but it was no use.

He pulled her close and whispered in her ear, "Stay quiet and nothing will happen to you."

"You're hurting me," Tess whispered. She knew Ian would stop this if he were close. She again tried to jerk her hand free, but he held on tight and pulled her outside.

They walked into the cold night air. The chill bit at her face.

"What do you want with me?" She demanded.

"Somebody wants to talk with you." The man said, still pulling her around the building. She would have yelled for help, but no one was in sight. The music inside played so loudly, she knew no one would hear her scream.

Her heart knocked against her chest and a ribbon of fear dribbled through her veins.

"Where's Ian?" Tess asked.

"You're Tess, aren't you?"

"You work for Barrington, don't you?" Tess asked.

193

"Such a shame about your father. Just when things seemed to be going well for him."

Tess pulled her arm back again, this time freeing herself. "What did you do?" For the first time since her arrival, she feared her father didn't die from an accident. She knew these men were to blame. "How did you know him?" Her teeth gritted together.

"You have a sister, don't you?" The man moved in close.

Tess nodded slowly. "You'd better stay away from my family."

"Shame what happened to her."

Tess felt panic rising up inside. *Where is Ian?*

"Evening to you, Miss Porter." A familiar voice echoed behind her, sending a rash of chills across her body.

She spun around on her heels and faced Barrington. "Where is he?"

"He? Who are you talking about?" His words came out slow.

"You know who I'm talking about."

"Have you reconsidered my offer?"

"What did you do to Ian?"

"Winter gets mighty cold around here. You ought to think about selling now before it's too late."

"Tell me where he is or I'll go get the sheriff." Tess wondered how much help he would be in this situation.

"The sheriff? He's right inside having a grand old time. Why would you want to disturb his fun?"

Two men walked up to Barrington and faced Tess. One of the men took out a handkerchief and wiped blood from his knuckles. His eye was swollen and the other man's lip was bleeding.

"Mr. Barrington," Tess said. Her lips tightened and a knot formed in her throat. "Where is Ian?"

Chapter Twenty-Five

Henry Barrington kept a smug look on his face as he stared at Tess, who was still waiting for an answer regarding Ian's whereabouts.

"I think I might have seen him go around the back of the building. Might be a little slippery back there. I would hate for him to fall and something happen," Barrington said.

Fear stifled her breathing. She bit her lip. Tess wasn't about to let that man see her afraid. "You'd better keep your hands off of him."

"Things might get rough for you this winter, Miss Porter. This is your last chance to sell. Don't make the same mistakes your father did."

She knew at that moment that Barrington was somehow involved in her father's death. "You won't get away with your crimes. I'll see to it."

"Crimes?" He laughed and Tess shivered. "Offering money for land isn't a crime."

"You know exactly what I am talking about." She stared at him for a few seconds. "Are we done here? I have an appointment to keep."

"Yes we are. You don't want to make him wait. He might need you," Barrington said, without cracking a smile.

The man scared Tess to the bone. She walked away, listening behind her, making sure none of the men followed her. She searched the vicinity around the side of the building. As she came around the back, she saw a patch of white skin showing through a heap on the ground.

"Ian!" Tess ran to his side and dropped to the ground. "Ian, can you hear me?"

When he didn't respond, she turned him on his back. He screamed in pain and drew his arm up next to his ribs. His eye was busted and his lip bloodied. She knew exactly who did it.

"I'll run get the doc. I'll be right back."

Ian grunted but didn't move.

Tess jumped to her feet, tripping over the front of her new dress. She turned the corner, bracing herself for Barrington and his men, but was relieved they weren't anywhere in sight.

As she entered the festival, she spotted Dr. Stein right away. She took a deep breath and walked across the room, trying not to make a scene. Tess put her hand on the doctor's arm to get his attention. "Dr. Stein, it's Ian. Something's happened."

"Where is he?" He set his drink on the table and followed Tess out of the building.

"He's out back."

The doctor approached Ian and knelt down next to him, checking his wounds. "Can you hear me, Son?"

Silence. Tess held her hand up to her mouth. Was he going to be okay?

The doctor touched his face and Ian winced in pain. "What happened?"

"I am sure it was Henry Barrington that put his men up to it," Tess said.

"Can you walk, Ian?" The doctor asked.

He took a slow breath. "I can try."

"We have to get him to my office."

Tess moved to the other side of Ian, placed her hand on his back, and helped him sit up. With each movement he cried out in pain.

The doctor stayed on the other side, moving him slowly. "On the count of three, we'll stand up together. Ready Tess?"

She nodded.

"One… two… three." Tess moved her head under his arm and held on to him, helping him balance.

"Give me a second to catch my breath." Ian took some shallow breaths. "Hurts to breathe."

"Your ribs are probably broken."

The walk back to the infirmary took several minutes. Ian took one agonizing step at a time until they were inside.

"Once we get him on the bed, you're going to have to help me. Sarah is at the festival," Dr. Stein said.

Tess nodded and helped Ian to the bed. He lay back and rested his head against the pillow. He grimaced as he relaxed and let out some air.

Tess' legs wobbled beneath her from carrying half the weight of the man much larger than she. She wanted to sit and rest, but knew Ian needed to be cleaned up.

She glanced down at her new dress, now covered in Ian's blood. Ruined. Tess bit her lip to keep from crying. She'd had enough of Barrington and his men.

The doctor reached for the scissors on the table behind him and cut Ian's shirt up the front. A large shoe print was mashed on the front of his shirt, no doubt from one of Barrington's men.

A wash of guilt ran over Tess. She wanted to turn away and give him the respect he deserved, but she kept her eyes on the man she was falling in love with. Would she ever know what he wanted to tell her?

A large purple bruise had already formed on his ribs underneath the footprint.

"Do you have running water?"

"Out back." Dr. Stein kept his eyes on Ian as he talked to Tess, asking more about his pain.

Clean towels were stacked neatly on a table by the back door. Tess picked up several, walked outside, and pumped water over them before wringing them out. When she returned to the room, it looked as though Ian's lip had swollen just in the past few minutes.

"I'll try not to hurt you," she said before wiping his face. Blood ran from his forehead. She pressed one of the rags against the wound and held it. With her other hand she wiped the mess from his eye, cheek, and lips. If she didn't know it was Ian, she would hardly recognize the man.

"This is my fault," Tess said, biting her lip to hold back the tears.

"No... no," Ian said, between shallow breaths. "You can't blame yourself. Barrington is angry with me."

"How could you ever have worked for such an evil man?"

He didn't answer, he only looked at her through swollen eyes.

197

"I'm sorry. I know you've changed. I know you regret your relation to the man."

"You're going to need a bandage around your chest," the doctor said. Tess was glad he interrupted their conversation. She didn't want to say any more hurtful things.

"Tess, I'm going to need your help sitting him up," Dr. Stein said.

Tess and the doctor once again lifted Ian into a sitting position. His face twisted as he sat up. As soon as he was up, the doctor began to wrap a bandage tightly around his midsection.

Tess returned outside and pumped the water out into a sink. She soaked the rags in the icy-cold water and lifted them up to wring them out before returning to the room.

When she got back in the room, Ian was lying down on the bed once again.

"The bandages will help you breathe a little easier. You're going to be down for a while."

"I can't. We have work to do on the ranch before winter sets in."

"You don't have a choice, Ian. Tess will have to learn how to run things."

Her eyes grew wide. Tess took a deep breath, held it, and stared at the doctor. She couldn't run it alone. She looked down at Ian and waited for a look of comfort, but none came. His eyes were closed as they continued to swell. She put the cold rag back on his face, hoping it would help.

"Now do you see why we need to leave this place?" Francine appeared in the doorway, sitting in her wheelchair.

Tess was startled by her presence. She would never leave this place. She couldn't go back to New York City. Not to her grandmother. She no longer was a part of her life. Denver City was her life. She took a deep breath and looked down at Ian. She stared at him for a moment. She knew then, Ian was her life.

***

"I heard what she said," Mrs. Barstall said, turning up the light on the lamp in the infirmary waiting room.

Tess stared straight ahead. "Francine doesn't understand."

"Is Ian ok?" the older woman asked.

"He will be. The men beat him up pretty severely." Tess wiped the sweat from her brow. "Where's Lizzie?"

"I had the maid put her to bed at my house. She'll take good care of the little one."

Tess remained quiet.

"There's something about the West. Something mysterious. It draws you in and steals your soul. Your sister doesn't see it, doesn't want it perhaps," Mrs. Barstall said.

"She's angry. Her husband, and now my father are gone." Tess said. She sat down on the settee across from the woman, who was proving to be more than a friend.

"Francine may never see it. But you do, don't you?" She kept her eyes on Tess.

She looked at Mrs. Barstall and nodded. The woman's demeanor had changed. It was calmer, quieter. She could see their friendship turning into something special.

"When I came out yonder west with my husband, I felt right at home for the first time. Nothin' has ever matched that feeling. I cain't leave this place."

Tess smiled. "It's almost like God is whispering my name and calling me to this land." A sense of peace washed over Tess. Knowing Ian was in the other room gave her the security she longed for.

"I want Francine to stay, but there are so many things she doesn't know. Might not ever know." Tess thought about her mother. Each time the idea came into her mind about her mother's occupation, she cringed. She didn't know if she could ever be fully honest with her sister about her occupation.

Tess now understood why her grandmother treated her with such contempt. She was the child of a lady of the night. Nothing could be worse. If she told her sister, would she treat her with the same contempt? Tess didn't want to find out.

An ear-splintering crash jerked Tess from her thoughts. Chunks of glass flew at the two women, and a brick, covered in paper, landed between them.

A shot of fear raced through Tess and she crouched down on the settee. After a moment, Tess leaned forward and picked up the brick. She carefully opened the paper.

"Leave now and spare your life."

Anger fumed inside of Tess. She stood up and brushed off her skirt. Tiny rips were forming from the shards of glass.

"Honey, don't go out there," Mrs. Barstall said. "No amount of anger will change their ways. It only makes things worse."

Dr. Stein ran into the room and surveyed the mess. "What happened?"

Tess ignored his comment and walked past him. She opened the door of the infirmary and walked out onto the front porch. She refused to hide. She would not be driven off her father's land. Her land.

***

"Sheriff, you can't deny that Henry Barrington had something to do with the attack on Ian Bidwell." Tess' voice grew stern.

"Miss Porter, Henry Barrington would never harm anyone." The sheriff sat down behind his desk and struck a match, then held it up under his cigar, puffing and spewing smoke in Tess' direction.

Tess took a deep breath and inhaled a cloud of smoke. She held her hand up to her mouth and coughed.

"If the smoke bothers you, Miss Porter, you can always leave." He continued to blow rings of smoke in her direction.

"Barrington sent his men out to do it."

"Henry Barrington's cattle have had free range around these parts for a long time. If someone started a war, Miss Porter, it would be your father."

"My father?"

The Sheriff continued, "He put up a fence, keeping Mr. Barrington's cattle out. They had plenty of water and meadow, until your father homesteaded."

"If my father didn't put up a fence, his own cattle would die of thirst. Mr. Barrington," she said firmly, "has more than triple the amount of cattle in his herd."

"Free range is what men do out in these parts. Neighbors don't take kindly to fences."

"I don't believe that's an excuse for violence. Two men attacked me at my father's house." She untied her bonnet and took it off. She lifted her hair and showed the sheriff her wound, still healing. "What do you make of that?"

"I don't believe you can prove any of this."

200

"How do you suggest I go about proving it?" Tess couldn't imagine what he expected her to provide in order to press charges against the men terrorizing her and her family, all in the name of land.

"Nothing you do will change the way things are around here." He kept his eyes on her. She knew exactly what he meant. Barrington probably paid him to keep his eyes closed and his mouth shut. Ian was right.

"Someone beat on Ian badly enough to cause broken ribs, a busted lip, and a cut eye. After Doc Stein cleaned him up, someone threw a brick through his window, with this note attached." Tess slammed the note down on his desk. He picked it up and read it.

"Maybe it was a joke."

"A joke?" Tess thought her conversation with the sheriff was the joke. "Are you going to do something about Ian and the brick?"

"I don't recall any complaints about a fight at the Harvest Festival."

"I'm complaining to you now." Tess felt as though she was getting nowhere.

"My deputies are always on the lookout for trouble. They didn't see anything." He threw the piece of paper back on the desk, leaned back in his chair, and stared at her.

"Are you suggesting I made that up? If you'll walk over to Dr. Stein's office you can see the damage for yourself."

"I don't believe that's necessary."

"What about the marshal, when does he come into town?"

"You're wasting your time, Miss Porter. He's a busy man." His conversation became more aloof than ever before.

"We'll see about that." Tess lifted the piece of paper off his desk and shoved it into her torn and tattered dress.

"Don't go doin' anything stupid. Might get you in some trouble," he yelled as she slammed the door behind her.

Denver City residents deserved justice.

Chapter Twenty-Six

Tess lifted the hem of her dress as she walked up the massive stairs at Mrs. Barstall's residence. She knocked on the thick wooden front door and waited for an answer. Moments later, one of the maids opened the door and invited Tess into the house. As she entered the foyer, she could hear Lizzie's giggles all the way across the house.

"I hope she hasn't been a bother," Tess said, as Mrs. Barstall walked in the room.

"Not at all. In fact, I'd love to keep her any time you need someone to watch her. The mister and I never had children, so her laughter has made this place come alive. All the staff seems to be enjoying their day a bit more."

"Thank you." Tess appreciated the woman's desire to help and be a part of their lives when they needed someone most.

"How's Ian doin' today?" Her loud voice echoed through the house.

"Better. The doctor said he could go back to the cabin, but he must stay off his horse and rest up. I suppose he will take care of Lizzie while I do things around the ranch."

"It's a good match," Mrs. Barstall said.

"He's only helping until I learn how to do things on the ranch and sell the cattle in the spring. Then I suppose he will join up with a cattle drive."

"I've seen the way he looks at you. Can't take his eyes off you, pretty thing." Mrs. Barstall said. "You're made for each other."

Tess felt the warmth traveling up her neck. "I don't know how to repay you for your kindness." Tess figured she better change the conversation or her entire staff would hear her words.

"You don't need to repay me. It was a real joy."

Lizzie's shoes tapped across the floor as she came running into the room. "Aunt Tessie!"

She leapt into her Aunt's arms. Tess lifted her and gave her a kiss on the cheek. She'd already fallen in love with the little girl.

"How's her mama doin'?" Mrs. Barstall asked.

"Every day is a bit better. She still has wooden splints on her legs, so we won't know for a while if she can walk. Dr. Stein is keeping her at the infirmary to watch her wounds as she heals."

"Glad to hear it."

Mrs. Barstall walked Tess and Lizzie out to the wagon. Tess lifted Lizzie up onto the seat and the young girl grabbed the reins and handed them gently to Tess.

As the two rode back to the infirmary, Tess couldn't help but wonder what life would be like with Ian. He was trustworthy and loved the Lord. What more could she ask for in a man? His handsome looks alone took her breath away.

***

Tess and Ian rode toward the foothills. Tess was thankful the cattle stayed near the watering hole, which was fed by the nearby stream of fresh water coming out of the mountains.

The sun slid behind the mountains and a cover of darkness lowered onto the land. They rode up and down the hills to check on the herd one last time before heading in to the house. As they crested the last hill, Tess gasped when she saw the cattle moving slowly toward the fenceline.

Tess looked at Ian and he flipped the reins on his horse and ran toward the moving animals. It had been several days since the festival and already Ian was healing fast.

As they neared the opening, a man stood up, just as several of the cows were being diverted through the fenceline.

Ian lifted his revolver from his holster and pulled back the hammer, aiming it at the man.

He gasped and put his hands up in the air.

"Tess, go get his horse and check through his saddle for any weapons."

She did as he said and rode around to his horse. Tess slid off her horse and landed on the ground. She marched over, lifted the flap on his saddlebag, dug her hand down inside, and felt for anything that could harm them.

"Nothing inside."

Tess hurried to the other side of the horse to the rifle tucked in behind the saddle. She pulled out the heavy weapon and struggled to hold it up. She continued to look for any other weapons, but found none.

She grabbed the reins on the horse and walked it back over to hers. Tess slid her foot in the stirrup, grabbed the saddle horn, and hoisted herself back up on Lady.

"You working for Henry Barrington?"

The young man nodded his head.

"Stealing cattle will get you hung. Dead. You know that?" Ian said, accentuating each word more than the last.

He nodded his head again.

"How old are you?"

"Turned fifteen last week," he said.

"Fifteen?" Surprise riddled Ian's voice. "You're a bit younger than I suspected." Ian lifted his hat up, smacked it against his leg, and placed it back on his head. "You're too young to be gettin' in this kind of trouble."

"Yes, sir."

"Where's your parents?" Ian continued the questioning.

"Died last year. I didn't have nowhere to go."

"You went to the wrong place. You need to get away from Barrington. He'll steer you down the wrong path and you'll end up hangin' from the end of a rope by the time he gets done with you. He's not out here doing the dirty work. He sent you here. Don't you see?"

Ian's shoulders rose up and Tess could see the tension on his face. Ian clearly wanted this boy to stay out of trouble. She wondered if he might be trying to find a way of escape for the young man. The same escape he was never given.

"Get on your horse and steer those cows back this direction. Then we'll tighten the fence back up and see what to do with you."

The boy nodded and climbed back on his horse. He went through the gaping hole in the fence and began rounding up the cattle.

Tess waited for Ian to come closer. He moved his horse alongside her, facing the opposite direction. She lifted the heavy rifle and handed it over to Ian. He slid it into the side of his saddle and looked at the boy.

"He reminds me so much of me when I was that age. I was full of fire and wanted to be tough. I missed my Ma so much, and couldn't find a job that suited me. I know this kid's stealing cattle, but I can bet you he's being strong-armed by Barrington. I know his tactics and I wouldn't be a bit surpiised if he talked this boy into takin' some of your cattle back to his ranch and rebrandin' 'em. He's too young to deserve to be hanged for somethin' like that."

"I see what you're saying, Ian, but I can't help but realize he agreed to take the cattle." Tess wanted desperately to understand this boy's reasoning for listening to Barrington.

"He agreed to take the cattle because he has nowhere else to go. You don't understand, when Barrington gets mad, he gets even. He won't take no for an answer. He'll either beat that kid to a bloody pulp or get rid of him if he don't do what's asked of him. Besides, that boy is probably hungry. Hunger can drive you to do some insane acts. Trust me, I speak from experience." Ian looked over at the boy, atop his horse, rounding up the cattle and pushing them back over onto Tess' land.

"I worked for the man for several years. He's 'bout the meanest man I know. He'd just as soon kill ya as he would be nice to you."

Tess tried to comprehend the violent, hateful nature of Henry Barrington. Didn't he have an ounce of compassion?

"If I do something, will you trust me on it and not question my motives?"

Tess watched Ian for a minute. He kept his eyes on the boy and looked back at Tess. "Yes, I will trust you."

His hand moved over and touched the top of hers. She felt the warmth travel up her arm. She wanted his hand to stay, holding hers. She'd never trusted anyone so much. Their eyes met and he leaned forward. Tess was ready. She closed her eyes and waited for the embrace.

"Mister?"

Ian jerked his head back and looked at the young boy. "Yeah?"

"I believe they're all back on your side." His voice cracked, most likely in fear of what was to come next. "What do you plan to do with me now? Take me to the sheriff, I s'pose."

"What's your name?"

"Kyle Watson."

"Kyle, you like workin' for Mr. Barrington?"

"No, sir." He gave a steady shake of his head several times.

"You want a good home and a livin' that would make your Ma proud?"

"I'd like that right much." A smile grew across his face at the thought. "I don't reckon that'll ever happen to me, though. I've done got myself into a bad situation."

"What would you think about comin' to work here for Miss Tess?" Ian looked at Tess and back at Kyle.

"Miss Tess?" He pointed to Tess.

Ian nodded. "That's right."

"Why would you do that? I just stole your cows."

"Yeah, but you put them back without any trouble."

"Why would you do that for me?" His eyebrows met in the center of his forehead.

"Because no one ever gave me a second chance," Ian said.

"I don't know what to say." He smiled again, this time all his teeth were showing.

"Say yes and get away from that thievin' man. The fewer men he has to do his dirty work, the more trouble he'll have getting things accomplished."

Tess smiled. She had to admit she was a bit fearful, but knowing Ian would be close by, she felt added comfort that he would be able to steer the young Kyle in the right direction.

"Let's get that fence mended and we'll get back to the house. It's gettin' dark," Ian said.

Kyle jumped off his horse and helped Ian tie up the wire, keeping the cattle from escaping again. Tess figured Barrington would be seething mad when Kyle didn't return.

***

The wind blew gently across Tess' face as she tilted back and forth in the rocking chair on the front porch. Lizzie slept soundly in her bed and Ian rested in the lean-to. She was grateful for the quiet time to think.

In the distance, a lone rider appeared on the horizon. She debated waking Ian, but feared it would be for nothing. Tess hated the fact that she didn't feel completely safe, but knew the reality of the situation.

As he neared, Tess recognized the Sheriff.

"Miss Porter," he said, stepping off his horse and dropping to the ground.

"Yes?" She stood up from her seat and walked down the steps. The sun blinded her and she raised her hand to shield her face from the light.

"I got some papers sayin' you gotta be outta here by month's end." He handed her a document.

Tess took it and unfolded the papers. "What's this all about?"

"Your brother's plannin' on sellin' to Barrington."

"I don't have a brother. My father had no sons." Exasperation over the matter was beginning to take a toll on Tess.

"It appears he did. Name's Isaiah Porter," the Sheriff said, pointing to the papers. "His signature's right there."

How can this be?

"You might as well go back to New York. Ain't nothin' out here for you and your sister now. Looks to me like your brother doesn't care a whit about neither of you."

"Where can I find this brother of mine?"

"I suppose he's back up workin' for Mr. Barrington. Ian knows 'em. Rode with him for a while now."

Tess choked back the tears. Ian was in this for his uncle. He didn't love her after all. She swallowed hard, trying to keep the tears from bursting out and flowing continuously. She trusted Ian. For nothing.

Tess watched the Sheriff climb back on his horse and ride away. He would finally be rid of her and her sister, and be able to make Barrington happy. She was sure there was a bit of flaunting as he handed off what she considered to be a life sentence. *Back to New York City.* The paper she held in her hands might as well have been a jail sentence.

Tess had never felt the kind of love growing inside of her for a man like she did for Ian—even with reservation. Why had she let her emotions and her feelings get out of control for this man? She needed to return to Franklin and become his wife. It was the only answer.

Tess returned inside the house and laid the papers on the table. She had no choice but to pack up and leave. At least her so-called brother had afforded her a month to find another place of residence.

Tess felt a wave of nausea roll across her stomach. She didn't want to face Ian.

Chapter Twenty-Seven

"You still work for Barrington, don't you?" Tess said.

"What are you talking about?" Ian took off his hat and stood by the door of the cabin.

"The Sheriff just left. He brought papers." She walked over to the table, lifted them up, and held them out in front of her. "Said a man claiming to be my brother was selling the place to Barrington. He said you knew he was my brother." Her face didn't resemble the soft, gentle features he left earlier this morning.

"What? Selling the place?" A rush of anger boiled inside of Ian. He trusted Isaiah to turn from his sinning ways.

"So you knew?"

Ian sighed and lowered his head. "Tess, I wanted—"

"Do you work for Barrington or not?" Tess' chin quivered as she spoke. She tightened her lips.

"No. I don't work for him anymore. I told you that." He set his hat down on the table and walked closer to her.

"I trusted you. I believed that you cared about my father." Tears streamed down her face. "How could you lie to me about all of this? You knew how much I missed my father and you took advantage of my grief."

Ian lifted his hand to wipe her tears. She locked eyes with him. He wiped her cheek with his thumb, drying the tears. He wanted to embrace her, let her know everything would be okay, no matter the outcome. He would take care of her and Francine and Lizzie, no matter what it took.

Tess pushed his hand away. "How could you be so cruel and heartless?"

"I do care about your father. He's the reason I came to know the Lord." Ian wanted so badly to hold her, let her know he was telling the truth. What could he do to make her believe?

"It's bad enough you lied to me, but now you bring God into this? I never even questioned your faith. I believed you."

"I don't know how to make you understand."

"Make me understand these papers?"

"What are they?" He took the papers from Tess and scanned them.

"My brother wants this land. He plans to evict us… me, Francine and Lizzie, from the property. I guess he's going to sell to Barrington once he gets his hands on this place." Tess walked over to the window and stared outside.

Ian remained silent. He knew nothing he said would make a difference right now.

She spun around and faced Ian. "What could you possibly come up with for hiding this from me?" Anger seeped out of her words.

"I wanted to tell you about your brother, believe me. I desperately wanted to tell you, but I made a vow to your father. He wanted to be the one to tell you and Francine."

"You expect me to believe that? My father is dead and buried. You could have told me. If I hadn't seen my own father in his casket, I wouldn't have believed, it either."

"It wasn't up to me to tell you. I kept my promise to your Pa." Ian walked across the room. "Your father came to a point in his life where he realized how much his actions affected you and Francine. He wanted to tell you, he did. But he realized that you might not come west to live with him."

"Sounds like a trap." She snapped.

"He wasn't trying to trap you, he was doing everything he could to form a relationship with you that he never had before. He loved you and Francine more than you could ever know."

"If he loved us so much, why didn't he take a chance and tell us before we came and let us decide the fate of our own futures? Now I'm miles from home. I'm not sure which is worse, a grandmother that despises me, or living in this place where no one cares about anything but the land. Lives are worthless here."

"All I know is that your father came to a place in his life where he knew that God wanted him to ask you and Francine for forgiveness. He knew how much his... indiscretions with other women would affect you. It pained him to know that you had a brother and you never knew him."

Ian would have given anything to take away the pain Tess was feeling. He wished her father had lived, so he could be the one standing here telling her. Ian didn't want any hard feelings between them. He felt a love so strong for Tess. He hated the idea that she was angry enough with him to think he would lie to her.

"When Isaiah arrived, your father was so happy. He had a vision for your family, one that would allow all of you to live together happily. Maybe it was unfair of him to get you all out here before telling you, but he had the best intentions. He finally realized how wrong and selfish he had been all those years."

Tess stayed by the window, as if she wanted to escape from his presence. "You masqueraded as a man who truly cared about me and my family. I trusted you and believed everything you told me," her voice raised. "I can't believe I was so naïve. How do I know you are even telling me the truth about Isaiah? Maybe this is all part of your ploy to get the land for Barrington."

"Tess—" Ian walked closer, but stopped. He didn't want to push himself on her. "I know about your mother."

"What do you mean?" She turned sharply and faced him. "What do you know?"

"I know what she did. For a living."

"How do you know?" Her countenance moved from anger to fear.

"Your father showed me the letter he wrote to you. He slaved over how to tell you. He knew it would change your life forever. Possibly the way you thought about yourself. He didn't want you to think you were worthless."

"You don't know any more about my mother than I do. How dare you speak to me of that woman."

Ian hung his head down for a moment and lifted it back up. "I don't know anything about the mother you knew, but I do know that your father loved your real mother more than any other woman."

"I think you need to leave."

Ian stared at Tess. He nodded his head and walked toward the door.

"For good."

Ian stopped and turned to face Tess. Could she really be telling him she didn't want him in her life?

"Tess, look—"

"I mean it, Ian. I'll find a way to pay you back for all your work. I don't know how, but I will."

"I don't want your money." He wanted her. All of her. He'd never fallen more in love with a woman. He wanted to be a part of her life. She was determined to follow through on her father's dream, in spite of all that she encountered. For the first time in so many years, he felt like he was home. With her.

"Tess, I love you." Ian walked over to Tess and pressed the palms of his hands against her shoulders. He wanted to hold her as his wife.

Tess spun around and looked him in the eyes.

"Ian, I would give anything to believe you. I've come to care for you. But, after this, it changes everything. I don't think I will ever be able to trust you again. I will have to take my chances and hope that I will be able to run this ranch by myself." Tess paused for a moment. "That is, until Isaiah makes me leave."

Ian put his hands down by his side and waited for a moment, hoping Tess would change her mind. He knew saying something else was futile. She didn't trust him, and what was love without trust?

Ian walked out to the lean-to and gathered his items. He was thankful the boy they just hired had gone into town. He could catch up with him there and explain the situation. Ian lifted his Bible off the makeshift bed and opened it up. It flipped open to the eleventh verse in the twenty-ninth chapter of Jeremiah. If there was ever a time he needed to see a verse, it was now.

"'For I know the thoughts that I think toward you,' saith the Lord, 'thoughts of peace, and not of evil, to give you an expected end.'"

Ian knew what he wanted his expected end to be. He wanted to hold Tess in his arms and look out the window of the cabin at the glorious mountains in the distance. He wanted to grow old with her by his side. He felt safe and alive when she was around.

He wasn't worried about finding work. He could always jump on the next cattle drive that came through town, or head out to work on the railroad springing up across the country. But for the first time in his life, he wanted to settle down and have roots with the woman he loved.

Ian stuffed his Bible in his satchel and walked out into the chilly air. He could see his breath in front of him in a cloud of white. Crystals formed on the ground in cities of ice. He took a deep breath and the cold air pinched his lungs.

Ian threw his knapsack over his horse, slipped his foot in the stirrup, and flipped his leg over. Still sore, he adjusted himself in the saddle, twisted the reins twice around his hands, and tapped his heels against Slater's side. She started walking slowly toward town. He pushed his hat securely onto his head and lifted his jacket up to cover his mouth. The wind picked up and blew strongly against him, blowing his heart and his dreams away.

***

Tess paced the room after Ian left. When he stood behind her, she wanted him to reach out and touch her, and hold on to her. She wanted him to wrap his strong, safe arms around her and tell her that everything would be ok.

But it wasn't, and it appeared he was the last person to tell her anything. She wanted to run outside and stop him from leaving. Everything inside of her commanded her to follow him, stop him, and turn him back around to stay.

Her heart longed for Ian. But how could she trust a man who kept a secret from her? Not just any secret, but one that would change her life forever. It was obvious his loyalties still lay with his uncle. For all she knew, Isaiah and Ian could be in on the trick to get her out of the cabin and take everything dear to her.

Tess sat on the edge of the bed and watched Lizzie sleep. Her slow, steady breathing was a comfort. She so desperately wanted the little girl to have a place to call home in the land she had come to love. The mountains stretched high in the distance. Denver City felt more like home than New York City, in the short time she lived here.

She moved over to the front door and placed her hand on the knob. Her hand burned to turn it, fling open the door, and run after

Ian. It was too late. He was gone, and what they had would never come to fruition.

Tess walked back over to the fire and lifted the fire prod and poked the burning wood in the fireplace. Sparks flew and flittered away into ashes. She lifted the letter from her father off the mantle and opened it up.

Tess read every word, soaking it in and trying to understand the meaning of it all. Did he really love her mother? She felt as though part of her died with the mother she always knew. She had always grieved over the woman, engulfed by sadness at her passing and the fact that they would never have a relationship. Now, she knew it was all a lie.

Whom could she trust? Her father didn't even send the letter about her real mother. She couldn't help but wonder how she would have reacted to the news if he had lived to tell her in person.

The night she accidentally stumbled upon the prostitute in town, Tess couldn't help but feel repulsed toward the woman. A woman just like her mother. How could someone be so immune to her body being a temple for the Lord that she could carry on the way she did? How could that same kind of person feel any love in their heart for another soul, even a child?

Or could they? Did her father save her mother from a fate worse than death? Did he take her off the streets and care for her in her dying days? Tess would never know. She wondered if she would ever know love and the fullness of trusting another human being.

Chapter Twenty-Eight

The dark, gray clouds hung low over Denver City. Winter was settling in on the area. Lines of smoke from the teepees in the far country, on the outskirts of town, were more prevalent than ever before.

"This winter will be bad," one of the elderly Indian men told Ian. His leathery skin hung from his dark face, and he wrapped himself in buffalo hide to keep warm. "I have seen this winter. It will bring more snow."

Ian had taken his warning seriously. He led his horse toward Thomas and Catherine's house. He hated to impose on the couple, but without money or shelter, he had no place to go. The bitter cold could freeze a man in a short time.

As he approached Josiah's store, he noticed the man out front, getting down from a wagon.

Ian stopped and dismounted from his horse. He walked around the side of the wagon and watched for a moment. Josiah slowly lowered one foot at a time, grimacing with each movement. Did he now regret his decision to follow the military up north to get rid of some of the Indians?

Josiah finally reached the ground and tried to stand up straight. His own weight must've been pressing down on his wounds.

"Looks like you took quite a beating," Ian tried to remain kind to the man, even though he despised what put him in that position.

"Ian, my good friend," Josiah said, squishing his face into a knot. "I think the return trip on the stagecoach might have been more painful than the arrow itself. The man that shot me had expert aim.

The arrow went through my chest, breaking a rib and pinning my arm to my side."

Ian stared at the sling wrapped around his arm. He remembered well the pain of being shot in the leg and the fiery sensation it brought.

"Glad to see that you made it back alive, otherwise."

"I thought about you many times since I left," Josiah said.

He wondered how he could possibly enter into that man's thoughts. He figured Josiah didn't listen any more to him than anyone else.

"Especially on the return trip."

Ian's interest piqued.

"I've fought the Indians before. I've never felt a bit of remorse for taking their lives and their supplies. Something was different this time. When we rode up on the camp, something inside of me rose up and scared me. I couldn't pinpoint it. Like someone was telling me to turn around and go back, stay away from these people."

Ian knew exactly what it was. The Holy Spirit. He'd experienced it many times before, since his decision to follow Christ. Had his prayers to change Josiah's heart been answered?

"At that moment, I wanted to flee. But I couldn't. I tried to push the feeling to the back of my mind and get rid of anything that made me feel such regret—like I'd never felt before. I couldn't very well turn around and leave the rest of the men after traveling all the way up there and promising to help get rid of the Indians."

Ian noticed he didn't refer to them as injuns this time. What was happening? What had changed?

"How did I figure into all of this?" Ian kept his eyes on Josiah.

"I thought about what you said. Your words about leaving the people alone continued to enter into my mind over and over as I rode north. I pushed those thoughts back as often as I could." A smile grew across his face and a laugh burst out of him. "I even stopped a time or two, considering turning around. I fought my instincts and continued on. If I had just listened to your words, I wouldn't have lost so much use in my arm, and I wouldn't be in such tremendous pain."

Although Ian's heart ached for Tess, he found joy in Josiah's comment. He knew God was present everywhere, but he couldn't help but get excited when he prayed about something and he saw results in such a short time.

"I'm sorry you had to go through all of that to learn that killing isn't the answer," Ian said. He knew that sometimes people had to take the long route to find God, just like he did.

"I wish I had listened to you, but it appears I needed to find out the truth on my own. When I saw the look on some of the faces of them men, I realized they were only actin' in self-defense. We're takin' everything they hold dear. I know there's no way to stop the movement of the White man across the plains, but little pieces of my heart began to feel somethin' fer these people." A look of question crossed his face, as though he didn't understand at all what was happening.

Ian understood. He had come to like the Indians he had met in the time he'd spent in Denver City. They seemed to be able to predict storms and teach others about survival in the harsh climate. Ian knew to listen when they warned of bad weather.

Ian couldn't believe the monumental change in Josiah. Could he come to the point of calling the man friend, and believing it?

"What're you doin' here in town?" Josiah asked.

"I'm headin' over to the preacher's. Need a place to stay." Ian looked down at the ground.

"I though you was out there with that gal, Tess. What happened?" Josiah showed a true interest in his situation.

"Let's just say my past caught up with me and it's made it tough for her to trust me."

"Why don't you come on over here tomorrow and help me out? I can't very well stock the shelves in this condition," he smiled at Ian. "My brother'll buy the store right out from under me if I don't pull my weight."

Ian nodded. "I could use the work. I can earn some of that money to pay you back for what I owe ya," he said, as he reached out and shook Josiah's good hand.

***

"Tess, what a lovely surprise," Franklin said. He leaned forward and placed a kiss on her cheek. "Are you alright? You look as though you've been crying. Leonard, see to Tess' things

217

immediately." He waved his hands in a quick motion toward the man.

Leonard nodded and removed Tess' shawl. He left the two standing in the foyer alone.

"Franklin, you asked me a question, and I've never given you an answer," Tess said.

"Let's sit down," he said, waving his hand in the direction of the parlor. "You look as though you need to rest."

"No, I'd rather stand." She shook her head before looking down at the floor and returning her gaze to Franklin. Never before had she sensed his honorable character like she did now. Her insides ached as though she couldn't move.

Tess placed her hand on his arm. "I... I will marry you." Tess pinched her lips together.

"Tess, darling," Franklin said, taking her hand in his own. "Of course I am happy with your answer, but are you sure this is what you want?"

"I've never been so sure of anything." How could she have been so blind to the truth? Why did she have to travel so far to see that the man she should marry sat right in front of her?

"We can send a telegram ahead to have my house prepare for the ceremony." He squeezed her hand. "Will that suit you?"

Tess nodded in agreement.

A smile lit Franklin's face. "Well, then, let's start planning."

Tess returned the smile. She wanted to feel the same joy and satisfaction that Franklin felt. A part of her almost felt as though she were betraying him by not giving the same amount of love he lavished on her. Maybe in time her love would grow. She could only pray.

"Your grandmother will be so pleased. She will be able to move all of her things into the house when we return."

"Pardon?" Tess looked up at Franklin. "What do you mean? She has a home of her own. She's perfectly capable of taking care of herself."

"Yes, but her creditors are ready to take the house. Didn't she tell you your grandfather left a mountain of debt?"

Like a blow to the stomach, Tess felt sick.

"It'll be grand to have your family under one roof. Francine, Lizzie, and the new baby are welcome to stay as long as necessary. You know I have the room."

He was right about the accommodations. The rented house in Denver City could fit twice inside of his New York City mansion.

"Let me inform Leonard of your decision." He kissed Tess on the cheek again and left the room.

"It's about time you made a decision," Eliza said, coming from the parlor. "I thought I'd have to stay in this wretched place forever."

"Grandmother?" Tess asked, "You weren't concerned about me or my future, were you? You only wanted a place to live."

"Your grandfather loved you. I could never understand that."

Her words felt like a sharp knife to Tess's heart.

"I raised you. I think you owe me something. You getting married to Franklin and insuring a home for me will be repayment enough." Her eyes narrowed as she spoke.

Tess searched for the words to respond to her Grandmother's spite. She was fully aware that no matter what she said, it would not change her outlook. Only God could do that.

***

For two days, Ian felt useless at Thomas and Catherine's house. He'd told Thomas he would stay with Catherine while he made his rounds visiting patients, including Francine, in the infirmary.

Catherine seemed to be well with the baby, but still unable to get out of bed for more than a few minutes at a time.

During the quiet moments, he told her of the events that transpired between him and Tess. Her absence was creating a void in his heart. Ian ached for her. He wanted to see her face and hear her voice. An unsettled feeling stayed on him. Several times, he wanted to sneak out and just see her face. It would only make matters worse.

Catherine seemed to have a good outlook on the situation, although he didn't agree that Tess would come to understand he couldn't break his vow to her father.

A chill raced over Ian and he stood up to move closer to the fire. As he passed the window, he noticed a blanket of snow on the ground. Snow continued to fall at a steady rate.

The door opened and Thomas came in, along with a blast of winter cold. "It's snowing quite hard out there. I don't believe I've ever seen it snow this hard."

Ian's thoughts turned immediately to Tess. Would she have enough wood to burn? Was she able to get out to the barn to check on the animals? Did Lizzie and she have enough food to last for several days in case the snow continued to fall?

Ian decided to take his chances and risk angering Tess, in order to make sure she and Lizzie would be okay throughout the storm.

He rode to Josiah's to pick up a few things before heading to the ranch.

The wind drove the snow hard against his face, like pellets of frozen sand. He pulled his scarf up above his nose to feel the warmth of his breath. His lips felt numb in the cold.

The snow began to fall harder, making it difficult to see very far in front of him. He searched for familiar trees and markings along the way. Many of the leaves were still on the trees, weighing the branches down.

He could hear a large branch crack from the weight of the snow and fall to the ground with a loud thump.

The snow accumulated on the ground so quickly, his horse strained against the movement. She had to lift her feet up, making the trek harder and more laborious. Her head moved up and down as she pressed on toward the cabin.

"Atta girl," he said, petting her neck. "We're almost there."

He could see the cabin in the distance, but the driving snow pressed against his body.

He couldn't see any lights on in the cabin and hoped Tess and Lizzie were inside still warm.

The wind howled in his ears and a shiver shook his body. The tops of his thighs were beginning to feel numb. He knew better than to head out in a storm like this, but he feared for Tess and Lizzie's safety. It could be days before anyone could get out to the ranch to check on them.

Thoughts of Barrington sending one of his men over to finish off Tess ran through his mind. Barrington or his men would figure out a way to make it look like it was an accident. Ian still believed Barrington had something to do with Ed Porter's death. He couldn't prove it, but something deep down made him believe Ed would still be alive if not for Henry Barrington interfering.

Ian noticed prints in the snow. Horse tracks. He stopped and looked around. Only one horse. At least he wouldn't be outnumbered. The prints were aimed right for Tess and Lizzie's cabin. Did Barrington send a man over here, as he suspected?

He reached around and felt for his revolver, strapped to his waist. He pulled it out and opened the cylinder to count the bullets. Six. He knew the ways of man and always kept his gun fully-loaded.

The footprints continued, but were already filling up with fresh snow. Was he too late?

As he approached, the snow continued to fall hard, making it difficult to see more than one or two feet in front of him. Ian stopped near the cabin and flung his leg over the side of his horse and dropped to the ground, landing in at least two feet of snow. He realized it must've snowed much longer out on the ranch than it had in town.

He slid his revolver back in the holster and tucked it behind his jacket, still accessible to him at a moment's notice.

Ian pulled on the reins and tied them to the front porch. The sound of footsteps came from inside the cabin. The smell of smoke hit his senses. He looked up at the chimney and a line of smoke ascended from the top.

As he reached the top of the stairs, he peered through the window and caught a glimpse of the back of a man.

Chapter Twenty-Nine

He waited until the man turned to the side to get a glimpse. His heart pounded against his chest and he feared Tess and Lizzie were already dead.

Ian backed up several feet on the porch and kicked the door in.

"What're you doin' here?" Isaiah yelled.

"Isaiah? What's going on?"

"I came here looking for Tess. I wanted to talk to her—"

"What'd you do with her?" Ian's voice grew tense. He clinched his fists.

"Nothin'. I promise." Isaiah said. A sternness rose in his voice Ian had never heard before now.

"I should've never trusted you." Ian chided himself for even considering that Isaiah might have good intentions. His eyes ran the length of Isaiah, searching for weapons. He wanted to be prepared. Ian hated the fact that he knew all-too-well how to size up a man, but it was still a part of his nature, and he didn't trust Isaiah.

"I know I did you wrong. I lied—"

"You did more than lie. You're costing Tess all she's ever wanted."

Isaiah nodded.

"Why are you doing this?"

Isaiah stayed quiet for a moment before answering. "We need to find Tess—"

"Give me an answer," Ian said. He wasn't about to let Isaiah distract him.

"When I got here, there were fresh tracks going out. She has to be out there somewhere. We gotta find her or she won't be able to find her way back in this blizzard."

Ian knew Isaiah was right. They didn't have time to spare. He'd find out the answers to his questions later.

"We'll go separate ways. If you find her, discharge your gun. That'll let me know and I'll find my way back here. I'll do the same if I come across her." Ian cringed at the fact that they might not be able to find her in the storm. He couldn't bear to go on, knowing she was dead. They had to find her.

***

"Tess?" Isaiah screamed. Since his mother's death, he hadn't felt such a sense of urgency and fear that tangled his heart. Why was he worried about a woman he'd never met? When Tess first arrived in Denver City, he didn't care about her or Francine. He only wanted his father's land. Vengeance seemed so close and sweet.

But after watching Ian go from a thief to a man bent on making things right, he wanted to get to know his sisters. Even if it meant giving up on selling the land for money—the one thing he wanted. Getting the land, and revenge, didn't seem to matter anymore.

"Tess?" He screamed again. He knew this land well, but the driving snow made it hard to see five feet in front of him.

The sun peeked out from behind the clouds for a brief moment, allowing Isaiah to see a brown shadow on a tree in the distance. He couldn't be sure, but it appeared to be a horse.

As he approached, he could see Tess slumped over her saddle. He could feel the beat of his heart pounding in his ears.

Isaiah slung his leg over his saddle, dropped off his horse, and ran to her side. "Tess? Can you hear me?" When she didn't respond, he pulled his hand out of his glove and slid it through her scarf, searching for a heartbeat.

Her neck was warm and her pulse felt strong. They could make it back in time. He just hoped she didn't have any frostbite.

"We're gonna get you back to the warm fire." Isaiah wanted Tess to live. As he pulled her from her horse and climbed up onto his, he opened his jacket and pressed her body against his to warm her.

Isaiah pulled his gun out of his holster and fired three shots in the air, letting Ian know Tess had been found.

***

Muttered voices awoke Tess. Her eyelids fluttered open and she squinted in the light that was filtering through the window. She took a deep breath before looking around.

"Tess," Ian said, sighing, "I've been so worried about you." He knelt down on one knee next to the bed.

Tess turned her head and stared at Ian for a moment before speaking.

Although the blanket was up around her neck, her fingers and toes stung. She pulled her hand out from under the covers. Her red-tipped fingers moved slowly, but didn't look as though frostbite had affected them.

"What're you doing here?" She looked around the room.

"I came out to make sure you and Lizzie had enough wood and food to last the storm."

"The last thing I remember, the snow began falling so fast," Tess said. "It went from sunny to a blizzard in such a short time." She lifted herself into a sitting position on the bed. "I checked on the cattle and by the time I headed back, the snowfall was so dense I couldn't see in front of me."

"You have to know these parts. A winter storm can strike fast," Isaiah said.

Tess stared for a moment before speaking. Her body still felt groggy and lethargic. She looked at Ian and asked, "Who is he?"

Isaiah hesitated, but walked closer to the bed and sat down in the chair. "I'm your brother, Isaiah."

She stared at him for a few moments, searching for any resemblance to her father. How many more lies would she find out about? Tess didn't like the fact that she would never be able to confront her father about the truth he kept from his family. "Who is your mother?"

"She died two years ago. We lived out east, in New York—"

"You lived near us?" Tess felt the fury rise inside of her. She clamped her jaw shut and gritted her teeth. How is it she lived near her brother, but never met him? Tess struggled to comprehend the situation.

"I never knew of you until I arrived out west. Our father sent for me, same as he did for you. I guess he planned to tell each of us 'bout the other when we got here."

224

"How long have you been here?" Tess tried to fit everything together in her mind. The time frame, the turn of events, her new brother, and the truth about her mother.

"Almost a year."

"Were you working for Barrington?" She kept her eyes on him, trying to determine if this was all a lie.

He nodded.

"Why?" She had to know the truth.

"I had nowhere else to go," Isaiah said.

Tess understood the need to earn money for food.

"But Pa died right before I arrived. Why weren't you at the funeral?" She asked.

Isaiah turned his face and looked toward the window. "Before you got here, Pa and I fought. He was angry with me. I took off hoping he'd forgive me. But, I never gave him a chance.

"I needed work, so I went to Barrington. I knew he'd hire me to get at Pa. It made Pa even angrier. I came to the house to reason with him, but he told me he'd have nothin' to do with me 'til I got away from Barrington. But, I couldn't leave. I owed him."

Tess knew how it felt to be ignored and thrown away. Her own grandmother treated her as though she didn't matter. Now it all made sense. All these years, she stayed angry with her son—her only son—for his affairs. Too many affairs. Tess felt sympathy for the young man across from her claiming to be her brother.

"You never worked it out?" Tess asked.

Isaiah shook his head back and forth. "There are days I wish I could take it all back, just to know that he loved me when he died. But I can't. I'll always have that hangin' over me."

Tess understood. She wanted more than anything for her father to be alive, breathing, and able to enjoy his family as a whole. Whatever that meant. Since she arrived, she found out that her mother was a prostitute, lost her brother-in-law, prayed her sister wouldn't die, and found out she had a brother.

"Why are you telling me this now, after all this time?"

"All's I ever wanted was a place to call home. My Ma could never afford to stay in one place. We moved all over the city, sometimes sleepin' out on the streets. I was angry at Pa for not helping us more. He wasn't there for me, or my Ma.

"I swore I would never live like that again. Gettin' the papers from Pa gave me assurance that I wouldn't have to go without again. You don't know what it's like livin' on the street." Isaiah turned his head and wiped his hand across his face. Tess figured the talk choked him up.

"This cabin is rightfully mine. He's just as much my Pa as he is yours." Isaiah continued. "When he died, this cabin and all of the land should've ended up with me. I don't want to spend the rest of my life running from place to place. I refuse to do it. I don't like to do this to you, but I have to evict you from this place."

"You can't do this. This home belongs to Francine and me as well. You don't know what you're doing."

"I'm just as much one of Ed Porter's children as you are. We may have different mothers, but this is our father's property, and I intend to sell this land to Barrington."

"I should have known better." Tess stopped talking for a moment. "Barrington put you up to this, didn't he? That's it. You're working for him and posing yourself as my brother."

"If you don't believe me, ask Ian. He knows the truth." Isaiah stood up from the table and walked to the door. "I'll be kind, you have one month to find a place to live. After that date, I'll send the sheriff out here to make sure you no longer take up this space."

Tess heard him loud and clear, but her heart refused to listen. She glared at Ian. "How long have you been in dealings with Isaiah?" Her eyes blazed with anger.

"Tess, it's not like that—"

"It is like that. It's bad enough you lie to me, but to continue to act as though you care about me and my father." A tear ran down the side of Tess' cheek and she wiped it away with still-numb hands. She didn't want him to see her pain, her grief.

"Tess—"

"Please don't say anything. You'll only make matters worse. I'll be leaving any day now. I plan to go back to New York City. Francine seems to be getting better each day. She should be able to travel very soon."

"What will you do?" Ian stood across the room with his arms crossed.

"I am planning to marry Franklin as soon as we return home. I can no longer see the point in not marrying a man I know will take care of me. He has proven his strong, honest character over and over again." Tess looked away. She had wanted so badly to be held by Ian one day, as his wife. But now she knew that would never happen.

"But, you don't love him. How can you marry a man that you don't love?" Wrinkles across Ian's brow. He walked across the room, closer to Tess.

"You don't know anything about love," anger seethed out of her words. "You only care about getting land for your uncle and filling your own pockets with money."

Ian's eyes grew large. His lips pressed together before speaking. "I've told you, I don't work for my uncle. I have no part of Isaiah's choices," his voice rose to a sharp tone. "I have no control over those men. I tried to talk sense into Isaiah, but he wouldn't listen."

"It's done. My decision has been made." Tess looked down at her hands. She squeezed them together. She wanted nothing more than to throw her arms around Ian, but how could she now? His betrayal was more than she could bear. "You must go."

Ian remained silent for a few seconds. "I'll not trouble you again."

He walked to the door and stopped, looking down at the floor. Tess watched him from behind, wondering if he would turn and confess. Instead, he opened the door and closed it gently behind him, never looking back.

The moment he left the room, Tess tumbled over in the bed and muffled her cries in the blankets. It was as though her heart left with Ian. How could she ever love Franklin after Ian?

The weight of responsibility fell on Tess, knowing she had to marry Franklin. It was the only way.

Chapter Thirty

Isaiah searched out the window from his hotel room, waiting for the marshal's arrival on the stagecoach. He'd wondered if the man would believe him when he told him Henry Barrington killed his father.

A part of Isaiah was awash in fear, worrying that the marshal would suspect him of foul play instead. Had Barrington lined the marshal's pockets with wads of cash, as he had everyone else in town?

The rumble of the stagecoach rolled into town and Isaiah took to the stairs, and walked across the street to the café, where they were scheduled to meet. He was careful not to be seen. He didn't want Barrington getting to him before he had a chance to say his piece.

The alley behind the café was quiet and desolate, just the way he'd hoped. He slipped through the back door and walked up two wooden steps when a large, stout man with shoulders the width of a door stood in front of him.

"What's your name, Son?"

"Isaiah Porter." He could hear his own voice trembling as the words came out.

"Marshal Nelson is expecting you." He moved out of the way and pointed to a small, dark room just inside.

Isaiah's eyes adjusted to the darkness, and he sat down in a chair across from a man, just as large as the last.

"You're quite brave to make an argument that the man who owns half this valley killed your father," Marshal Nelson said, adjusting himself in the chair.

"Yes, sir." Isaiah nodded. He'd let the Marshal do the questioning. He wouldn't add any more than what was asked.

"I came quite a long way to hear this story. Out with it."
Marshal Nelson nodded his head once.

The man didn't mince words, he was ready for business.
Isaiah was glad. He wanted this over with, one way or another.

Isaiah sat for a minute, trying to figure out where to start. He
wanted it off his chest. "Not long after I moved to Denver City, Pa
and I argued. I needed a place to work, needed food. That's how I
tangled up with Barrington. He gave me a job, said he'd use me to
get at my Pa. Barrington thought maybe I could talk him inta
sellin'."

"But your Pa didn't want to sell, did he?" The Marshal asked.

Isaiah shook his head. "No. Fact, he didn't want to ever
leave. Said he'd found home." A knot formed in his throat and he
swallowed hard to push it down.

"Go on." Marshal Nelson folded his arms across his chest.

"Barrington brought me to my Pa's cabin a while later, when
Pa wasn't cooperating. We tried to talk to him again. I tried to reason
with him. He wouldn't listen. That's when I saw the look on
Barrington's face."

"Look?"

"Yes, sir, he filled his head with rage and lunged at my Pa. I
hollered at him to stop, but he didn't." Isaiah stopped and tried to
take a deep breath and keep his tears from coming, but he couldn't.
He wiped several away and took a deep breath before continuing.

"He, he pushed my Pa so hard, he hit his head on the mantle,
and again when he fell down. On the hearth. I tried to wake him up.
But I couldn't. I couldn't." He pulled in a deep breath before sobbing
into the palm of his hands.

Isaiah felt like a small child, weeping at the feet of a grown
man. He felt responsible for his father's death in some way.

"Are you prepared to go to trial with this information?" The
marshal asked.

Isaiah nodded.

"Barrington will probably hire the best lawyers, like he did
last time."

"Last time?" Isaiah looked up at Marshal Nelson and creased
his brow.

"This isn't the first time he's been accused of murder," Marshal Nelson said. "Why do you think I came all the way out here on the short telegram that you sent?"

Isaiah shook his head.

"He had some pretty good lawyers. Let's hope this time we can nail him."

"Right." A rush of disbelief hit Isaiah.

"Look, kid, I know you've beat yourself up over this. But, you couldn't have done anything to save your father. If Barrington wanted him dead, he would've killed him one way or another. It's a wonder he hasn't killed you and your sisters."

"She's had someone out there, protecting her." He thought of Ian and all that he'd done for him and his sister. He practically owed him his life.

"You were smart not telling anyone your plans. You don't know whom to trust," he said, standing up from the table. "I'll need a more formal statement once we get him into custody. Watch your back, he might be angry enough to send his men after you."

Marshal Nelson left the room. Isaiah knew they would head out and arrest Barrington right away. He just hoped the man didn't get loose, or he might not live to see another day.

Isaiah wanted so badly to tell Ian and Tess, but he knew it might jeopardize the situation. He'd just have to wait.

***

The morning sun shone bright on the vast Colorado Territory landscape. The frost dried in tiny clouds of fog, rising from the ground in the warming sun.

Tess loosened her bonnet at the base of her neck and let it fall against her back. She opened the doors of the church sanctuary one last time. Already Mrs. Barstall made her way to Tess.

As she approached, the woman embraced her. "A young lady came by here lookin' for you. Kinda reminded me of myself back in the day."

Tess crinkled her eyebrows and wondered who could be looking for her. "Who?"

"Said her name was Matilda—"

"Oh, my goodness." Tess' hand went up to her mouth. "Where'd she go?"

230

"Don't know. I went around the side to look for you and she disappeared."

"She came from down on Holliday Street, didn't she?" Mrs. Barstall asked, tilting her head to the side.

"How'd you know?" Tess watched her intently, hoping she wouldn't be as judgmental as she knew some of the others would be.

"Honey, do you remember that tintype I have hangin' in my house? Ya know, the one with a lot o' leg?" She nudged Tess with her elbow in her usual fashion.

"I do."

"I keep that up as a reminder."

"A reminder of what?" Tess asked.

"A reminder of the way I used to be." Mrs. Barstall pulled Tess' hands into her own. "I ain't no crystal-clear, snowy-white gal. I used to entertain men for a livin'."

Shock raced through Tess. How could this woman, so wealthy and opinionated, with plenty of clout in the community, be a former prostitute? Tess shook her head.

"That tintype serves as a blatant reminder of my former life. It doesn't define me. I define it. Matilda will find her way back. When she does, I'll be here. Ain't nobody gonna run her off. Not if I have anythin' to do with it." She winked.

"What about your husband? What did he think of your old life?"

"Honey, that's where I met the man. He had some straightenin' up to do, too."

All this time, Tess's admiration for Mrs. Barstall had grown. Surprisingly, her admission didn't make her any less of a Christian woman in Tess' eyes. She respected her more for her unwavering honesty.

She stared at her for a moment, wondering if she would ever be able to accept her own mother, although she was a prostitute, and forgive her father. Tess still didn't know if that day would ever come.

***

Tess looked back at the mountains before climbing into the stagecoach. Their strength and majesty touched the heavens. Her heart would ache for this land, no doubt about it. More than anything, she would ache for Ian.

231

"Your sister and grandmother are in the coach, ready to go," Franklin said, touching Tess lightly on the small of her back. "Lizzie seems quite excited to be riding again." He smiled wide.

Tess nodded. She looked around again, hoping to see Ian standing nearby, trying to stop her. But the streets were empty. She'd said her goodbyes to Catherine and Thomas and Mrs. Barstall. There was nothing left to do.

Tess lifted her dress and climbed up into the coach. She sat down on the hard seat and waited for Franklin to join them.

He stepped inside and tapped the top of the coach with his cane. It lurched forward and Tess covered her mouth, stifling her cries.

"Are you sure you want to return?" Franklin asked. He must've sensed her trepidation.

"Of course," Tess said. "New York City is where I belong." She glanced at her grandmother. Her sour face continued to enrage Tess. She knew she'd have to learn to deal with her in one way or another. Tess peered out the window and aimed her eyes in the direction of the ranch, which was slowly fading in the distance.

*****

A knock on the door startled Ian, and he rose from the floor of Thomas and Catherine's house to open it.

Barrington's former hand, the young Kyle, sat up and rubbed his eyes. The young lad had stayed alongside Ian.

"Stay here. I want to make sure it ain't my uncle lookin' for you," Ian said.

Kyle nodded and stayed put.

Ian opened the door and felt a rush of surprise. "Isaiah, what're you doin' here?" He wanted to slam the door and never lay eyes on the young man again.

"Barrington's in jail." A smile crept across the young man's face.

"What're you talkin' about?"

"Marshal Nelson rode into town yesterday. I told him what happened to my Pa. They arrested him for murder—"

"Wait, slow down," Ian said, pulling Isaiah into the house. "Sit down a minute. How do you know it was murder?"

Isaiah sat down as Thomas walked out of the bedroom and stood near the fireplace. He remained silent as the two men talked.

232

"I was there."

"Why didn't you say anything before now?" Ian paced the floor. His mind churned with the new information.

"I couldn't. I knew the sheriff wouldn't do a thing. So, a while back, I sent word to Marshal Nelson. Didn't know when he'd come west again. I didn't want to take a chance on Barrington finding out and gettin' to me, Tess, or Francine."

"Why didn't you tell me about this?" Ian leaned down and pressed his hands against the table.

Isaiah cleared his throat and looked down at the table. "I was plumb scared."

Ian nodded. He understood. Barrington could drive fear deep into a man. He ran his fingers through his hair.

"I need to go tell Tess and Francine," Isaiah said, standing up.

"They're gone, Isaiah." Ian crossed his arms on his chest.

"Gone? Where?" His voice rose higher.

"Back to New York City."

"It can't be."

"You took their land. What else could they do?"

"I gave Tess a month. I figured she'd stay and this whole mess would be over by then."

"She had no reason to stay." Ian hated the fact that even he couldn't keep her here.

"We have to do something. We can't just let them go," Isaiah said, a frown darkening his face.

"There's nothin' that can be done. It's over." Ian picked up his hat, plopped it on his head, slid on his boots, and left the house. He knew he'd never see Tess again.

Chapter Thirty-One

"So, why are you still here?" Thomas said, walking into the church sanctuary.

"What're you talkin' about?" Ian asked. He sat down in the back pew and stared at the pulpit.

"Why aren't you going after Tess?" Thomas sat down in front of him and turned to his side to face Ian.

"Why would I go after her? She wants nothin' to do with me."

"Do you really believe she doesn't care for you?"

"She never wants to see me again. What more proof do I need?" Ian said.

"If you don't go after her, you will regret it for the rest of your life," Thomas added.

Ian knew the truth in his statement. "I have nothing to offer her."

"Tess doesn't want fancy things, Ian. She wants a man that will take care of her and love her for who she is. I saw the way she looked at you. There's no mistaking the love she has for you."

"I just don't know if she can forgive me for harboring the secret about her brother," Ian looked down at the floor. "So many times I wanted to tell her. I knew she needed to know, but I promised Ed I wouldn't say anything."

"Don't you see?" Thomas said. "That's what she loves about you. Your honesty. She just doesn't know it yet."

Ian looked up to a smile crossing Thomas's face.

"I guess it's somethin' to think about."

"Don't let her get away." Thomas stood up and walked out of the sanctuary.

The quietness of the room filled Ian's senses. He enjoyed Sunday mornings, but had to admit he loved time alone in the sanctuary. It gave him time to think.

***

Ian pulled his hat down to shield his eyes from the morning sun. Although they stopped for just a few hours during the night, Ian wondered if they would make it in time to stop the stagecoach.

"Gettin' mighty nervous, ain't ya?" Isaiah said, looking over at Ian, laughing.

"A bit." He smiled in return. "We're almost to the way station. Maybe all that ridin' last night'll pay off."

"I hope so," Isaiah said. "Not sure how many more nights I can go chasing down Tess."

The two rode onto the dusty streets of Fremont's Orchard. Although a rendezvous point for mountain men, Indians, and weary travelers, the stop was a small town. Ian hoped they'd be able to find the stagecoach before it left again to go east.

The two stopped and Ian glanced around the town, hoping to find the station house. Isaiah pointed to a sign on a window. "Stagecoach" was written in large, white lettering across the wavy glass.

Ian's heart sank. No sign of the stagecoach. Had he arrived too late?

He hopped off Slater and flipped the reins around the post in front of the station. When he opened the door, he spotted a young man behind the counter.

"Just wonderin' if the stagecoach going east already left?"

"Yes, sir. 'Bout two hours ago. The man on board said he wanted to get a head start."

Ian knew it had to be Franklin. "Thanks," he said. Ian grabbed the doorknob and leaned his head against the door before opening it. Was he crazy for going after Tess? Would she even want him? Doubt continued to fill his heart. Maybe he and Isaiah should turn around and go home.

As he walked out on the porch, Isaiah yelled to him. "There's a coach right there." He pointed across the street.

Ian ran down the stairs and jogged across the dusty roadway. The driver climbed down from the top and dropped to the ground.

"Where ya headed?" Ian asked, out of breath.

235

"Denver City," I'd offer ya a spot, but I got a full load."

Ian nodded and turned to walk away. He should've known better.

"Lady's got a couple broken legs. Poor thing. I gotta help her get up in the seat."

He stopped. A grin grew wide across Ian's face. "Broken legs, you say?"

"That's right." He faced Ian and looked at him with a crooked grin.

"You takin' a pretty brunette with a set of brown eyes that can knock you off your feet?"

"Sure thing. Little bit feisty, too. Said she had somethin' to get back to. Real quick like." He stopped loading the coach long enough to laugh.

"Somethin' or someone?" Ian pursed his lips.

"Now that ya mention it, I think she did say someone." He climbed up on the coach and secured one of the trunks. "There she is now." He pointed as he hollered down to Ian.

Ian turned around. He pulled on his brim, shielding his eyes from the sun. Tess stood in the distance with her back to him. Wisps of light brown hair glittered in the sun and blew in the gentle breeze. Lizzie bounced up and down at her feet and Ian gave a chuckle.

"Ian!" Lizzie spotted him, and her voice carried across the distance. Tess turned around. She smiled and followed Lizzie, now running, to Ian's side.

Before she spoke, she blinked a few times and smiled again. "What are you doing here?"

"I heard they make a mean cup of coffee at the diner across the street," he said.

Tess laughed.

"I came for you," he added softly. "But, I didn't know if you'd have me."

"I was wrong," Tess said. A tear formed in her eye and Ian reached up to wipe it away. "I was wrong about everything. I understand now why you couldn't tell me about my brother. I was so angry I couldn't see past my hurt. I thought you were keeping a secret from me. But you were just trying to keep a promise."

"Your father meant everything to me," Ian said.

She nodded.

"Regardless of your parents' choices, you're a beautiful woman. God knows your heart."

"I know that now," Tess said.

"How'd you figure all this out?" Ian said, running his hands along the sides of her arms.

"Mrs. Barstall. She has a past, but she's not afraid of it. She helped me see God's grace and mercy."

"How 'bout you come see your land."

"But, what about Isaiah?"

"Ya' mean that fellow over there?" Ian pointed across the street and Isaiah lifted his hand in a wave. "You finally got some land to call your own."

Tess looked up at Ian. "Our own?"

"Your Pa worked hard for it," Ian said.

"What of Barrington?"

"Looks like there's enough evidence against him to send him away for a long time. I don't think he'll be a problem anymore."

Ian lifted his hands and rested them on her cheeks. "I ain't gonna let anything interrupt me this time." He leaned down and pressed his lips against hers. They were soft and warm.

"I love you," Ian said, pulling her head into his chest.

Tess smiled and knew she'd come home.

Epilogue

"Look," Tess said, holding up an envelope. "A letter came from Franklin."

"What'd he say?" Francine asked.

Tess read for a moment and a smile grew across her face. "He got married." She wanted so badly for him to be happy. Did he truly find someone to love?

"Married? Who'd he marry?" Francine asked. She stood up and lifted her cane to her side, leaned against it, and limped over toward Tess.

"Miss Lundberg," Tess answered.

"Who's Miss Lundberg?" Catherine asked. She poked at the wood in the parsonage fireplace, trying to stoke it up, and keep the room warm.

"Our Sunday school teacher in New York City," Tess said.

"I always thought she was a sweet woman," Francine said. "I think she taught my class for at least ten years."

"They'll be happy together." Tess wanted so desperately for Franklin to be with someone that passionately loved him, the way she loved Ian.

When she decided to return to Denver City, Franklin understood her love for Ian, and supported it. It made her departure from him so much easier. "It would be hard to find a better man."

"I can't believe he allowed Grandmother to live under his roof, even after you parted ways."

Tess and Francine both giggled. "Grandfather did a lot for him when his wife died. Franklin told me once that he didn't believe he could've made it through without him."

"I'm sure Grandmother is still angry with us," Francine said.

"Franklin can handle her pretty well," Tess said. She added one more ribbon to her hair. "I'm so glad you stayed."

"I had to. I wanted to be close to my sister and brother."

Warmth traveled across Tess. Never did she believe she'd be able to stay in Denver City, and with family.

Outside, snow fluttered to the ground in light flurries. A dusting of white covered the frozen ground.

The door flew open and a gust of wind blew in some snow. Mrs. Barstall sauntered in and slammed the door behind her.

"I thought there was gonna be a party today," she hollered.

"Soon, very soon," Francine said. "We just have a few more things to do."

"Well honey, you'd better get busy. You got a church full of people waitin' for a weddin'.

A baby's cry sounded in the other room. Catherine stood up and disappeared to her bedroom. She returned a moment later, cuddling a tiny boy.

Tess pulled back the blanket and touched the tip of his nose. "He's so precious."

Mrs. Barstall pulled Tess to the side and said, "Your friend Matilda said she'd be there waitin' to see ya."

"I'm so glad she's coming," Tess said. In time, she knew Matilda would feel more comfortable in church. Tess knew that God placed Mrs. Barstall in their lives for a reason. The two women had already formed a lasting friendship.

"Lizzie, are you ready to go?" Francine leaned over slowly, and pulled on one of her ringlets.

The young girl looked up at her mother and grinned. Her pink dress touched the floor, and the sash was half as big as the young girl. "Do I get ta go first, Mama?"

"After me," Francine said.

"You're so pretty, Aunt Tessie." Tess leaned down to kiss Lizzie. She touched the edges of her simple wedding dress.

Tess stood up and looked in the mirror. She lifted her mother's locket off the table and stuck her fingernail between the two sides, popping it open. Tess looked at her father's photograph on one side and her mother's on the other.

Francine stood near. "I can't believe the resemblance."

Tess took a deep breath and tried to keep the tears from falling. She ran her finger over the small photograph and snapped the locket shut.

Mrs. Barstall took the necklace from Tess' hand and clasped it behind her neck. Tess tucked the locket into her dress and pressed it against her heart.

"I'm ready," Tess said.

***

Tess slid her hand into her brother's and drew in a deep breath.

"You're the most beautiful bride I've ever seen." Isaiah leaned forward and kissed Tess on the cheek.

Lizzie bounced up and down in front of the two. "Okay, Lizzie, it's time."

They opened the sanctuary doors and Lizzie took off running down the aisle. Laughter erupted as she pounced up several stairs.

Ian stood at the front of the church, near the pulpit, waiting.

"Ready?" Isaiah asked before walking Tess down the aisle.

She nodded and the two walked arm-in-arm.

Tess reached Ian and turned to face him. His blue eyes dove deep into her soul.

"You take my breath away, Miss Porter."

She grinned at her groom. "I'll always be here to make sure you breathe, right along side of me."

***

51779036R10145

Made in the USA
Charleston, SC
03 February 2016